BLIND VIGILANCE

SYDNEY RYE MYSTERIES, BOOK 13

EMILY KIMELMAN

EK

Blind Vigilance
Sydney Rye Mysteries, Book 13
Copyright © 2020 by Emily Kimelman

All rights reserved.
No part of this book may be reproduced in any form or by any electronic or mechanical means, including information storage and retrieval systems, without written permission from the author, except for the use of brief quotations in a book review.

Heading illustration: Autumn Whitehurst
Cover Design: Christian Bentulan
Formatting: Jamie Davis

For Lauren Troppauer Gavioli, the most courageous woman I know. Vulnerability is your super power. Thank you for being my friend all these years. Thank you for being you.

The only morality of the algorithm is to optimize you as a consumer, and in many cases you become the product. There are very few examples in human history of industries where people themselves become products, and those are scary industries – slavery and the sex trade. And now we have social media.

— Christopher Wiley, Cambridge Analytica Whistleblower and author of *MindF*ck: Cambridge Analytica and the Plot to Break America.*

CHAPTER ONE

Dan

Blood. It's blood. The dark stain circling Sydney is *blood.*

Fuck. Fuck. Fuck. I grab my phone, unlock it, navigate to favorites, and touch Mulberry's name without even fully registering the thought.

It rings. *How am I going to explain knowing Sydney Rye needs help?*

I'm thousands of miles away, stationed on a private island in the middle of the fucking Pacific. And yet—

"Hello?" Mulberry's voice, gravelly with sleep, cuts through my thoughts.

"Sydney is bleeding."

My phone beeps. I'm getting another call.

"What?" Mulberry's voice clears as sheets rustle in the background.

A dog barks. I focus on the monitor with the live feed of Sydney's room. Blue is up and going wild. Sydney, her shoulder length hair splayed out on the pillow, the white of the hotel sheets only a few shades lighter than her blanched skin, remains motionless. *Shit.*

I didn't even need to call. The dogs would have alerted Mulberry. *Foolish. Careless. Shit.*

"What's going on, Dan?"

I don't answer.

The door between Mulberry and Sydney's rooms flies open—I watch it on the screen and hear the hinges swoosh over the phone line. Reaching out, I slide my finger along the stylus bar to raise the volume. Mulberry stumbles into Sydney's room, unsteady on just his one leg.

She didn't lock the door. That isn't like her. Except it was Mulberry on the other side. A subtle invitation?

"Fuck!" Mulberry's voice echoes between the phone and computer speakers. He lunges toward the bed.

Sydney lies on her back, a dark stain spreading around her hips. Mulberry drops the phone when he grabs her shoulders, his broad back blocking Sydney's face from my view.

I swivel to a different monitor and bring up Mulberry's phone screen. I dial 911. Someone has to. I can always be counted on to do what needs doing. Overstepping saves lives.

"What's your emergency?" the Miami 911 operator asks.

I clench my fist on the glass surface of my desk. *Answer her, you asshole.* Mulberry doesn't follow my mental command. *Fine.* I take full control of the phone. "My wife is pregnant and bleeding. We're at the airport Marriott, room 523," I say, my voice even and clear. I say it like it's my baby. Like it's my life. Not something I'm watching on a screen. My eyes flick back to the live feed of her room. "I can't wake her."

Dear Jesus. Mulberry sits on the edge of the bed, face tear streaked.

Sydney isn't moving.

She isn't moving.

Don't let her die.

EK

Sydney

"It's time to wake up, Joy." James smiles at me, his hand warm in mine.

"Wake up?" I ask. He nods. "Wait." Tears thicken my voice. "This isn't real?"

He shrugs, eyes sad. "It is, but you're sleeping. And now you have to wake up." James smiles; it's subtle, not like the grins he used to offer so freely. There is a film of sorrow around him now. We didn't understand the price of joy or its fleeting nature.

"I'm so sorry you're dead," I say. The words are like glass in my throat, leaving behind a thirst that a million gallons of water will never quench.

His smile widens, and he reaches up to swipe a tear from my cheek. "Me too, me too..."

I awaken from the dream in a wash of confusion. Blue's nose is wet against my hand. Mulberry looms over me, his fingers digging into my shoulders. "Get off." I raise my arms to push him away. They are heavy... too heavy.

I'm cold.

This is shock.

"Sydney!" Mulberry is yelling.

"What?" My mouth is full of cotton, that raging thirst still there.

"You're bleeding."

He swings his arm down to indicate my lower half. I struggle to lift my head. There's a red stain around my hips. *The baby.*

Panic seizes my chest. "Mulberry," I eke out.

He's holding his phone now. "She's awake," he says. "She's lost a lot of blood."

Blue whines softly next to me, and I meet his eyes. "I'm okay," I promise him, my speech slurred. My eyes slip closed, and the darkness takes me again. But this time, I'm alone. James is gone.

Really gone.

Sharp pain strikes through my chest like a lightning bolt, and I hear the sizzle of the electric current, feel it writhe through me. Love will destroy us if we let it.

EK

Dan

They take Sydney out on a stretcher. Mulberry has the presence of mind to close the hotel room door, locking the dogs inside. He forgets to grab Sydney's phone, computer, and bag. *That won't blind me though.*

Blue sniffs at the bloody sheets before herding Nila and Frank into Mulberry's room through the still-open connecting door.

I watch Mulberry's text scroll across the screen—he's letting Anita know they are on the way to the hospital. I use my app on Anita's phone to turn on the cameras and microphone. Her face fills one box and her rumpled sheets the other.

Dark brown eyes flanked by thick black lashes read the text. Her lips part, and the wrinkle she gets between her brows when she's upset appears. Anita clamps her teeth down on her bottom lip, worrying it as she responds to Mulberry's text. *I'll meet you at the hospital.*

His phone is in his pocket, but the siren wails through the speakers. I'm leaving the sound up in case the paramedics say anything important.

Anita takes her phone with her into the bathroom and puts it on the counter so that one camera darkens and the other shows the light fixture and mirror.

I silence Anita's phone and turn away from the screen, offering her some privacy. On a different monitor, I shoot Anita a quick text to remind her to take Sydney her phone and computer—I'm sure she'll want it. I'm being thoughtful.

My phone chimes to remind me I have a message. *My mom.* I glance at the transcription. *Hi honey, just calling to check in. Call me back when you can. I know how busy you are, so don't feel any pressure. There is something kind of (unintelligible) so call.*

The siren turns off, and there is motion in Mulberry's pocket. Anita throws her phone into her bag. I turn up the volume on Mulberry's device, straining to make out what is being said. I grab my headphones and slip them on.

Sorry, Mom, you'll have to wait.

EK

Sydney

"She's going to be fine, sir."

My eyes are glued shut, but it's bright out there.

"What about the baby?" Mulberry's voice—edged with anxiety—asks.

"We'll know soon."

I want to speak, but I can't. I want to scream, but I have no voice. I want to sit up, run out of here, be away from all of this... but I can't move.

I hear James's voice. *Relax, everything is okay. Rest.*

And I slip back into darkness.

EK

"Hey." Mulberry leans over the bed, his face coming into view. "You're awake."

I blink. He turns and grabs a cup of water, offering me the straw. I suck, my head feeling light and my body weak. The water slips down, soothing my burning thirst.

Lying back against the pillows, I close my eyes. "The baby?" I ask.

"It's fine," Mulberry says. Relief hits me like a ray of sunlight bursting through cloud cover. "Hold on, I'll get the doctor."

He leaves, and I cradle my stomach, gratitude welling inside me. Tears burn my eyes, and I let them flow, don't even try to stop their slow march down my cheeks.

Mulberry comes back. "He will be here in a minute." He sits in the chair next to me and points to a bag next to the bed. "Anita brought your phone and stuff. She had to run but plans to come back later."

I nod, too tired to speak. A knock at the door and a doctor walks in. "Good to see you awake. I'm Dr. Hope," says the tall, bronze skinned, graying man. He smiles like he's heard everything one might say about an OBGYN named Hope so there is no need to add to the repertoire. I rub at my eyes, pulling myself together.

"The baby is fine for now, " Dr Hope says from the end of the bed. "You've had a subchorionic hemorrhage, so we need to take some precautions."

Mulberry squeezes my hand so hard I wince and try to pull it away. He looks at me and then down at our hands. "Sorry," he mumbles and lets go.

"I'd like to keep you overnight, and then bed rest for the next few weeks while we keep an eye on this."

"Can we move her out of the city?" Mulberry asks.

Dr. Hope nods slowly. "Yes, she should be fine to leave the hospital tomorrow, just no carrying any heavy bags. Did you lose your home in the storm?" His brow furrows as he references the hurricane that recently tore through Miami, leaving it devastated.

"Yes," Mulberry lies easily. We didn't have a home here. The only thing we share is a fraught history and the new life growing inside of me. "What does bed rest mean exactly, like how much movement?"

"She doesn't need a bedpan or anything, but restrict movement as much as possible."

Mulberry nods, mulling this over with a furrowed brow. "So, she should get a wheelchair at the airport. And she should stay still. But a couch is okay?"

"Yes, that's fine."

"I'm right here," I point out. Mulberry turns to me, all male confusion. "You two are talking about me like I'm not here." I switch focus to the doctor. "What is a subchorionic hemorrhage?"

He clears his throat. "A hemorrhage that forms between the placenta and uterine wall. You had a medium-size hemorrhage. Lots of women go on to have healthy pregnancies, but the blood loss is frightening for the patient."

"Why didn't she wake up?" Mulberry asks. "It took a lot to get her to come to."

"Again," I say, my voice tight, "I'm *right* here."

"Sorry." Mulberry sighs. "I'm upset."

"That doesn't give you the right to stop treating me like a person."

His lips thin, and color raises into his cheeks. "I'm worried about *you*. I am very aware *you* are a person."

"Good. Feel free to use my name."

A tight smile tugs at his lips, and he raises one brow. *Which name?* his expression questions. I return my attention to the doctor who seems used to couples squabbling. "Why bed rest?" I ask.

Mulberry stiffens next to me. Dr. Hope cocks his head, surprised that

I'm questioning his prescription. "We want to avoid this happening again."

"Are the hemorrhages caused by movement?"

"We don't fully know what causes them, but rest is important during the early months of pregnancy."

"Exercise is almost always a good thing," I say.

"Are you really arguing with him?" Mulberry asks, his voice growing louder.

I glare at him, and his eyes narrow to mere slits of anger and frustration. "It's *my* body."

"It's *our* baby."

I may punch him in front of the doctor. I don't want to, but I might have to. "I'll let you two discuss," Dr. Hope says, removing himself from the room posthaste. *Smart man.*

"I will go insane sitting around for months, Mulberry; you know that."

"I guess you'll have to dig deep."

I bark out a laugh, and the tension around his eyes lessens. He reaches out for my hand, and I let him take it.

I take a deep breath. "Here's the deal. I'm going to do my own research. But from everything I know about my body, being still isn't good for it."

"Maybe this is its way of saying it wants you to slow down." Mulberry drops his gaze to our linked hands. "Your body may need something different than it ever needed before."

Hold up. What are we talking about?

He looks up at me. Yellow bands of color radiated from his pupils, carving a path through the green irises. I drop my gaze. He wants things I can't give him.

The door opens, and a nurse enters. "Hello, Tara," she says, using my alias. "I'm Maud. I'll be your nurse for the next twelve hours. How are you feeling?" She walks up to the machine next to me and checks the IV.

"Fine," I say.

She looks at her watch and then across to Mulberry. "Visiting hours are over in fifteen minutes. Just a heads-up."

"I'm her husband," Mulberry says.

The nurse shakes her head. "Not according to my paperwork, honey." She smiles but isn't falling for anything.

"We're engaged," he says. *Damn, he's good at lying. When did he get so good at that? Maybe always and I just never noticed.*

"Don't lie to me," the nurse says, not falling for any of it. "I've got five kids."

"Five?" I sputter out.

She pats my hand. "It gets easier," she says before returning her attention to Mulberry. "Tara needs to rest, and while you two might be having a baby, it seems you're also having some disagreements." Mulberry's cheeks brighten. Oh my God, she's making him blush. This woman is my hero. "So get ready to hit the road, son."

With that she leaves the room. I'm grinning. "I'll be back first thing in the morning," Mulberry promises. "I'll take care of the dogs; you don't need to worry about them."

"Thanks."

He stands, looking down at me. I tilt my chin to maintain eye contact. "You scared me." His words hit me right in the chest.

"I'm sorry."

He nods then turns toward the door but pauses when he reaches it, refocusing on me. "I'll see you tomorrow."

I nod.

He opens the door and leaves. I reach for my phone, grateful that Anita thought to bring it for me. Time to turn to Dr. Google...

CHAPTER TWO

Lenox

A unicorn stands with its head bent, the mythical creature's horn directing the viewers' focus to a gangly foal at her feet. Mountains in gold and green rise up behind the new mother. Intricate flowers, each petal shimmering in pale pink, create a border around the central image of the tapestry.

I cross my arms. "$23,257," I offer, a specific and final amount.

The salesman doesn't respond immediately; he wants more. *Doesn't everybody?* But my voice leaves no room for bargaining. We've gone back and forth over several cups of tea—the mint scents the air, along with the wool rugs. Fiber dust motes drift in the shafts of sunlight that filter through the stained skylights.

One of my first regular clients, a rug salesman's wife, liked to get fucked on her husband's stock. The scent of this showroom brings the sweet perfume of her to my nose, reminding me that I, too, was once stock to be bargained over and sold.

The dealer and I have reached the end of negotiation. He must decide: should he sell to me or wait for another offer?

A low thud vibrates through the room. Someone in the market dropped something heavy. And though only a few feet separate us from the busy passageways beyond, the tapestries on the walls and rugs layered on the floor keep the sales room suspended in near silence.

"That is a good deal," Petra says, her heels quiet on the rugs as she moves across the room.

She stares at me with an intensity that sends shivers down my spine. Now that Petra no longer pays me, it's as if her gaze has become that much more riveting. She has me, yet her longing grows.

Petra has never claimed to love me. And while I spent a brief moment in my youth thinking I loved her, my heart is my own again. It sits to the left of my spine and beats with the will of a warrior, the tenacity of a street dog, and the ice-cold certainty of a vigilante. It is mine, and so it shall remain. It is the only sure way to survive.

"You drive a hard bargain," the salesman says.

"You have no idea," Petra purrs, circling behind me and running a hand up my spine. Her nails scratch through the layers of coat, sports jacket, and shirt to leave a trail of heat. "He is very hard."

I suppress a laugh as Petra stalks to the salesman. "Leave us," she says.

The merchant glances at me, and I keep my face unreadable. He looks back at Petra—whose back is to me so I can't see her expression—but it makes the man leave his own shop.

Petra stands in a band of sunlight. The black knee-length cashmere coat absorbs the light, but the sheer stockings reflect it. Her green eyes, catlike in shape and temperament, smile.

Petra is good at smiling with just her eyes. The stern line of those luscious lips—painted harlot red—tighten my stomach. "I want you," she says, her voice even. The woman never plays coy, never acts shy.

I let a smile twitch across my lips.

"I don't want much." She takes a step toward me, showing the flash of red from the bottom of her black pump that matches her lips. "Just a kiss."

Her lip trembles as if she is afraid I'll refuse her, and she bites down on it with white teeth, her eyes turning soft. But not pleading. She won't beg... yet.

Petra needs to be on the absolute edge to beg.

I glance at my watch—a gold Rolex gifted to me by another client—and then back to the rugs. I could have her there in six minutes, but to do it right, to *really* make her scream, would take seventeen.

I only have fifteen. I'll make it work.

I always make it work. I'll have Petra on a lovely vintage Oushak rug and, before we leave, I'll have the tapestry too.

EK

Petra's arm rests in the crook of mine as we leave the restaurant. A fine mist thickens the air and sparkles in the streetlight's glow. A cool breeze blasts down the street, and Petra grips my arm, her hair whipping around her shoulders.

We make our way to the Paris Hotel—one of the oldest and grandest in Istanbul. We've come to see Yusuf Polat, who keeps a suite here. The doorman bows to us as he opens the door.

Water shimmers in Petra's chestnut hair like dew in a spiderweb. She smiles at a bellboy, and he blushes. *Poor thing.*

"Good evening," the front desk attendant greets us. "We are expecting you, please." She waves a graceful arm to another bellboy. "Mustafa will show you up." Mustafa bows and takes us up in the elevator.

To think there was a time when people could not operate elevators on their own. During that period, people of my skin color would not have been welcome in this hotel unless as an employee. Now I enter as an honored guest. We shall see if I make it out with such auspicious reverence.

EK

Yusuf reminds me of the *Star Wars* character, Jabba the Hutt. Except the beautiful young woman attending him is not held by a literal chain around her neck but rather the invisible economic bonds of class, birth, and sex.

I watched *Return of The Jedi* mostly naked in a British tourist's hotel room, the curtains drawn tight against the bright beach sun trying to blast into the dark, intimate world we'd created. *Marigold*. Lovely in her fifties, she told me I was beautiful enough to be on film. Her skin smelled of sunscreen and the hotel's jasmine-scented soap. She ate her toast dry with black coffee and laughed easily. Marigold remained a client for years.

A weight swings from my heart at the memory of that day, of her, of the me I used to be. When I see a young woman forced into the same profession, flashes of my past work life evoke a mix of nostalgia and relief. I *chose* to sell my body to climb out of poverty. I held on to my dignity, creating a strong and thriving identity that still serves me today.

This girl, with her sallow skin, dark circles, and slumped shoulders, teeters on the edge of total destruction. If the drugs don't swallow her, then that viscous inner voice will tear her to pieces. Princess Leia knew she didn't belong in chains. This girl looks as if she believes she was born to wear them.

I inhale slowly through my nose, taking my gaze from the ornamental whore to the beast of a man sitting on the love seat beside her. His pudgy fingers, decorated with fat gold rings, dig into her thin thigh hard enough to leave fresh bruises. They will match the ones on her arms that she's covered in makeup but still shine through.

"Petra." Yusuf smiles broadly and stands. His silk Versace shirt, patterned with gold lengths of twining rope, gapes open to his stomach—tan, hairy, and shiny, as if he is sweating or had just rubbed on oil.

Petra shrugs out of her coat, and one of Yusuf's guards, a mountain of a man in a sharkskin suit, steps forward to help her. Mountain's diminutive counterpart—the physical opposite but wearing the same suit with its bulging sidearm—stands just behind us with his hands loose at his side. Ready to kill.

Yusuf takes Petra's hand, and they kiss cheeks. Petra turns to me. "This is my partner, Lenox Gold," Petra says. I bow my head as Mountain moves behind me, a silent request for my overcoat.

I slip it off my shoulders and let the man take it, acting as though the weight of it, the extra layer between me and the scum in this room, wasn't a slight comfort. Yusuf holds out his hand, and I meet it with my own, placing a subtle smile on my lips and bringing a light of vague interest into my eyes, ignoring the slick feel of him.

The best whores are the best actors.

"Please," Yusuf says, "what can I get you to drink?"

"Red wine," Petra says. I nod that I'll have the same.

Yusuf waves a hand at Tiny, and he stalks to a bar, his suit glinting with each step. Yusuf returns to his seat, not bothering to introduce the woman next to him. She doesn't meet our eyes, just stares down at her hands lying limp against her bare thighs. The dress she's wearing is black and clingy as a bathing suit.

"Sit," Yusuf invites, gesturing to the two armchairs that face the love seat. I wait for Petra to settle into the gaudy gold and red thing before taking my place beside her.

"Chivalrous," Yusuf comments. "Did you learn that as a gigolo?"

He says it as if to elicit shame. *Sorry to disappoint, Jabba.* "My mother always taught me to respect women, treat them with delicacy, while also recognizing their incredible strength. They are creators, after all, Yusuf. We merely provide the seed."

"But without the seed, a plant cannot grow."

"Without the soil and sun, it will never survive." I smile.

Yusuf barks out a laugh. "I like him." He flings an arm around the nameless creature next to him.

Mountain hands us our wine, and Yusuf's grin slowly fades. "I like you." He says it to me this time instead of addressing Petra. "But I don't like you coming into my city and doing what you're doing."

"Yusuf." Petra uses that purr of hers, the one that raises the hairs on men's arms... and other parts as well. "I've worked in this city for a decade, and you never had a problem with me before. I still pay my dues."

He blinks slowly, the fat around his eyes tightening as he stares at her. "Ian is very upset about his brothers." Murdering a man's family does often upset them.

"Business." Petra shrugs. "You understand." She raises one brow, as though they share knowledge of past deeds done.

"What you're doing isn't business. It's charity."

My voice catches in my throat, holding it in, not letting my own beliefs and emotions into this moment. Yusuf runs this city's underworld, and if we want to survive not just tonight but the years ahead, we either have to negotiate with him... or end him.

"Yusuf," Petra uses his name again. "Charity?" She shakes her head. "Happy whores make happy customers. Also, better working conditions allow us to have a higher level of entertainment. And—" She sips her wine. "—keeps Joyful Justice off our backs."

Yusuf sucks at his teeth. "I don't like it." He frowns. "You used to work with the McCain brothers. Now you turn on them." The lines around his mouth deepen. "You start letting girls out of contracts." The girl next to him flicks her gaze up to Petra just for a second, but Yusuf senses it. His hand grips her shoulder, and she curls deeper into herself. She won't be safe anywhere until this man is dead.

"You worked with Omer for many years," Petra says, her voice light but edged with warning. "And that did not stop you from moving up."

Yusuf shifts in his seat, leaning further back, feigning a relaxed and powerful pose, but the man does not like having his inglorious past put in front of his face. *Petra, be careful. A puppy will let you rub its nose in its mistakes, but a full-grown pit bull will not.*

"You have higher ambitions then?" Yusuf asks, the warning in his tone absolute—*do not answer wrong, or I will kill you now.*

Mountain and Tiny are still behind us. They have not moved, but they don't have far to go for their weapons.

"I only wish to make the most money that I can with the least amount of hassle," Petra answers. "As always."

Yusuf shifts his gaze to me. "And what about you, Lenox Gold? Do you have ambitions?"

"Of course. I am a man."

Yusuf bares his teeth in a grin. "What do you want?"

"I wish to create a profitable business and healthy work environment for my employees."

Yusuf coughs a derisive laugh, his belly shaking from the sound. "Employees." He sits forward, putting his elbows on his knees. "Call them what they are, Mr. Gold. They are whores." He says the word as if it is a wine he wants to fully get the taste of, swirling it around in his mouth, enjoying the subtle flavors. I offer him a friendly smile. His eyes narrow. "You don't like women?"

I allow a flash of a grin, a hint of my true wolfish nature to peek from behind the blinds. He will trust a man who likes to fuck because he believes that none of us can control our inner beast. What men like Yusuf never learn is that leashing the beast heightens its appetite and pleasure.

"I enjoy consensual sex with women," I answer, cool as a sunset cocktail on the bow of a yacht. "Very much so." My voice drops an octave to a velvety, dark place that every sensual being knows and desires.

Yusuf laughs. "Consensual. You are very modern, aren't you, Mr. Gold?" He grips the girl's leg again but maintains eye contact with me, daring me to challenge him. To see which of our wolves can tear out the other's throat first.

I sip my wine, my expression once again that gentle friendliness that has served me so well. Yusuf shifts his attention to Petra again. "I will need a higher royalty," he announces. "You're hurting business all over the city, starting to get whores talking about rights." He says *rights* like it's a foul-tasting oyster he has to spit out or risk infection.

"But, Yusuf," Petra keeps her voice friendly, "we already pay you 10 percent. With overhead, you leave us so little," she pouts.

"What do I care?" Yusuf drops the words like stones into the bottom of a well—deep, big plops. At least we know there is water down there.

"You see no reason to care," I mirror his language.

"That's right. Your business margins are not my problem."

"Not your problem."

He nods, enjoying the mirroring. So many men do. I wait in silence, knowing he'll speak again. "I don't like what you are doing or the way you are doing it."

"Our methods are not to your liking."

He nods, agreeing with me... himself. "It does not make sense to treat them so well."

"Why should we treat them so well?" I smile gently. *I hear you.* That's all anyone wants... to be heard. Understood. Empathized with. If you give a man empathy, you earn his soul. The devil is so good at bargaining because he knows what his victims truly want. The key to any good negotiation is to find out what your counterpart wants, empathize with them, then show them how giving *you* what you want can better fulfill their needs.

"Exactly! Letting whores out of their contracts, that looks bad for all of us."

"Bad for everyone."

His nostrils flare. "It riles up the workers."

"Riles up the workers."

"Makes them think they are important and can stand against us."

"Gives them a false sense of importance."

"That's right!" Yusuf glances at the girl next to him. "Take Anna here." The girl flinches as if someone might actually *take* her. "She's a good girl. But what if she worked at one of your places? Would you treat her right, keep her in her place? Or let her cry and beg off?"

I nod slowly. "It seems like you want to make sure that your business practices won't be undermined by the changes we've implemented."

"Right!" I wait, letting time slip by, letting silence work its magic. "Giving in to Joyful Justice is no way to defeat them."

"We can't defeat Joyful Justice by giving in to them."

His mouth spreads into a cat-who-ate-the-canary smile. "You've got it." He glances at Petra. "Your man here knows what he's talking about."

Petra sips her wine and offers a friendly smile. *We just want to find a way to live together in this crazy world.* "It seems like you want to destroy Joyful Justice," Petra says.

"Of course I do." His eyes narrow. "Don't you?"

I shrug. "They have backed off since the McCain brothers left Petra's organization."

Yusuf laughs. "You are a slick one, aren't you, Lenox Gold?"

"You seem to think I'm trying to trick you."

"No." His brow furrows as his ego rebels.

"Sorry." I raise my free hand. "I just said it seemed that way. I must have misread the situation."

"That's right. You did." He calms.

"It looks like what you want isn't a bigger percentage of our business but for your business to remain the same. You want the status quo to be maintained."

"What if I want both?" He leans back again, putting a fat arm around Anna.

"You want us to return to standardized practices and give you a larger percentage?"

"That sounds good to me."

"Our business is a problem for you."

"It's *a* problem. Giving in to Joyful Justice's demands is dangerous and shortsighted."

"Dangerous and shortsighted," I mirror.

"Exactly! Next thing you know, they'll be demanding that we shut down altogether."

"It seems like you're concerned about future problems with Joyful Justice."

He leans forward then, faster than a man of his girth should be able to move. "I don't worry, Mr. Gold. I prepare."

I nod, using my imagination to try to slip into his skin. *If I was Yusuf, ran illegal trade in Istanbul and environs...* "You are always prepared."

"Yes, always." A bead of sweat slips from his hairline down the side of his face. "So you will give me my 20 percent and stop letting whores out of agreements. Then maybe, *maybe,* I will let you continue to work in *my* city."

"How are we supposed to do that?" *Ask a calibrated question when a demand is made.*

He raises both brows. "Not my problem."

"There are other services in the city that have rules similar to ours."

"High-end escort services. That is very different."

"How is it different?"

His nostrils flare again, and he shakes his head. "I'm done with this conversation."

"What if we could help with Joyful Justice?"

He raises his brows, a sneaky smile cresting his lips. "I have that in hand. You don't need to worry about them."

"We will need to think about all this," Petra says, standing. "Thank you for your time."

"Come back with your new percentage, or don't come back," Yusuf warns, also standing. Anna and I are the only two still sitting. Our eyes meet for a brief moment, but hers dart away quickly.

"How much for her?" I ask, cursing myself but knowing I can't leave without her.

"Who?" Yusuf sounds genuinely confused.

I look up at him. "Anna."

He glances at her. Yusuf shakes his head. "She's not for sale."

I smile. "Yusuf, everyone has a price."

He likes that—the idea that people and morals can be bought and sold. "Make me an offer."

I stay seated, letting him feel bigger than me. "$1,000." I start with a low, round number.

He snorts and turns away, pacing toward his armed guards. "Not even close," he throws over his shoulder.

"What if I promise to treat her 'right'?"

Petra catches my eye but gives nothing away. She won't undermine me in front of Yusuf, but her heart does not bleed like mine. This is foolish.

I stand and join Petra. Yusuf looms behind the love seat, his hands on Anna's shoulders. She stares glassy-eyed at her lap. "She is one of my favorites," Yusuf says. "Never knew a man before me."

"You are lucky," I say.

"I am powerful, and I take what I want."

"Yes," I agree. "Very powerful."

He straightens, relinquishing the girl. "I will give her to you, a gift." He smiles. "A thank-you for the increase in profit sharing and return to normalcy at your establishments."

"Thank you," Petra says before I can speak. "Come," she says to Anna. The girl looks up at Petra, her eyes wide with astonishment and fear. She doesn't trust this turn of events. None of us do.

CHAPTER THREE

Dan

"How did you know she was bleeding?" Mulberry's question is reasonable, his voice calm. But the truth would sound nothing less than crazy... stalkery... creepy... unacceptable. I'm not in love with her. Not anymore. I'm just... I keep track of everyone.

But they can't know that.

"I had a dream." I keep my eyes on the external camera feed from his phone. Mulberry's hair brushes the edge of the lens, so I'm looking at the hospital hallway through wispy dark strands.

"A dream?" He sounds incredulous now. *Fair.*

"Yes, I woke up absolutely sure she was in trouble. I can't explain it. What happened?"

"Dan," Mulberry's voice drops as a nurse passes him, "you used my phone to call 911." I let his own words sink in. *I did what you could not. I acted when you froze.*

"I was worried. You screamed and dropped the phone." My turn to sound incredulous. "I was scared."

He sighs and spins to the wall, leaning against it. "You can control my phone?"

"Of course I can. Mulberry, I can control every piece of equipment associated with our organization. You know that."

"I guess..."

"It is vitally important for security."

"What about privacy?"

Ah, the age-old question: What do we give up in exchange for security? The social contract—every justice system—exists in an attempt to answer this question. "Have you read Hobbes?"

"The Hobbit?"

I snort. "No. But kind of actually..." *There are themes about justice and the social contract in Tolkien's classic epic.* I shake my head. *Not now.* "Thomas Hobbes, the English philosopher. He came up with a theory that, in order to survive in a hostile world, we must enter into a social contract in which we give up some of our liberty in order to enjoy the security of a powerful state. Basically, the rule of law protects me, and I follow the rule of law." Not going to mention Hobbes theory that it should be a single ruler in charge of everything...

"Dan, I've read Hobbes." Mulberry's voice is tight with annoyance. "Are you watching us through our phones? Yes or no?"

"No." The lie justifies the outcome here—Machiavelli is underrated in my humble opinion.

"But you can watch and listen to us?"

"Yes." I clear my throat. "Mulberry, I can watch almost anyone in the world through their phone." I say it low, quiet. *Let that sink in.* "Part of my job is to make sure that no one is watching you through your phone."

"Except you?"

I can taste the bitterness in his voice on the back of my tongue. Fuck him. I saved Sydney's life. I bite my tongue hard enough to wince. *Don't say anything you'll regret.*

"How is Sydney?" I finally ask, already knowing the answer. I glance over to her screen. She's reading about bed rest. Wait... what the fuck is that? I expand the live code feed. I'm not the only one watching her phone. My eyes narrow. My fingers find the keyboard, and I'm on them, chasing the little fucker around her phone. They are hiding in the messages... yes. There it is. A text from... no, this doesn't make sense. *How are you hiding yourself?*

"Dan!"

"Haley, disconnect call." My computer complies and ends the call with Mulberry. I need to concentrate if I'm going to remove this spy... this intruder. A smile pulls at my lips. I do love a challenge. A chase.

EK

Vibration wakes me. I jerk to attention, knocking over a half-empty cup of coffee. *Fuck.* It flows across the desk toward one of my keyboards. I grab up the mug and swipe at the liquid with my shirt hem, staunching its advancement.

I scan the office for a more permanent solution. A roll of paper towels lies on the coffee table in front of the black leather couch, along with a bunch of other half-finished mugs of tea and coffee. *I really need to clean up.* The vibrating stops, and my phone chimes that I have a message.

I grab the paper towels and soak up the rest of the spill before checking my phone. Mom called again. It's after nine at night here, so six in the morning in Jersey. My sleep schedule is totally screwed up.

I hit reply, rubbing the sleep out of my eyes and checking to make sure my work eradicated the intruder on Sydney's phone. A strange bug: echoes of Homeland Security's clunky footprints but with the shine of Fortress Global's camouflage.

"Dan." I can hear the smile in Mom's voice when she answers.

"Hey, Ma, how are you?" I yawn and lean back in my chair, stretching my back. Falling asleep at my desk is doing a number on me physically.

"Well..." I don't like the length of the pause. "Tell me about you first."

"I'm good." I sit forward and open up her email. It's been a while since I checked on Mom's messages.

"Your start-up is still doing well? You're busy."

"Yes, but I always have time for you, Mom."

"I don't want to distract you. I know what you do is important." She has no idea what I do. I lie to protect her. Story of my life.

"Mom, what's going on?" There is an edge of annoyance in my voice that I don't like. "Sorry, you're worrying me." I sit back and stare out the glass wall in front of me to the command center of Joyful Justice. Below my office, the rows of computer banks are half full. Rachel, my second-in-command, is leaning over one of the newest recruits, pointing at the screen. On the double-height wall of monitors are a few maps but no active missions. It's all recon right now.

Mom sighs, focusing my attention. "I've been diagnosed with cancer. Breast. So... well, it's stage 3. I should be fine. But I might not be." The floor drops out from under me. I'm floating above the command center with no safety net. "I'm sorry, Dan. I don't want to be a distraction." *How in the hell did I miss this?*

"Mom, wait." I hold up a hand as if that can keep the oblivion from swallowing me.

"I start chemo today."

"Today? Why didn't you call me earlier? I'll fly out now." I'm at least twenty-four hours away from New Jersey though. I'll never make it for her appointment.

"I did call, honey." Her voice is quiet. "You don't need to come all this way. I'll be fine."

"I'm coming, Mom."

After we hang up, I stare down at the phone in my hand. I wasn't paying enough attention. That isn't like me.

Steps sound on the spiral staircase leading to my office, followed by a knock at the door. I don't respond. The door opens anyway, and I swivel around.

Rachel has both hands on her hips and is filling the doorway. She wears her uniform of board shorts, a button-up shirt, and a bandana keeping her short hair off her face. "You have barely left this room in two weeks, dude! I'm dragging you out of here." Rachel's brown eyes are narrowed with determination.

"My mom..."

"What happened to your shirt?" she asks, glancing around the room. "This place is insane, Dan. You know I understand getting sucked into a project, but you *need* fresh air—"

"I have to go now." I stand.

Rachel throws her hands in the air. "Thank you! Let's go for a walk. Have you eaten?"

I shake my head. "No, I have to go to New Jersey."

"New Jersey?" Her confusion is complete.

"My mom. She's sick." The words are a fist to my Adam's apple. She can't die. No. No. No. My hands clench into fists. *No.* I will not allow it.

CHAPTER FOUR

Sydney

James links his arm through mine as we stroll down the street. It's a gorgeous sunny fall day, and the trees are bursting with color. "So, what are you going to do?" he asks me.

"I don't know," I answer, my tone grumpy and petulant.

James laughs. "You don't want to go to Costa Rica or the island. So where do you want to go?"

I shrug. "I should go somewhere safe, I guess."

"Where is safe?"

"Where no one knows me. A place where no one would expect me to go."

"What about Spain?" James asks, excitement edging his voice. "You could go to Barcelona and learn to flamenco."

I laugh. "That has got to be the antithesis of bed rest."

James laughs. "Bed rest sounds like a bunch of bullshit to me."

"Me too," I agree. We stop in front of a brownstone and look up at the glass-fronted doors. The sun glints off the polished-wood frame. James pulls me down onto the stoop. "I just don't know what to do."

James puts his arm around me. "Trust yourself, Joy. That's all you can ever do."

I shake my head. "I've made too many mistakes." My voice is small, scared. *I got you killed.*

"There are no such things as mistakes, just lessons you need to learn."

"I guess I'm a bad student because I can't seem to get anything right."

He shrugs and laughs. "Not with that attitude you won't."

A knocking sound distracts James, and he turns to look up the stoop to the doors. "Time to go," he says.

"Already?"

"I'll see you soon." He kisses the top of my head. Blue's wet nose on my knuckles pulls me fully from the dream.

"Hey, boy," I say, rubbing his snout. His tail thumps loudly on the floor.

The knocking sounds again, and Blue urges me up with a snout push.

I find Anita at the door. She's wearing a bright blue tunic and white jeans, and she's holding a paper bag of takeout. "I brought wonton soup."

"Sounds good. Thanks." I step aside so she can enter the hotel room.

"How is bed rest going?" Anita asks, putting the bag of food down on the desk while I put the security latch back on the door.

"I'm probably going to murder Mulberry," I say, sitting on the bed as she starts pulling out cartons of food. He brought me home from the hospital and circled me like a mother hen until I made him leave.

"Where is he now?" Anita asks.

"I told him to fuck the fuck off."

"You've always had a way with words."

I huff a laugh. "He is all for me taking naps, so I took one." I yawn, my eyes tearing a little with exhaustion.

"Well, you'll be in Costa Rica soon, and then you'll have plenty of people who are not Mulberry to wait on you." She looks over her shoulder and grins at me.

I wince. "I'm not going to Costa Rica."

Anita raises a brow and cocks her head, turning fully to face me. "You're going to the island?"

"No."

"Where then?" She crosses her arms in front of her chest.

I stand up from the bed and pace to the window. Sunlight glints off a plane's wing as it climbs into the gauzy clouds. I grew up in the flight path of a military base, and I'd often see giant cargo planes making their approach. They seemed to be impossibly large and to move impossibly slowly; it was a wonder they could fly at all.

"I'm going to Spain," I tell Anita.

Her clothing rustles as she steps up next to me. "Spain?" Her voice is neutral. "What's in Spain?"

"I've never been there. I don't want to go to Costa Rica, and I don't want to go to the island. I want to be alone, just for a few weeks. I'm not saying I'm going to move there forever or disappear. I just need some time."

I turn back to the room and stare at my duffle and the clothing spilling out of it. Blue sits by the door, Nila and Frank on either side of him, waiting patiently for me. Blue is still the biggest of the three dogs, with the height of a Great Dane, the long elegant snout of a Collie, and the markings of a Siberian Husky, he watches me with his one blue eye and one brown interpreting every move I make.

His daughter, Nila, inherited the pure white coat of her mother—a Mastiff from the mountains of Kurdish-controlled Syria—and the bright blue eyes of her father. Her gaze radiates a fierce intelligence. Her brother, Frank, is a dufus. He inherited Blue's height and markings, but has not filled out yet. His giant paws make him clumsy and his sweet nature makes him a terrible guard dog. Both puppies' snouts are shorter than Blue's, and their bodies stockier. They were hoping for a jog, but I won't get to run, not for a while. Frustration tightens my hands into fists.

"I don't know if this is the best time for a vacation, Sydney," Anita says, annoyance edging into her voice now.

"I'll be careful, I promise. I'll have Blue with me."

"What about Nila and Frank?"

"I'm going to send them on ahead to Costa Rica."

"Have you talked to Merl about that?"

I look over at her. She meets my gaze unflinching. "He'll watch them for a few weeks; it's not a big deal."

"Okay."

"I don't want my baby born into this," I burst out.

"Into what?" Anita asks, keeping her voice calm.

I pace away from the window toward the bed and start shoving my clothing into the duffle. Frustration's close cousin, anger, makes my movements jerky. "Into all this violence. Into all this..." I stop. I don't know how to express what I want for my kid. *My kid.* Jesus.

"I don't want to move to Costa Rica or an island in the middle of the freaking Pacific to be coddled by a bunch of people who think I'm a hero. I don't want to be surrounded by people who look at me like I am anything more than a flawed human." I look up from the duffle, which is now fully stuffed with my clothing. Anita is watching me, sunlight spilling around her where she leans against the window. "I need a break from Joyful Justice."

"But, Sydney—"

I hold up a hand. "This isn't me running away. I just want space. I want to be by myself. Maybe just for a month. Maybe more. I don't know."

"Okay." Anita looks down at her feet. "Fine. But just a gentle reminder that people are trying to assassinate you."

"I don't think that's true."

She meets my gaze. "You don't?"

"No. I don't think Robert is dead." Anita's eyes fill with sympathy. I shake my head and zip the duffle closed with a sharp zing. "I'm not in denial because I loved him or anything crazy like that. It just doesn't make sense to me. I mean—" I shrug and let out a breath of a laugh. "—I can see why someone would *want* to kill Robert, but the motives we've been offered don't make sense to me."

Robert's son, Fernando, who he just learned about recently, runs a criminal organization with his mother, Natalia—a former FARC rebel turned international drug dealer. Fernando wanted Robert dead for personal reasons that aligned with his business goals of destroying Joyful Justice. Fernando and Natalia are part of a criminal cabal that wants to end our crusade to exact justice with a two pronged approach—kill off key members of the organization and destroy Joyful Justice's reputation.

Fernando lured Robert, Anita, and me to the hurricane refugee center where a woman, the week earlier, had killed several people claiming Joyful Justice gave her the assault rifle she used—their first move to tarnish our reputation as a principled, organized vigilante network. Joyful Justice would never hand over a powerful weapon to a distraught person and suggest they kill indiscriminately to assuage their own pain.

While we were there, paid plants in the crowd began chanting Joyful Justice slogans before starting a riot—another attempt to make our organization look dangerous. My mother, April Madden, arrived with a bus load of Her Prophet followers—women and men, but mostly women, who believe in a burka-clad prophet who emerged from the Syrian bloodlands claiming to bring a message from God that it is time for women to rise up against the patriarchy. To release the wolf inside them and refuse to be subjugated. My mother, April Madden, has traveled the country spreading "the word".

Several vans of incels—self-described involuntary celibates who blame women for their misery and believe they are entitled to the use of any woman's body—arrived next. Turning it into a full on shit show.

In the melee, a sniper shot Robert, and he fell into the toxic waters of a canal, disappearing into its murky depths. So...I don't *know* that he died. He's like a cockroach, impossible to kill...at least that's what I've always thought.

"It is more effective to destroy Joyful Justice's reputation than to kill us off one by one. You can't destroy an idea, Anita, not with a gun. Besides, Robert was hardly an official member of Joyful Justice. The whole thing smells funny to me. And in my experience with Robert, nothing is as it seems."

Anita nods slowly. "Nothing is ever as it seems anymore, Sydney."

"What does that mean?"

Anita sighs and pushes off from the window, headed toward the food. "Everyone is in their own reality now. With social media, we all just get the feeds that are augmented for us. We think we *choose* them but we don't. Every action we make across any device is combed, analyzed, and then an algorithm gives us more of what we 'want'...more of what advertisers want us to see. There are forces doing their best to destroy Joyful Justice's reputation."

Anita looks up at me, her eyes holding a challenge. Anita will fight that war until it's won. "These are the data wars, Sydney. It's different than anything the world has faced before. False narratives and propaganda are easy to disseminate. Each message can be tailored to your world view. Killing Robert makes sense to me for one reason."

"What's that?" I ask. Anita opens a takeout container and tears into a pack of chopsticks.

"Because Robert had a lot of experience with propaganda. Fortress Global provided all kinds of security for its authoritarian clients, including weapons-grade communications. If you're a dictator, you want your people to keep loving you; makes it easier to stay in power."

I nod. "That makes sense." Anita hands me a carton of food and chopsticks. The scent of sweet hoisin hits my nose, and my stomach growls.

Anita smiles at the sound. "Eat," she says, waving at the box in my hand—it's full of steaming buns. "When Robert destroyed Fortress Global and started Dog Fight Investigations, he took one department with him whole."

"Which one?"

"His data team." Anita picks up another carton and opens her own set of chopsticks. She leans against the desk. "Data, Sydney, is the 21st century's most dangerous weapon. Not only because it makes it so easy to manipulate people but also because it turns them into the product."

"What do you mean?" I sit on the bed and bite into one of the buns. It's sweet and salty and so damn good.

"Your data becomes the product. *You* are the product for social media companies—they sell information about their users to advertisers, to anyone who wants it. The buyers can then use that intimate knowledge to sell you anything from a," she waves a chopstick in the air, "mystery novel, to a vision of the world where fascism is freedom. There are few industries where people are the product, and they are not auspicious—slavery and sex work, which as you know often turns into its own form of slavery."

"Yes," I agree, my appetite evaporating.

"Sorry." Anita gestures at my food. "Eat, it's important."

My eyes narrow. "Are you and Mulberry in cahoots?"

She laughs and digs into her own takeout box. We eat in silence. Frank sets himself up on Anita's foot, hoping for some scraps. Blue and Nila stay by the door, throwing disdainful glances at Frank's blatant tactics.

I finish a bun and hand the box to Anita; she passes me another one. As I take it, our eyes meet. "You told me before that you'd support me no matter what I decided, that you'd help me disappear if that's what I wanted."

Her eyes turn grave. "I will," she promises. "Freedom is often more important than life itself."

"I'm not planning on dying, Anita."

"No one is, Sydney. No one ever is."

CHAPTER FIVE

Lenox

A message alert chimes. I reach over and pull my phone from its cradle. *Anita.*

I put in my code and read it. *Call when you wake.*

Petra shifts next to me, rolling over and throwing a thin arm across my chest. Her pale skin stands out against the darkness of my own.

I slide out from under her embrace and head to the bathroom. Freshened up, I go into the kitchen and start a pot of coffee.

It's dreary and wet this morning, colder than early fall usually is in Istanbul, but climates are shifting the world over. The street below our window shines with last night's rain. The grocer on the corner, Ahmed, is opening his shop. The gate rises with a rattle, and he pauses to blow on his hands before unlocking the door.

The coffee machine gurgles, and I glance back to it before gathering milk and sugar.

I take a cup into the bedroom. Petra enjoys it light and sweet... nothing like her personality. She blinks her eyes open as I place it on the side table. A smile curls her lips. "Thank you, my pet," she says. I brush a kiss across her forehead before returning to the kitchen and my own mug of coffee.

I go to the safe, removing my laptop and other communication equipment, and sit on the couch. I set up the hotspot and key in my code. Petra comes out of the bedroom, wraps her arms around my shoulders, and kisses the side of my neck.

"Have you decided what to do with the girl?" She stands, her arms slipping away. "We paid a heavy price for someone so useless to us. You showed Yusuf a piece of your true self. And now we owe him."

"I could not leave her there," I answer, pulling my laptop from its bag and putting it on the coffee table, leaving my lap free, anticipating that Petra will want to climb into it. She comes around the couch and stands in front of me.

"It has only been a day, Lenox, but you cannot leave her at The Dragon's Cage forever." We dropped her at one of our clubs before heading home. She left Yusuf's suite with just the dress she wore and barely spoke two words the entire cab ride. We both knew she did not want to be a sex worker.

"I know. I'm sorry that it'll cause us trouble."

Petra rolls her eyes. "Lenox," she purrs, "you are such a good negotiator if you keep your heart out of it. Please." She steps closer and puts a knee on the couch by my thigh, leaning over me. "Do not do something that stupid again."

I smile as she throws her other leg over my lap and rests her weight onto me. "I will try."

She puts a hand on each cheek and stares down at me. "I worry about you."

It's as close to "I love you" as we'll ever get.

I tilt my chin, and she lowers her mouth to meet mine. We kiss deeply, her hips shifting on my lap, and she lets out a soft moan. "Go get in the shower," I tell her. She raises a brow. "I must make a private call."

She laughs and stands. "You are too much, Lenox Gold."

The shower turns on as I boot up my laptop. *You awake?* I text Anita. It's 8:00 a.m. in Istanbul, so after midnight in Miami. *Yes*, she responds quickly.

I put in my earbuds and dial her number, using the app that Dan installed on my computer. It allows for private conversations away from prying eyes and ears. "What's going on?" I ask when she picks up. Last we'd spoken, everyone was back at the hotel safe and sound after a harrowing escape from a gang of incels at a refugee center in hurricane-ravaged Miami. Everyone except Robert Maxim, who apparently was shot and killed. I'll cry a river next time I cut an onion.

Anita sighs. "It's been a bloody crazy forty-eight hours."

I respond with an affirmative sound but don't speak. She needs space to talk.

"First I get a frantic text from Mulberry saying that Sydney is bleeding profusely, barely conscious and headed for the hospital. She's okay—it was a complication from the pregnancy," Anita is quick to add. "And the baby is fine."

Good. Though a miscarriage could be a blessing. I have no idea how she will raise a child. Our enemies will work hard to destroy it, and therefore Sydney. It makes her extremely vulnerable.

"So I get to the hospital and everything is fine. Sydney is, of course, being a pain in the ass." There is a note of humor in her voice. "Then I get back here, and Dan calls a few hours later to tell me his mother is sick, he's headed halfway across the world to be with her, and he is leaving everything in Rachel's hands."

"Rachel?" I turn the name over in my mouth. "She took over as his second-in-command after..." I leave the unfortunate incident of the infiltration and blackmail of Dan's team hanging in the air. Anita and I both know what happened. There is no need to rehash it. My eyes drift to the window. Ahmed is building a tower of oranges now.

Without that infiltration, I wouldn't be here. I wouldn't have met up with Petra again. I wouldn't be in charge of a network of brothels. Ian McCain's brothers would still be alive, and Yusuf wouldn't be *my* problem.

"Yes, that's right," Anita confirms my assumption about Rachel. "So he is flying to New Jersey right now."

"I see, and you are still in Miami. Sydney is with you?"

"Yes, but she is, get this, going to Spain."

"Why?"

"Fuck if I know."

"Anita, you sound frustrated."

"I am! Sorry to yell. Sorry, Lenox." She sighs. "We need to have a council meeting. I've spoken with Merl briefly. Mulberry is going to head to Costa Rica and help out there and also just get out of the way." She gives a sharp laugh. "He's all kinds of messed up about Sydney going to Spain. She said she needs a break from everything."

"I imagine. That makes sense for both of them. The looming responsibility of motherhood coupled with the physical limitations of her growing pregnancy will be an extreme challenge for Sydney. And for Mulberry, I can see it must be very frustrating to be so emotionally involved with someone so incapable of vulnerability."

Anita laughs. "You are..." Her voice fades away into a breathy laugh. A smile tugs at my lips. "You're right. Very well put, Lenox. You should have been a therapist."

"My profession is not so different. I've always done more listening than anything else."

She laughs again. "That makes total sense." Her voice sounds more relaxed. Listening can ease so much stress and pain. But it is difficult for many. I wait in silence to see if Anita has more she needs to share. "Would a council meeting in two hours work for you?" Anita asks.

"Yes." The shower turns off, and I hear Petra moving around in the bathroom. "Talk to you then."

We hang up, and I return my equipment to my bag. Petra comes out dressed for the day in tight jeans, a beige turtleneck, and stockinged feet. "Will you run down and get some fruit? I crave papaya, and we are out," she says, pouring herself another cup of coffee.

"If you wish." I move toward the door, swiping my phone, gun, keys, and wallet off the table by the door. I put the small pistol into the belt holster at my low back and pull my shirt over it. When I turn back to Petra, she is standing at the kitchen bar, watching me with that strange intensity. Our eyes meet, and unspoken truths flitter in the air between us.

We've made promises to remain loyal to each other in practical ways, but the vulnerability that Mulberry begs from Sydney is not on the table.

Neither of us have offered or asked for that depth of connection. Are either of us even capable of it?

"I'll be right back."

She smiles, her lips bare and eyes still puffy from sleep.

I wonder if that deeper connection can sneak up on you, lie in the grass waiting as a snake does, enjoying the warmth of the sun, then strike, poisoning and paralyzing from a place that moments ago was utter stillness.

EK

"Ahmed, *Gunaydin*," I say as I approach the fruit and vegetable stand. The sun has peeked from between the clouds, and I didn't bother with a jacket. A cool breeze whips through my thermal shirt, and I shrug off the chill.

Ahmed turns from where he is crouched, organizing watermelons. A thin man with narrow shoulders and thick black hair that catches the light like a record, he grins when our eyes meet.

"Good morning!" He knows I've exhausted my Turkish. He stands and turns to a stack of papayas. "Very fresh today. And Frida, she made you some more yogurt."

"Wonderful, thank you, and please thank your sister." He moves to the small fridge behind the counter and pulls out a jar, placing it next to the old-fashioned cash register.

"I think she will be sorry she missed you." Ahmed waggles his eyebrows and bursts into laugher.

I shake my head, ignoring the insinuation as I pick out a papaya. His sister is barely eighteen and mad for me. Petra says I encourage her, but really all I am is polite. Placing the papaya on the counter next to the yogurt, I pull out my wallet.

A bill slips free and flutters to the ground. As I bend to pick it up, I hear the sharp sound of glass cracking, and Ahmed sucks in a breath.

I glance up to see him tip to the side. My heart thunders. Staying low and hidden behind the fruit display, I crawl around the counter. Ahmed lies on his side, his eyes wide and fearful. The man's hands grip his stomach. Blood seeps from between his clenched fingers.

Ripping my shirt over my head, I press it to the wound with one hand while wrestling my phone free with the other. "Hold this," I tell Ahmed. He wraps his bloody hands around the shirt.

Dialing 112, I press the phone to Ahmed's ear. Using my free right hand, I pull the gun from my waist holster.

Ahmed speaks in pained tones.

"Ahmed?" Frida's head pops over the counter. Her eyes widen.

"Get down!" I command. She doesn't move. "Now!" I seethe. Her eyes move off her brother to me.

Frida's oval face, framed by a navy head scarf, is pale. Her eyes land on the pistol in my hand, and she jerks as if slapped. "You shot him?" Her voice is a bare whisper of pain and fear.

"No, get down!"

Instead, she turns and runs into the street, screaming for help. No one shoots her. Sirens stir to life in the distance. Yogurt drips off the counter and mixes with the blood on the floor.

I rise to my knees, keeping my head down. The shooter is probably in the building where Petra and I have an apartment. It's got the best advantage. Taking my phone back from Ahmed's ear, I hang up on emergency services—they are on their way—and call Petra.

She doesn't answer. I can see our window, but the sun glints off it, obscuring any activity inside. I dial her again, and this time there is an answer. "Lenox Gold," Ian McCain's Irish brogue reaches across the line.

"Ian," I say, scanning the shop, shutting down all emotion. The best actors can turn it off as much as on. I start to crawl toward the back door, keeping close to the fruit displays so that a sharpshooter won't be able to see me.

Frida is still screaming, and the sirens are growing closer. I reach up and turn the knob of the back door. As it swings open, a brush of cold air caresses my naked chest, raising goose bumps. The storage room. I've never seen a truck pull up to the front of the shop, so deliveries must come through the back.

I crawl in and shut the door behind me, cloaking the room in darkness. "You want Petra back?" Ian asks.

The air is thick with the sweet scent of fresh fruit and the crisp coolness of produce. "She's alive then?" I ask, switching to speaker so that I can turn on the flashlight. Ian laughs as I run the beam over shelves lined with cardboard boxes.

"Yes, she's alive," Ian answers. "I plan to have some fun with her." The insinuation is clear, but Ian continues. "I'm going to fuck her like the bitch she is." My body stiffens, but I keep moving. Sometimes we must remove ourselves from our body and allow it to work without the conscious mind interfering.

"What do you want?" I ask as my light hits a back door. I move toward it, one hand holding the phone, the other gripping my pistol.

I turn the deadbolt and yank the door open. Sunlight streams in with no shadows from unseen attackers. But there is a truck, old and battered and just begging to be stolen—as if Ahmed needed anymore crap luck today.

"What do I want?" Ian asks. "I want my brothers back!" His voice rises in anger. *Anger leads to mistakes.*

Glancing around the storage room, I spot a red toolbox. A screwdriver waits in the top compartment. "But since that's impossible," Ian goes on, "I'll take Petra's life, after I've used her up." I find a wrench under a greasy rag in the bottom.

"If you kill her, what will that do?" I ask, moving out the door into the now sun-filled day. It warms my bare skin, and I squint against the glare.

Ian laughs as I pull open the unlocked driver's side door of the truck. "Revenge, obviously," Ian says. "What possible reason would I have to let her live?"

"She is valuable to me."

He laughs again, a big, broad sound that rolls out of the phone as I lower the visor. *No key.* I wedge the screwdriver into the key cover.

"How valuable?" Ian asks, his voice dipping lower.

The key cover comes off in my hand, and I use the screwdriver to pull the plastic away from the key mount. "How much do you want?" I ask.

"You think I want money?" Ian asks. "Do you think there's a price, a monetary price that can make us even?"

I put the screwdriver down and pick up the wrench, opening it to fit around the ignition turnstile. "If it's not money you want, then what?" Sweat trickles down my nose, and I swipe at it. Despite the chilly day and my bare skin, I'm hot.

"Come back to your apartment," Ian says. "We will negotiate. Yusuf says you're quite the negotiator." I clamp the wrench onto the key mount and turn. The engine rumbles to life.

"Come back to the apartment? What will stop you from killing me and Petra?"

Ian laughs again. "Petra's not worth risking your life over?"

"You're not asking me to risk it. You're asking me to offer it up on a silver platter." I take the phone off speaker and hold it between my ear and shoulder as I pull the truck out into the road and start down the alleyway.

"I'll catch you eventually. If you come now, I'll let you both die quickly."

It's not a bad offer, not really, but one of the key tenets in negotiations is to never take the first offer. I turn onto the main road and start navigating away from the apartment. "How about instead, you let her go and I let you live?" *Open with a big ask...*

Ian chuckles softly. "You're in no position to negotiate. Come here now, and I'll be kind enough to kill you quickly. Make me hunt you down, and I promise you'll regret it."

"You'll make me regret it?" I mirror him.

"That's right."

"It seems like you think I deserve a painful death."

"I do."

"You're angry," I surmise.

"I'm beyond angry. I will have my revenge on you. I will take it on Petra now. She will be dead before sunrise. She'll be begging for it by nightfall. You could change all that. You are choosing her death for her."

"Only God can choose our death, Ian."

"That's wrong. Only God can choose where we go after we die. Men decide each other's departure every day. You chose for my brothers. Petra's in my hands; you will be as well soon." His breath is heavy.

"I will be in your hands soon," I mirror again.

He laughs, and I hear movement on the other side of the line, as though he is walking through the apartment. "I'm going to go now. Your woman awaits my attention. See you soon, Lenox."

He hangs up. I take the phone from my ear and throw it on the passenger seat, concentrating on the traffic ahead. I have until nightfall, perhaps even until sunrise to save her life.

CHAPTER SIX

Lenox

The door slides to the side, and a pair of brown eyes blink at me through the opening. I tilt my head and raise a brow, indicating for her to open the door.

The locks disengaged with a solid clunk of metal, and Anna opens the door of The Dragon's Cage. She gives me a shy, confused smile. Probably wondering why I'm here so early in the day and why I don't have a shirt on.

I don't answer those questions. I offer her a reassuring smile as I step into the building, closing the door and setting the locks. "Is Johnathan up yet?" I ask. She shakes her head. "Okay."

I move through the bar area, its silk-draped walls and plush furnishings recently installed. The brothel doesn't open for hours, but most of the girls and our manager sleep on-site.

Ian knows this location. It used to belong to him, but he'd never recognize it. The air is perfumed by an incense infuser, and the bar is stocked with top-shelf liquors. When he and his brothers ran it, the women were prisoners, the drinks half poison, and the air fetid.

We removed the former manager and put one of my lieutenants in charge with plans to train one of the women to run it. Her maternity leave began last week, so we had several months to set up our systems. *We still do*, I remind myself.

Petra and I always expected Ian to come after us. Petra worked with the McCain brothers for a decade before attempting to enlist me in their plans to destroy Joyful Justice. Instead, I convinced Petra to join me in bringing freedom and justice to the sex trade.

There is nothing inherently wrong with selling one's body for pleasure. Criminalizing the sale of women's bodies is another form of patriarchal control. And because it is illegal, women need protection not only from clients but also law enforcement creating an even larger loss of power.

This is why for a long time I only traded men. But Petra convinced me that the only way to truly change the business was from the inside. And so I agreed to take over the brothels and trade routes she'd run with the McCain brothers.

We always knew Ian would come for his revenge. This is not a surprise, and we are not without resources or protocols in place. Like Yusuf, we prepare.

I pass the bar and enter the long hall lined with closed doors that lead to the workers' rooms. It's quiet since the place only closed about five hours ago.

At the end of the hallway, I knock on Johnathan's apartment door. When he answers his hair is mussed from sleep, his pale brown eyes puffy. "Lenox." Johnathan's eyes lower to my chest. "Why are you at my door half naked at this ungodly hour?" His British accent manages to make the question sound respectable.

Fascinating how our brains perceive trustworthiness in the vocal tones of our conquerors. The British empire at its height ruled over a quarter of the earth's population. Only 10 percent of those 430 million people lived on the island in the Atlantic that we know today as the United Kingdom. The empire oppressed native populations and ravaged their lands for resources; yet the world over, a posh British accent is associated with trustworthy stewardship.

"I need clothing and cash," I tell him. "Then we will evacuate."

His eyes sharpen. "What's going on?" He steps back to let me in. His living room is sparsely decorated—the new furniture is set to arrive next week. A stack of books sits on a worn coffee table next to the slouchy couch.

Our shared passion for reading is one of the things that bonded us more than a decade ago when we first met on the French Riviera. We were both working the season—he as the full-time companion of a royal dame, and me as an independent contractor seeing several clients.

Johnathan disappears into the bedroom and comes back moments later with a white, long-sleeved shirt and a hoodie. "Not the hoodie," I tell him. "Give me the nicest sweater you have, something cashmere."

He gives me a look that says, *Really, now?*

"I'm a dark-skinned man. I need to look wealthy, or I'll look dangerous." Cashmere, like British accents, is trusted.

He nods, his brow furrowing, and returns to his bedroom to fulfill my request.

The sweater is tight across my chest, but the soft violet speaks of long, liquid brunches on sunny afternoons. "Start the evacuation process," I say. "Phoenix Rising."

Johnathan blinks a few times, his cheeks coloring, before turning to his phone. He sends the message to our other brothels and safe houses then heads down the hallway to start waking up the girls, following the steps we have in place.

Alone in the apartment, I call the Joyful Justice emergency line. It rings once before the line fills with soft static. "Phoenix Falling," I say into the void, then hang up.

I take a deep breath and wait for the return call.

Anita rings me. "Are you in a secure location?" she asks, all the frustration and exhaustion that edged her voice earlier gone despite the later hour.

"Yes, but Ian has Petra."

Anita sucks in a long, slow breath. "What do you need?"

"We are evacuating all the known locations in Istanbul until we know how much muscle he brought with him. I'll need an extraction team to get Petra back. I believe they are holding her in our apartment." *Holding isn't the correct word for what they are doing...*

"Dan is in the air but sent me a link to surveillance in your apartment. I'm sending it to you now."

My phone pings with the message. "How does he have surveillance of my apartment, Anita?"

"I don't ask Dan questions like that... anymore. I find I don't like the answers. But I do enjoy the safety that comes with the knowledge."

Anger sputters in my chest, searching for an outlet, but I quash it. These are my allies. "I don't like it."

"You will when you watch it. You're right that they are still in the apartment. Petra is unharmed as of now." Relief engulfs me, and suddenly it feels like I can breathe again. I hadn't even realized how strangled I felt. "I'll have Rachel deploy an extraction team to location..." I hear keys tapping as she looks up the code for our Istanbul rendezvous points. "Location Zed."

A stall at the Grand Bazaar... close to where I bought the unicorn tapestry. "Got it. Location Zed." It will take the team at least a few hours to assemble and meet me.

"I'll have Rachel update you as necessary." She pauses for a moment, the phone microphone rubbing against fabric as if she's adjusting it before her voice comes back. "Good luck, Lenox."

"Thank you." *I'll need it.*

The building is coming to life as Johnathan wakes the workers. There are footsteps and tinkles of nervous laughter.

I check the text Anita sent and click the link. My iPhone uses my face as the password, and the screen fills with a view of the living room I've never seen before. It is as if I'm a fly on the top of the window frame. Petra sits on the couch, her face calm and still. Ian paces behind her. Two large men sit at the kitchen barstools, guns holstered, and bodies relaxed.

I turn up the volume on my phone when Petra begins to speak.

"Don't worry, Ian," she says. "He will come."

"And if he doesn't?" Ian stops his pacing to stare down at Petra. She looks tiny—all thin bones and feminine curves—next to him. Ian is a large man, over six feet by a few inches, with broad shoulders. His leather jacket shines in the light as if it's new. His hair is the same pitch-black as the leather and cut short. A sheen of sweat glows on his pale face.

"Lenox is a good man," Petra says, her tone unconcerned, as if she is just laying out fact. "He will do what good men do. Try to save the woman in distress." It does not sound like a compliment.

Ian shakes his head. "You better be right. If this fails, you'll pay for all your mistakes, Petra."

She waves an unconcerned hand at him. "He will be here."

I take in a slow, even breath. Johnathan comes back into the room. "We are ready to go," he says. His color is still high, eyes bright with the excitement and perceived danger of the moment.

"Good. Go."

"What about you?"

"I will see you soon," I promise. "Be safe, old friend."

His eyes narrow, but he doesn't contradict me. "Be safe."

Johnathan closes the door behind him, and I return my attention to Petra—a snake in the grass or a gazelle trying to talk her way out of the lion's grip. I will listen and learn.

Listening is so powerful. Especially when the speaker doesn't know you can hear.

EK

Location Zed is the storage area of a towel and bath goods merchant deep in the bowels of the Grand Bizarre. Stacks of striped Turkish towels in dreamy peaches and pale pastels gives the dim space a sense of promise. *Good times with sun and surf will come soon.*

The owners—a mother and daughter—leave me with an elegant glass of mint tea to wait for the extraction team. I pull out my phone, unlocking it with my gaze, and return to watching Ian and Petra.

I'm confused. My early assumption of betrayal is challenged by the reality that they could have easily taken me in the apartment. If Petra is indeed on their side, I've been a fish with a hook in my mouth for months, lazily swimming into shallower waters, making it easier for them to yank me out. Yet, this morning, Petra sent me down to the market, providing what proved to be an avenue to escape.

Maybe she is not betraying me—that she's following some other plan.

I want her to care for me. To be loyal.

I want her to fight for me as I will fight for her.

We met again because she was plotting against Joyful Justice—not knowing my affiliation. Petra chose to join with us once we settled our differences. She agreed to change the way she ran her business. Or did she lie, pretending and waiting for my defenses to lower?

Ian rifles through our refrigerator, turning back to one of the men. "Liam," he yells. The large man looks up lazily, his big body still relaxed, taking on none of the urgency of his leader. "Did you take the last cola."

It sits on the counter in front of Liam, the accusation impossible to deny. "Sorry," he says, his voice a low baritone that hardly reaches the speakers.

Ian stands, holding a carton of milk. "Am I supposed to drink this?"

Liam doesn't respond; the question does seem to be rhetorical. Ian is vibrating with anger. He hurls the carton of milk at Liam, who dodges, the carton exploding against the wall behind him. "What the fuck?" Ian yells. "How long is this going to take?" He turns his wrath onto Petra, who glances over her shoulder at him, her air of nonchalance a sharp contrast to his temper.

"Ian, I told you he will come. Stop your worrying." Petra's eyes flick to the camera. *Does she know it's there?* "Lenox expected you to make a move, but he did not expect to fall in love with me." She drops her gaze. "As I promised, he will come unprepared. He will throw himself on the bomb for me. I tried to stop him from going out, but the man loves his morning papaya."

She is lying to Ian.

It is as natural to her as breathing. How can I tell the difference between the truth and her self-serving fabrications?

"How can you be so sure of your own powers when you can't even get him to stay in bed instead of going grocery shopping?" There is derision in Ian's voice.

"I am sure of Lenox Gold."

Ian slams the fridge closed and glares at Liam, who drops his gaze. Liam is wearing a black leather jacket and jeans, like his boss, but he is a larger and softer man. The other henchman stares, bored, out the window while eating from a bag of nuts.

Ian focuses his attention on the nut eater. "Conner."

The large man turns his head toward his boss. "Yeah?"

"Stop eating those. You're already a fat fuck."

Conner, who is even bigger than Liam, so that his black leather jacket looks like a cow dressed up like a bull, puts the nuts down.

Ian comes out from behind the kitchen bar and approaches Petra. "Maybe you are in love with Lenox and not the other way around?"

She shakes her head, a smile crossing those cruel lips. "I am not capable of such depth of feeling, Ian. You must know that about me by now." She leans back into the couch cushions, appearing totally at ease.

"I never thought you'd kill my brothers." Anger edges Ian's voice, and his fists clench as he places them on the back of the couch.

Petra pouts, angling her head to better look him in the face. "I told you that was Lenox. I never wanted them dead."

"You want your lover dead now?" He leans over her, trying to intimidate her with his size.

Petra does not answer for a long moment.

My heart hammers. What is she up to? Why am I turned on by her duplicity? Am I so unworthy of love that I want it desperately from a woman who will see me dead?

"I don't want him killed." She looks up at Ian. "But I know that you will never give up. I'd rather lose him than watch my back for the rest of my life. Besides, his way of doing business isn't as profitable."

Ian nods, smiling, understanding and believing in greed. Petra is a master at mirroring—better than me. She is showing him what he wants to see. Reinforcing his viewpoint. Most women learn it more easily than men. They are trained from birth to reflect what society wants to see. It is how they survive.

Ian turns away from Petra, and she looks back to the window... at the camera. Her eyes are hard. But she seems to be looking straight at me. The hairs on the back of my neck slowly rise.

Hearing footsteps on the far side of the storage room, I jerk my gaze up from the screen and pull the earbuds free. A light knock on the door settles my nerves a little. Killers don't usually knock so politely, but my hand hovers near my weapon as I rise to answer.

It's Palma, the towel merchant's daughter. She is a foot shorter than me, her thin face framed by a bright pink head scarf. "Do you need anything?" she asks.

"No, thank you."

She bows slightly and leaves me alone again. A ping on my phone draws my attention. It's another link from Anita with the dossier on the team members en route. I settle back into the hard, wooden chair between the piles of cheerful towels to read.

The leader, Hans Steiner, is a retired officer from the Jagdkommando—the special forces arm of the Austrian army. The photo shows him staring into the camera, a man in his early 50s whose piercing blue eyes penetrate through the screen.

I sip my tea and glance around the room. When I return my attention to the phone, it has gone blank—one of Dan's security measures. Whenever we are looking at personnel files, the phone deactivates unless it sees my retinas. If anyone hacked into my phone, they'd never find the files. If they hold it up to my face to force my passcode, all I have to do is show teeth and it will open, but to a decoy phone that looks like any normal businessman's device.

I scan over Han's list of specialties: extraction, explosives, leadership. He will be a powerful ally.

I open the next file. Ramona Jones, a former rodeo champion who grew up on the circuit—both her parents champions as well. In her photo, she is looking past the camera, her thick brows pulled together in thought, a halo of thick curls blowing in the wind.

She went into the US army at twenty-one and left it ten years later—honorably discharged but pissed as hell.

Recruits find their way to Joyful Justice from many paths, but often the women have suffered a sexual assault. Our name and the vengeance we offer is whispered about in support groups. Many women can't go back to life as it was before the incident, so they choose to join us and fight to stop it happening to anyone else. I suspect Ramona Jones is one of those women.

Sophia Boucher... *Butcher.* She is French and pretty as a picture with a button nose, wide eyes, and long waves of golden hair. In the photo attached to her file, she has a silk scarf draped around her neck. A former pilot for the French Air Force, she lost an arm in Afghanistan, which led to an honorable discharge.

This is another road that fighters take to reach us. When they've been cast off as unfit by other armies, we still find use for them. You do not need all your limbs to fight for justice, certainly not to thirst for it.

They should be here soon.

Whether Petra is setting me or Ian up, I need to get her back. I need answers.

CHAPTER SEVEN

Sydney

There is an armed guard at my mother's front door wearing a checkered button-down shirt and a pair of jeans that fit like he's some kind of cowboy. His blazer does a piss-poor job of covering up the gun under each arm. Where did she find him? Is he a hired gun or a devotee to my mother's cause?

He nods to me and Blue as we move down the hall toward him. He's not one of Robert's men—all polished black outfits and dead eyes. Robert was shot and fell into a canal teeming with toxic chemicals and flesh-eating bacteria. *He won't be providing security for anyone anymore.*

I push the thought aside, not fully believing it. Either my instincts are right and Robert is still alive, or I'm in denial that a man I've always considered indestructible has finally been destroyed. By his own son no less. It's one of those things I can't look at fully or I might feel something too deep and dark to ever come out the other side.

My mother's head of security, Veronica, opens the apartment door and smiles at me, then down at Blue. "Welcome," she says. Veronica is not your average head of security. A self-identified witch, she wears long, flowing tunics and a head wrap. Today they are a brown green that matches her eyes... and some of the outer rings of bruising on her face.

The air has an acrid scent to it, and smoke rises around Veronica like she is some kind of apparition.

She holds up a smoldering bundle of herbs. "It's sage," she explains. "It cleanses and heals." *Ah, now it makes sense... not.*

Veronica invites Blue and me in, waving her hand toward a velvet couch; its rich navy plush reminds me of a red mohair I owned back in New York. Inherited from my grandmother, along with her rent-controlled apartment, the red majesty of its presence was like a wealthy aunt who'd fallen on hard times but refused to take off the tiara.

Veronica steps to an elegant, smooth-finished cherry sideboard and snuffs the sage out into a bowl. She picks up a teapot nestled in a hand-crocheted cozy as I settle on the couch. Blue sits next to me and leans against my leg.

I recognize the canary-and-peach striped cozy. My neighbor in New York, Nona—also inherited from my grandmother—stitched it. I'll have to ask Mom how she is doing. Guilt churns in my stomach. Nona loved me, and I let her think I died. She might be gone by now...

"Would you like some raspberry tea?" Veronica asks. "It's very good for pregnancy. Tones the uterus."

B'scuse me? "Sure..." She smiles at the uncertainty in my voice before turning back to the sideboard and pouring the tea. Steam curls into the air.

"Where is Mom?" I ask, scanning the apartment. It is one of two that take up the second story in a converted mansion in Coral Gables, a small city that functions as a posh section of Miami. What was once a large house for a single family is now apartments. Outside the tall casement windows, denuded palm trees stand like mutilated Barbies. While Coral Gables didn't get hit with flooding from the hurricane, the winds took off a lot of roofs and stripped all the greenery away.

"She'll be out in a minute. She's getting dressed."

"How are you feeling?" I ask as Veronica settles on the other side of the couch, passing me a cup of tea and cradling her own.

She winces and smiles. "I hurt, but I'll be fine." During the riots where Robert was shot, Veronica threw herself in front of a van to save my mother. I killed the driver—a murder that hasn't crossed my mind until now. What kind of a person kills with such ease? What kind of a mother could they possibly be?

The man deserved it, I think. A self-professed involuntary celibate, he and a group of other incels attacked my mother and her followers. It's only been a few days since the brawl that broke out between the two groups at the hurricane refugee center.

The image of Robert disappearing under the murky, toxic canal water flashes through my mind—the bloom of blood on his chest, the splash his body made when it hit the water, the way he sank as though the depths welcomed him home. I shake my head, trying to dispel the image.

I blow on the tea Veronica handed me before taking a sip. It's earthy and slightly sweet.

The bedroom door opens, and Mom steps out, bringing the humid, scented air of a recent shower with her. She's wearing a white blouse and khaki pants. A gold chain disappears into the neckline. I'd bet money a cross hangs at the apex. Her hair is still damp and pushed carelessly off her bare face. She gives me a big smile, and I stand, putting my tea on a side table to accept the hug she offers.

"I was so happy when I got your text saying you wanted to come see me," she says, leaning away but keeping her hands on my shoulders. Mom is slightly shorter than me, but we have the same eyes—an otherworldly mercury gray that instantly identifies us as family. James had them too. I almost start to tell her about the dream but stop myself. The skin around her eyes tightens. "What is it, honey?"

I take a deep breath and pull away, folding back down onto the couch and bringing my tea close, a defense against her watchful gaze, a scalding weapon if I need one...

"Nothing." I smile up at her, and she lets it go, turning to a nearby armchair and sitting.

"Would you like tea?" Veronica asks her.

Mom waves her away. "You're not getting anything for me. Don't be silly."

"I noticed the tea cozy. Are you still in touch with Nona?" I ask.

"Oh." Mom turns and looks back at it. "Yes, she's doing well."

"Do you travel with it?" I glance around the rental again. I recognize other items—a painting that hung in the entryway of the house I grew up in, another that was my maternal grandmother's. "Wait, are you here full time? I thought this was just a short-term rental. Are you living in Miami?"

"We moved in a few weeks ago." Mom smiles. "Just made sense with how much time I was spending in Florida. Though I've hardly been here what with all the speaking engagements."

"Oh..." I don't even know where my mother lives. My head suddenly pounds.

"So," Mom says, crossing her legs, "how are you feeling? I was so sick with your brother I could barely move." She grins as if that's a positive memory.

"I'm fine," I say, leaving out the whole hemorrhage thing. "Just tired and a little nauseous now and then."

"Have your partner bring you crackers in the morning before you even lift your head," Veronica advices. "That really helps."

I nod, like I have a partner and a morning routine that might include them bringing me crackers. A subtle chime rings from inside Veronica's tunic. She reaches into one of the large pockets and pulls out her phone. "Time to take my medication," she says. Her face twists with pain as she stands. Mom gets up and tries to help her, but Veronica shakes her head. "I'm fine." She points to her seat. "Visit with Sydney. I'll be back in a little while."

Mom rubs Veronica's arm, her face all sincere concern. Veronica smiles back at her, adoration glowing in her gaze. I look down at Blue, uncomfortable with the reality that people think my mom is some kind of messenger from a higher power.

"So," Mom says, taking Veronica's place on the couch and pulling one leg up so that she can more fully face me, "I want to hear everything."

Blue sighs and rests his head on my thigh. I lay my hand on his ruff and massage him as I turn to her.

"I'm leaving, Mom, going somewhere I'll be safe." The words taste like ash in my mouth. I don't deserve to be safe. "Where the baby will be safe." *That's better.*

Mom sighs, relief wafting off her. "That makes me so happy." She laughs, reaching for my hands, scooting closer. "Of course, I'd like to be with you as much as possible. But I really want you to be safe." Mom grins. "All any mother wants is for her baby to be safe."

I guess. Wait. What is that smell? I narrow my eyes, and see guilt behind my mother's smiling gaze. Under the flowery perfume of her recent shower, a sharp scent lurks. As soon as my mind registers it, that's all I can smell. *Alcohol. She's drinking again.*

EK

"She's drinking again," I hiss at Veronica when she shows me to the door. The taller woman meets my gaze, but her eyes are unreadable. "That doesn't concern you?"

"All is as it should be."

I shake my head. "No, it's not. She is *not* a good drunk."

"Your mother is on her path."

I take a step back, my anger needing more room to rage. "She might be on *her* path, but she is holding up a freaking flag, telling everyone that *her* path is *the* path. When really, she's a wandering drunk in the woods. I've seen her fall off cliffs. I won't watch again."

"Understood."

"What does that mean?"

"I can see you're upset."

"Well, you're really fucking observant."

Veronica slow blinks at me. *Slow blinks. At me.* I throw up my hands. "What's your plan? Are you going to follow her off the cliff? Or are you going to jump off it for her?"

That was a low blow. She saved my mother's life. I'm an asshole. Fuck.

"I wish you well in your travels, wherever they may lead you."

I swallow and nod. She is dismissing me. "I just hope you are as willing to save the poor idiots who think my mother is some kind of messenger from God as you are willing to save my mother."

She doesn't respond, just looks at the door, then back at me. *She and Merl would get along.*

I leave. What else can I do? I walk past cowboy security man, out the front door of the old mansion, and head for the airport. I have Blue, my duffle, and a one-way ticket to Barcelona.

My phone rings as I get in the Uber. It's Mulberry. I take a breath, bracing myself. He did not take it well when I told him I planned to leave. The fact that I didn't say goodbye this morning *might* be why he's calling now.

"What in the actual fuck, Sydney?" Mulberry yells when I pick up. "Did you plan to say goodbye? Or are you just running off without even a word? A word!"

"I told you I was leaving." I struggle to keep my voice down. Mulberry blew up at me this morning already. So I didn't come and say goodbye before heading to my mother's. Sometimes when you act like an ass, people don't want to be around you. I should know. "I'll see you soon."

"Soon!"

Big vocabulary this one.

"Calm down."

"What? Calm down! The mother of my child is running off to God knows where when she is supposed to be on bed rest. You show up this morning before I've even had my coffee to tell me. Then just—" He's sputtering now, unable to get any words out for a minute. I concentrate on evening my breath. "You just disappear. And I'm supposed to calm down! I'm not calm. I am freaking out."

"Look." I keep my voice low. What with the driver just a few feet away, I don't need to start screaming. "I understand you are invested in this situation."

"Invested!"

"But this is *my* life. *My* body—"

"It's not just you in that body anymore."

I take in a deep breath through my nose and close my eyes. After counting to three, I open them again. "You dumb fuck." I say it low, but the Uber driver's eyes jump to the mirror. "I am fully aware of what is happening to me. What *you* need to get is that *you* don't have a say here.

You care. I get that. I appreciate it. I know what you want. You've been incredibly clear. But I don't know what *I* want. And it will be impossible to figure that out without some space to think and just be."

"Be!"

"Stop yelling," I grind out.

"Sorry! But..." He sighs. "Why, please, just." He is stuttering again. "People are trying to kill you. Kill all of us. Can't you please just go somewhere safe?"

"I am." *Barcelona has a very low rate of violent crimes.* "Besides, you know I'm hard to kill."

"Please," he's begging now, and I can't have that. I just can't.

"Stop it. This is necessary."

"I don't think I can lose you."

"You won't have to," I promise. Both of us are good at lying. The perfect parents. I should pick up an apron for me and a fedora for Mulberry—we can be the Cleavers.

He sighs again. "I wish you'd come and said goodbye. That you'd tell me where you are going. It hurts that you won't."

"Sorry. I didn't want to have to punch you." I smile. He chuckles low in his throat. It's a sexy sound, and a zing of regret pulses through me. *No.* I need space to think. To figure out what I want and need. To figure out how I'm going to do this… any of it.

My phone beeps that there is someone on the other line. "I have to go. I'm getting another call."

"Let me know once you land, please. Just let me know you're safe."

"Okay." I switch to the other line—an unknown Miami number—before Mulberry can say anything else.

"Hello, my name is Teresa Johnson. I'm Mr. Robert Maxim's estate attorney and the executor of his will. Do you have a moment to talk?"

My mouth goes dry. "Sure," I say.

"I have a letter from Mr. Maxim for you."

"Of course you do," I say with a laugh.

"He wanted me to give it to you in person. Are you in Miami?"

"I'm just leaving."

"I see. When will you be back? The transfer of assets is easier if you can sign some paperwork in person."

"Transfer of assets?"

"Yes, Ms. Rye."

I wait for her to say more, but when she doesn't, I prompt her. "What assets?"

"I'm uncomfortable saying more over the phone, having no way of knowing Mr. Maxim's wishes as to your knowledge of his bequest prior to reading the letter he left you."

This is so Robert Maxim. Fucking with me even from beyond the grave. The guy is unbelievable. "I'm on my way to the airport."

"May I suggest you come to my office first? You won't need to fly commercial ever again, Ms. Rye."

I take in a deep breath. "He left me a plane."

"Much more than that. Much more."

Robert fucking Maxim.

EK

Teresa Johnson's blush pink suit flows over smooth curves, the pants narrowing to hug her ankles and accentuate the heels the woman is walking around in as if they are her slippers. The hair defies the laws of nature—a perfect platinum bob that frames her heart-shaped face with its pouty lips and perfectly applied makeup.

Next to her, I am a hot mess. A tire fire of a woman with my worn jeans, scuffed combat boots, and bare skin. At least my T-shirt is new. Her secretary offers to take my duffle bag—her kind eyes appearing not to judge me. "I'm good," I tell her. "It's not heavy."

Blue taps his nose to my hip, and I lay a hand on his head. "Coffee? Tea? Sparkling water?" Teresa offers as she moves around her yacht-sized desk, gesturing to one of the leather contraptions she's using as guest chairs.

"Just water, please," I say. "Some for Blue as well if you have a bowl."

"Of course." Teresa smiles at Blue, and the secretary leaves, presumably to get the water.

I sit in the chair, slipping deep into the low-slung thing. My boots barely reach the floor. I scoot forward, resting my elbows on my knees. Teresa sits across the expanse of glass desktop, her ankles crossing under it, her hands folding onto the black leather blotter. A slim envelope lays between us. "I'm glad you could come here first," she says, smiling perfect teeth at me.

"Sure." I give her a tight-lipped smile back. "Is that the letter?"

"Yes." She slides it across the desk to me. I have to stand a little, an awkward movement to grab it. Why does she have these stupid-ass chairs? Just to fuck with her clients?

She holds out a silver letter opener; it glints in the sun pouring through the window behind her. I wave her off, ripping the letter open with my hands.

Dear Sydney, if you're reading this, it means I'm dead.

Nice opening, Robert. Go on...

You know how much I've come to admire you over the length of our friendship. And you know I've hoped for it to be more.

He is not guilting me in his death letter, right? That's *not* what is happening right now. I roll my eyes. He's not even dead. I'm pretty sure.

I've always understood your hesitation to allow me to be more to you than a friend and benefactor. But please know that my love for you is the purest thing I ever felt. In the time I spent on the planet, my love for you is the greatest gift I received.

Shut the fuck up, you asshole. I glance up at Teresa. "Can I have a moment alone?"

"Of course." She stands just as her secretary returns with the water. I take the glass she offers me. She puts a dog bowl on the ground. Blue looks to me for permission, and I grant it. He laps at the water while the two women leave. I stand up out of the stupid-ass chair, putting my glass on the desk, and pace to the window, leaning against its sun-warmed smoothness for a second before returning to the letter.

We never became lovers, Sydney.

Oh, really, thanks for the update, dead guy.

But I loved you truly nonetheless. And that is why I am leaving you the majority of my fortune.

It is suddenly hard to swallow.

My homes, my stake in our shared company, my planes, my investments, and other assets.

What an asshole.

Don't worry, I'm taking care of my ex-wives. But you are who I care about, Sydney. You and your child. I want you to have the choice of freedom if you want it.

I know how much Joyful Justice means to you, how much you enjoy the work.

His smile, soft and careful, flashes across my mind. Stupid, stupid man.

Your dedication to your vision of what the world should be like is part of what drew me to you. But unlike so many people in your life, Sydney, what I truly loved about you... was you. The way you eat your pancakes in the morning, the way you turn your face into the sunset, closing your eyes and letting the beauty wash over you. The way you push your body to perform, trusting it to carry you forward. Your relationship with Blue and then his puppies. Your loyalty and faith are part of it, but there is something intrinsically you that I adore, admire, and love deeply.

I hope you are happy in life. I hope that you raise your child with that same love and lust for justice and existence even as it is... We cannot wait for perfection to enjoy this lifetime. You brought me great joy. I hope that the protection and love I offered in life is easier to accept now that I'm gone.

When did you become a philosopher, you asshole? A tear lands on the paper in front of me, and I grit my teeth. Fucking hormones.

Turning away from the window, I return to my side of the desk and chug the rest of the water. It goes down, washing the emotion with it.

My gaze returns to the window and the city beyond. Blue tarps are pulled across missing roofs, and windows are boarded with plywood. And here I stand in a fucking tower of safety, about to be showered with the kind of extraordinary wealth that could cushion the rest of my days. Yet, I throw myself constantly into the fray... throw myself in front of bullets. My hand comes to my belly, to the scars there... to the life under those scars.

I glance down at the letter again.

See you next lifetime. Eternally yours, Robert.

Grief grips me, sucking me under the waves, shocking in its ferocity. He's gone. He's really fucking gone.

Robert fucking Maxim.

CHAPTER EIGHT

Dan

I pull out my phone as Mom disappears into the kitchen. *No new messages.*

I open the Facebook ads app and check my advertising spend and reach for the day. My new "Be Brave" meme with the photo of a woman holding up a bottle of water to a burned koala bear's lips is doing well. It's reached a half million people in the last twenty-four hours at a very low spend. People love cute animals. They love to share images of humans helping cute animals.

I'll get into the dashboard later to check on my latest profile scrubbing.

I switch to my tracking app. Sydney's phone is off. She must be in the air. Mulberry is still in Miami. Anita said he planned to fly to Costa Rica today though. I'll keep an eye on that.

The extraction team is en route to Lenox, and he has reached location Zed.

"That's nifty," Mom says as she comes back into the kitchen, gesturing to the pop socket on the back of my phone. It sticks out so that I can slip my pointer and middle fingers on either side. I close the app and put my phone down on the couch next to me.

"Thanks," I say, taking the cup of tea she offers. "It makes it easier to hold. I can get you one."

Mom waves a hand. "Oh, I don't need that. I don't use my phone that much."

Only about forty-five minutes of screen time a day. Mostly she watches TV the old-fashioned way or listens to music on Alexa while she reads real books. She refuses to use the Kindle I got her for Christmas, preferring the smell and feel of paper. Though she's told me several times how much she appreciates the gift, I know from the spyware I installed that it ran out of batteries several months ago and has not logged onto her network since.

Mom sits on the other end of the couch, sunlight from the bay windows slanting across her pale skin—it looks thin and translucent. The circles under her eyes tighten something in my chest. She smiles at me. "Don't look so worried, Dan. I'm going to be okay."

She holds her teacup with both hands, and steam drifts up around her face as she blows on the hot liquid. "I know you will," I say. "When is your next treatment?"

"Well—" She sips the tea and smiles. "—I had the first yesterday, after we spoke. So two weeks." *I can't believe I missed this.* "I'm happy you're here, honey." She beams at me, the lines that bracket her mouth deeper than my last visit two years ago, but she is still so beautiful it makes me ache just a little.

Mom never remarried after Dad died from a sudden heart attack. No time to say goodbye. No time to watch the lines deepen, the skin turn transparent. I sip my tea, tasting the familiar comforting chamomile—heavy with honey and lightened with milk.

I force a smile and meet my mother's gaze. She breaks eye contact and looks down at her mug. "You shouldn't put your life on hold for me; that's not right." She meets my gaze again. We share the same eye color—a unique pale green that always draws attention. *I guess you two aren't related,* people have always joked.

"I can take some time off."

"I know you're important."

I huff a laugh, my eyes darting to my phone as a message lights the screen. "I'm not that important, Mom."

She stiffens at that. "Yes, you are."

I put my tea on the coffee table and pick up my phone. Anita checking to see that I made it. I reply that I have, then return my attention to Mom.

"I want to be here. You're the most important person in the world to me," I say.

Mom's eyes well, and she presses her lips together, trying not to cry. I reach out, and so does she, our hands intertwining. "Thank you," she says, her voice low.

I nod, my throat too tight to speak. I can't lose her. I just can't.

Through the rushing in my ears, I hear tires in the driveway. More than one set. Brakes screech.

I'm standing and moving to the big bay windows that look out onto the circular drive before the thought to do so fully forms. *Oh shit.*

"Dan, what's happening?" Mom's voice pitches up.

I'm staring out the window at the black and whites and the spinning colors in the front yard. They fill the driveway and spill out onto the suburban street.

I turn back into the room and grab my bag off the couch, slipping it over my shoulders and tightening down the straps. "Stall them," I say, bending to kiss the top of her head. The scent of her, the same floral perfume she's worn my entire life mixed with the stringent spike of antiseptic, fills my senses. This *can't* be the last time I see her... but it might be.

Mom looks up at me, her eyes glistening with unshed tears. She's afraid for me. "Dan," she whispers. A fist tightens around my heart. I'm hurting her.

"I'll be okay, Mom. I'm sorry."

She doesn't believe me. I shouldn't have come.

As I head to the hallway, she stands in the living room, hands twisting. The knock comes at the front door. Gesturing with my chin, I encourage her to answer. She sniffs once and then hurries out of sight.

I pull up the hatch to the crawl space and leap down into the darkness and musk. I lower the door.

"My son?" Mom asks, her tone confused and protective. Mom, sweet Mom.

In the pitch blackness of the crawl space, I fish my phone from my pocket and turn on the flashlight. The beam illuminates the narrow dirt-lined space. I lower to my hands and knees, fitting the pop socket between my teeth so that I can use the light and my hands at the same time.

The moist earth soaks through my jeans as I crawl to the far back corner. Pulling away the thick tangle of sticky spiderwebs exposes the wooden doorway. My escape hatch, prepared back in my youthful hacker days.

The FBI never came for me then, but even a decade and a half ago I knew one day they'd get this close. I'm one of the best, but we all have weaknesses. And the law doesn't give up. That's one of the things I admire about it.

Heavy-booted footfalls sound above as I yank open the low-framed door. Scurrying sounds echo in the dark. I raise the flashlight. A rat disappears around the bend. I lick my lips, tasting the dank air.

Fingers crossed that the tunnel hasn't collapsed in the years since I dug it.

Plant roots dangle from the ceiling, brushing against the back of my neck and sending shivers down my spine. The flashlight cuts through the darkness, revealing the narrow passageway in stark light, driving creatures slithering and scurrying.

I take shallow breaths. My pack scrapes along the roof, raining dirt onto my back and thickening the air. The passage is barely wide enough for my shoulders. I didn't count on becoming so much bigger.

Reaching the end of the tunnel, I push at the hatch above. It barely budges. It *should* let out into the furthest reaches of my mother's backyard. She hasn't sold any of her land. *That I would have caught. How did I miss her cancer? Don't think about that now.*

I reposition myself to get better leverage on the hatch and push up with my shoulder, using my legs. It shifts more, giving way and letting sunlight eke into the space. It's probably just covered in fifteen years' worth of dirt and leaf fall. I should get a landscaper out here to do some work. Assuming I'm not in jail and mom is alive. *Stop thinking!*

The hatch flops open, and I stand up into the sunlight, taking a big lungful of sweet, fresh air. Looking back at the house, I see uniformed officers circling the place. I hunch low, trying to hide in the trees. Someone yells from inside the house, drawing the circling cops' attention.

Another yell echoes down the passageway. *They found it. Time to go.*

My bag strapped close to my body, I move through the woods, vines catching at me and springing back. I spent much of my early childhood playing in this copse of trees at the back of the property. A stream runs through it in spring and fall, but in the cold hush of winter and the dry spells of summer, the land is hard packed.

The leaves are just starting to turn now, and there are thick pines to help hide me, but I'm dressed in jeans and a blue long-sleeve shirt—not exactly camouflage.

I reach the end of the property and discover that Billy Brush's backyard is fenced now. *Dammit.* I run along the high wire fence built to keep deer out, following it toward the road. I can circle around to Milton Field's yard. There is yelling in the woods behind me. They've followed the tunnel and found my exit. I glance back but don't see any uniforms yet.

A dog barks. *Fantastic.*

I run faster, my breath still even. The few weeks I took off from physical activity have not left me totally useless, that's good. A hole in the fence up ahead sends a shot of adrenaline through me. As I duck down to squeeze through, the broken wire catches on my shirt, tearing it. Crap. I pause to unhook the jagged metal from the material and see the first hint of movement in the trees behind me.

Billy's yard—or at least it used to be Billy's yard, it's now owned by a new family—slopes down to my right toward the main road. The ranch house is to my left, its driveway connecting to the cul-de-sac beyond it. If I race straight across their 2.4-acre lot, I can cross into a larger wilderness area that has trails running through it and a play structure.

There is yelling behind me again, and I turn back to see movement on the other side of the fence. The dogs will track me no matter which way I go.

A white Subaru is parked in front of Billy's former house. I bet the keys are in it...

I sprint toward the Subaru. "Stop!" a voice yells behind me.

Crap. It will have to be plan B. I stop, putting my hands in the air and dropping to my knees. *I am not a threat.*

Footsteps run up behind me. A hard kick to my back flattens me to the ground. I curl into a ball as another kick hits my legs. "You dumbass!" one of the cops yells.

A blow to my lower back, below my backpack, arches me, and a different foot thunks into my newly exposed stomach. Vomit surges out of me, splattering the boots in front of me.

"Motherfucker!"

A blow to the base of my skull explodes dark spots across my vision. Screaming starts up—it's not me. "What are you doing?" It's the new owner of the house.

I blink up to see four cops around me now, the light through the trees dappling their uniforms. One of them raises his foot, and I shield my face again, but he smashes down on my cheekbone. Lights explode behind my closed lids.

This is not going well at all...

CHAPTER NINE

Lenox

The sun sets and darkness folds around the buildings. Our van idles outside the apartment building. Ian, Conner, Liam, and Petra are still in the living room.

Ramona turns in her seat, fidgeting, her eyes darting to the tablet I'm holding with the surveillance feed and then to the sidewalk where Hans and Sophia pretend to be lovers on an evening stroll. The pair stop in front of the apartment building doorway to whisper and touch.

Hans speaks over the radio, his accented voice coming right into my ear. "We saw nothing to indicate they have additional measures in place. Lenox, you should go now."

"Roger," I say.

Ramona nods, her body vibrating with leashed power.

I move across the street, the tablet tucked inside my overcoat, rubbing against the bulletproof vest. My earbud still hears the feed from the living room. The moon glows white and full, casting a pale blue over the cement and reflecting off the parked cars.

I glance up at it, sensing a largeness that is beyond myself. My mother flashes across my memory. The warmth of her eyes and her cool hands on my forehead. It's been a lifetime since I lost her, since she was taken from me. A lifetime, and yet the pain can be as fresh and dangerous as the new moon.

Men like Ian McCain and his brothers, men like Yusuf, they breed a belief in the right of the powerful to exploit the weak that is deadly. It killed my mother. It sent Ramona here to be by my side. It drives us all in its own way.

All my adult life I've sought to avoid it. By only selling men, I could tell myself that I was not the problem. By joining Joyful Justice, I could tell myself that I was doing everything I could to stop it. By standing next to Petra in our new venture, I could tell myself that I was doing everything in my power.

And now, as I step across the street and approach the door, as I prepare to kill these men and "rescue" Petra, I must be honest with myself. This is not what my mother would want for me—spending a lifetime entrenched in an un-winnable war. No amount of revenge or action will bring her back. I must release the anger and pain around her death and choose my path with clear focus.

But first I must learn if Petra has betrayed me. Like a blindfolded man in a field full of swords, I will have to use my instincts to discover the truth. Is Petra my ally or my enemy? My lover or my betrayer?

The glow of Han's phone illuminates Sophia's face as she looks at me. The blue cast of the phone similar to that of the moon, but brighter and harsher. She looks like stone, a beautiful illuminated sculpture. A deadly design.

I open the apartment building door. Hans and Sophia move in with me. Ramona will remain outside to watch our backs. I've spent the day listening to Ian and his henchmen—who can only be described as mentally challenged—and from what I gathered, they do not have backup. They believe Petra is on their side. They can't see past the mask. Can I?

EK

The door bursts open, the wood splintering and hinges cracking. Hans stays low as he rolls a canister of pepper spray into the room. It hisses and makes a tinkling sound against the hard wood.

Hans flattens against the wall. His silver hair pokes out from between the bands holding his gas mask in place.

Coughing echoes inside.

I watch the tablet in my hand through my own mask. Petra has dropped to the floor, flattening herself in front of the couch, hands on the back of her head—just like a good captive should. The bloom of acrid smoke thickens. Ian, Conner, and Liam pull their weapons, backing away from the spinning, hissing can of gas.

Ian leads them behind the counter in the kitchen, and they duck down, out of line of sight from the camera and the front door. "Behind the kitchen counter," I say quietly into our comms.

Sophia and Hans go first, moving in unison, like ballroom dancers performing a standard. The gas flows and ebbs with us, circling our bodies and gathering at our feet. Petra coughs behind the couch, out of sight.

The shorter end of the L-shaped kitchen counter is right in front of us, the men behind it protected—though their location made obvious by their wracking coughs. The back of the couch faces the longer end of the counter, and the now empty stools. My gaze darts to the window the couch faces, where the camera is hidden. I can't make out where it is... and I don't think it's just because of the smoke.

Ian pops up, red eyed and wild. His gun explodes in the small space, the sound ricocheting as fiercely as his bullet. It thunks into my chest, blowing me back a step. Sophia's silenced weapon whispers through the smoke, exploding into Ian's brain and spattering it across the white counters behind him.

His body lurches to the side, his weapon discharging again. The wayward bullet strikes the window—creating a spiderweb of cracks joined at a central hole that sucks the pepper spray out into the night.

My breath echoes in my mask, the pain in my chest radiating but dull.

A hand comes up from behind the kitchen counter. "I give up," a voice chokes out. "Please don't kill me."

"Throw your weapons away," Hans orders them. Two guns skitter out from behind the counter, followed by a switchblade and a smaller pistol.

"Stand up slowly," Hans commands. "Hands on your heads."

The two goons' fingertips appear, followed by hands, wrists, and elbows, then tear-streaked faces and broad shoulders. Finally, round bellies are exposed. "What do you want to do with them?" Hans asks me.

I don't have an easy answer.

We have no way to hold them. But we can't release them. Clearly they want to live and are no longer bound by loyalty to Ian, but once our guns are down, their fear will dissipate. "Take them down to the van," I say. "I will meet you at location D."

Hans gestures with his gun for the men to come out from behind the counter. They keep their hands up as they move around. Sophia covers them, and the four move out of the apartment.

I need to speak with Petra alone.

My eyes flick to the couch she still lies behind, her coughing easing as the smoke clears out the ruined window.

"Stand up," I say, my voice steady.

She rises slowly, and I walk toward her, so now just the couch separates us. "You betrayed me," I say behind my mask.

Her eyes are red and swollen. She takes in a deep breath, then coughs it out. "No." Her voice is hoarse. "I did what I had to do to save you after that bonehead move with Anna." She shakes her head. "It was the perfect opportunity to get Ian out of hiding. And now we are free to take on Yusuf. We will take the whole city."

Her eyes burn with ambitions beyond mine. "Ian needed to be dealt with." She waves at his body. "He was an idiot, but his anger made him erratic and difficult to pinpoint. Now he is out of the way. We no longer need to worry about him."

"Does your ego know no bounds? You think I will just trust you. Just—"

"Lenox!" She coughs, her thin body hunching into itself.

A pang of regret pulses through me. I should get her out of here. Get her to cleaner air. I rip off my own mask, some chivalry inside me refusing to retain my advantage, instead following the trap of honor to a burning throat and stinging eyes.

"Do not play the fool," Petra says. "Do not pretend you do not know how I feel for you!" She stamps her foot, impetuous and powerful—how does she pull it off?

I step closer to her, my movement another subconscious footfall. I want to grab her, but stop myself. My throat burns from the remaining gas still in the air.

She tilts her chin to look up at me. I am bigger and stronger. I could hurl her across the room. I could *hurt* her. I fist my hands. "We are not in love."

"Wrong." Her eyes narrow. "*You* are not in love, Lenox, or so you think. But I'm..." Her voice catches, and she blinks, the fire in her eyes shifting from a flame to a burning coal. Her voice quiets, the passion still there but also a new... vulnerability. I open my mouth to say something, anything, to stop the words I expect to leave her mouth. She speaks first. "I am in love with you."

I shake my head and take a step back. I don't want to hear it. Can't hear it. Refuse to believe it. She is a liar. "This is not what people in love do."

"We are not people, Lenox. I am me, and you are you. We are not to be understood by others. No one can see me like you."

"I can't see you." I sweep an arm out, indicating the blood-spattered kitchen, the stinging air, the trap she laid. "I did not see this coming."

"You saw enough to know to come for me."

"I don't want Yusuf's power. I don't want to run this city's underworld." I stop short from saying I don't want her. It's a lie. A lie I can't even tell myself, let alone her. Why do I still want her? She is manipulative, infuriating, and dangerous.

"What about me? Do you want me?" Petra asks, that note of vulnerability sneaking back into her voice.

"I don't know." *Why can't I just say no?* She's a drug, a powerful hallucinogen. I need to stop this madness, break free from her control. But...

"You're lying."

"I don't want to take over Yusuf's role," I say again, my throat tight and voice harsh. "We need to stick to what we can control. This is not our place. We cannot change everything here."

"We can do anything we want."

A voice inside me cheers at her bravado, at her certainty. But a louder, saner sense is telling me to run from her. To leave this city, leave this woman, and never come back.

"We can change the world." Petra starts to round the couch. "But now we must go. Before the police arrive. Before we have to answer too many questions. Come." She reaches my side and holds out her hand. "Let's go."

I stare down at her outstretched fingers, at the fine lines radiating across her palm. I meet Petra's gaze again, still red-rimmed from the pepper spray. The cracked glass of the window behind her a fitting back ground to this spider of a woman.

My heart thumps, and blood rushes in my veins. My nervous system urges me forward. She's right. We must go. I put my hand in hers. She closes her fingers over mine, and I tug, yanking her off balance. She hits my chest, melting against me, looking up, her eyes pools of watery green mystery.

"I can't trust you," I say, but the words sound false. My hands running up her back, pulling her closer, defy me. I close my burning eyes and inhale her scent—coughing on the gas still floating in the air.

"You don't have to trust me. You know me." Petra pulls back to look up into my face. Her smile is playful, but the tremor in her voice begs me to agree.

I crush my lips against hers, needing the contact, the sweet breath of her, the fire that she ignites in me, the bravery she exhibits every damn second of her godforsaken existence. When I pull back, her gaze is glassy, her smile lazy... *Yes, I control you too.*

We turn as one and leave the apartment, the crunch of broken wood from the ruined doorway our swan song.

CHAPTER TEN

Dan

My eye is swollen shut, the side of my head an aching mess of pain. My wrists are cuffed to a metal loop on the table, so that I have to sit forward in the plastic chair.

I rest my head—the good side—down on the Formica tabletop. The cool surface feels good. The blood crusted in my hair itches, but I don't have the energy to scratch it.

I must have fallen asleep, because when the door shuts, I jerk upright, bursting dark spots across my vision and radiating fresh, nauseating waves of pain through my head.

"Ouch," a woman says as she steps into my spinning vision. She's petite with dark chocolate-brown hair laced with caramel highlights. She squints almond-shaped eyes at the side of my face.

"Ouch is right." I try a smile. It hurts, and I wince.

She winces too, her eyes narrowing further. The woman reaches into her navy suit jacket and pulls out a pair of glasses. "Who did this?" she asks, pushing her shoulder-length hair behind her ears as she leans closer.

"Who didn't?" I try to smile again and am rewarded with the same wince. Her eyes meet mine for the first time. She blinks behind the lenses, and I blink back. She's gorgeous. Fuck me.

Clearing her throat, she stands upright, the pale cream satin blouse she's wearing under the suit jacket catching the florescent lights the way satin is supposed to. "I'm Dan," I say.

She suppresses a smile and raises one finely arched brow. "Yes, I know."

I shrug. It hurts but not as bad as smiling. "And you are?"

"Special Agent Consuela Sanchez." She turns around to take the other chair in the room, and my eyes land on her pants. They fit nicely. Not suggestive or meant to attract attention but also not baggy—she's not advertising or hiding, just wearing a pair of pants. Wearing a pair of pants over one hell of an ass. Jesus, I can't believe I'm checking out her ass at this moment. But as she turns to sit, a soft wave of regret pulses through me. I *was* enjoying the view.

Her eyes are waiting for me when I get back to them. She arches that brow again. "You're a hard man to find."

I don't answer. It wasn't a question.

She places her right hand on the table—elegant and small, the nails slick with clear polish. My eyes are drawn back to her face.

"Dan Burke. Your first arrest for violation of the Computer Crimes Act was when you were fourteen."

I reach up to scratch the blood in my hair. My finger hits a laceration. The pain wobbles my seat and spots my vision again.

Consuela's eyes are slits, and her lips are pressed into a tight line when I refocus on her. She didn't want me beat up. I don't think it's an act. She looks genuinely pissed.

"I could use a doctor," I say, remembering this time to keep from smiling. It's hard around Officer Consuela Sanchez. Ah, the name rings a bell inside my head. She started the task force to track the Her Prophet and incels. She was demoted, and I stopped tracking her. Guess I should have kept that file open longer.

"Yes." She nods, and hair sneaks out from behind her ears at the movement. It's thick. The kind of hair I could dig my hands into...

"What kind of Special Agent are you?" I ask, playing dumb.

She doesn't smile. "Homeland Security."

I nod, and my vision swirls. Sanchez stands. "You need medical help before we can have this interview." There is bitter regret in her voice.

"I look forward to seeing you again," I say as she opens the door. Sanchez looks over her shoulder at me, her hair hiding her jaw, but her eyes are bright, burning with intelligence. She looks suddenly like a predator. She's been hunting me.

Special Agent Sanchez wants me healed so she can be the one to tear me apart.

"Same here," she says, her voice an octave lower. My vision pinpoints, and I use what presence of mind I have left to lower the good side of my face down onto the table before blackness takes me.

EK

"How long until I can talk with him?" Sanchez is somewhere close, speaking in a low voice. *Where am I?*

The attack comes back to me in stark, flashing images: Four police officers standing over me, the dappled sunlight hitting their uniforms, the sweat glistening on their faces, the puffed cheeks... the rage. The kicking. A woman's high-pitched screams. I jerk at the realness of the memory.

My eyes shoot open, adrenaline spiking. My heart thumps in my throat. An incessant beeping maintains the same beat.

A man wearing pale blue scrubs appears at my side, pushing buttons on a machine. He silences the alarm, then turns his attention to me. His hair is auburn and styled in a coif.

Auburn's jaw works on a piece of gum as he smiles at me. "You're awake," he says, like that's a good thing.

"Yes." My voice comes out as a croak. Auburn turns away for a moment. He twists back and offers a cup with a straw poking out. I sip lukewarm water. My burning throat delights in the wash of hydration. I close my eyes, concentrating on the effort of sucking.

I try to bring a hand up to take the cup and hear the rattle of chains, then feel the chill of metal against my skin. I'm cuffed to the bed.

Auburn takes the drink away, and I open my eyes. "That's good for now," he says. "You're getting fluids from the IV, and I don't want to overwhelm your stomach right now." *Right, we wouldn't want to overwhelm my stomach. It did get the shit kicked out of it super recently.*

"How am I, Doc?" I ask.

Auburn frowns, his brown eyes welling with sympathy. "Not great, buddy." For some reason, him calling me buddy doesn't bother me. *Oh, I'm high.* I giggle, which makes me laugh. Which hurts.

"Ow," I complain.

Auburn leans forward and adjusts my pillow, helping me sit up better. He smells like peppermint—must be the gum he's chewing—and Purell—must be the hospital we're in. I'm in a hospital chained to the bed. *Whoopee. Oh, and I'm high. Whoopie-doo-da-day.*

Auburn steps back, and Sanchez comes into focus. She is standing by the door, arms crossed, a wrinkle of concern between her brows. "Hi," I say, a smile passing over my lips. It doesn't hurt as much. Looking at her feels *good*.

Wow, I am hiigghhh.

"What are you giving me, Doc?" I ask Auburn but keep my gaze on Sanchez. Why would I ever look anywhere else when I have that cute little frown to stare at? She pushes off the wall and approaches the bed. Her hips sway—not because she's showing off, just because that's how her body moves. *Moves.* Moves. That word is funny, so I giggle again.

Which makes her frown tilt on one side. *She thinks I'm cute.* Right back at you, *cutie*. My smile hitches higher, pressing at the injured eye. Oh, it's not swollen shut anymore. That's good. *How long was I out?*

"You're on a morphine drip," Auburn answers my question. "I'm Richard Fern, your nurse. Doctor Travis will be in to see you during rounds."

I spare him a brief glance but am drawn back to Sanchez. She's standing at the end of my bed now, her manicured fingers resting on the plastic footboard.

"What time is it?" I ask.

Richard glances at his watch. "It's just about 7:00 p.m."

I try to do the math. I got to my mom's around 10:00 a.m. her time, spent about an hour or so with her before getting chased and the crap beat out of me. So... I can't do the math. Ha. "You're not going to interrogate a man in my condition, are you, Sanchez?" I ask, smiling, teasing. "I'm high as a kite and have been unconscious for some length of time." That covers it.

She frowns again. "I'm not going to interrogate you while you're under the influence." Sanchez shifts her focus to Richard. "When will the meds wear off?"

"If I turn the drip off, he'll be sober in fifteen, but—" His gum pops. "—he will be in a ton of pain."

"I do not like the sound of that," I say, swinging my attention to nurse Fern. *Fern, dern, stern... Sanchez is kind of stern.*

Richard purses his lips. "Me either, buddy."

"Yeah." I turn back to Sanchez. "That's not nice."

"We need to speak. Time is of the essence," she says.

My brain floats on a placid lake, but her words send ripples of worry through it. What's so urgent? I mentally flick through Joyful Justice's critical missions. There is nothing planned for at least ten days that I can see... Of course, I'm not at my *absolute* best at the moment. *Best, test, nest, jest.*

"Give us a minute," Sanchez says to Richard.

"Okay, but," he addresses me, "if you need me, Dan, just push this right here." He points to a button in the plastic bedrail to my left... the one I'm not handcuffed to.

"Thanks, Richard." *Fern, dern, lern, pern... Those are not all words...*

Fern the Nern turns off my meds and leaves, then it's just me and Special Agent Sanchez. She moves around to the right side, sitting in the large armchair for family to spend the night.

A memory blazes across my consciousness: Mom in a chair like that after my tonsils were removed, the skin around her eyes tight with worry, her hair tangled from sleep. But she's smiling at me, her gaze warm and loving... trying to hide the fear. Trying to protect me. Always.

Please let her live.

My throat tightens.

These meds make everything funnier *and* sadder. I swallow the emotion and focus on Consuela Sanchez.

"Last time we spoke, right before I passed out, you were reading me my rap sheet," I say.

Her lips twitch to one side into a half smile, and victory surges through me. *I want to make her laugh.* "We only got to my first arrest. Want me to give you the other three? All when I was a minor, mind you." *Minor, mind you. Minormindyou.* I giggle again, and Sanchez's half smile becomes full—still no teeth, but this woman is warming up to me.

"Yes, you really shaped up when you went to college."

I nod. "Upstanding citizen. So, why did you send some local Jersey cops after me—"

"Why'd you run?" she cuts me off, her voice low, eyes suddenly sharp.

Oh. Watch out, Danny boy. Sanchez is a predator, remember?

I smile my harmless smile, the one I've perfected. *I'm easygoing.* She is not buying it. The smile does feel lopsided. My whole head feels lopsided.

Sanchez wets her lips, drawing my focus. *Wow.*

"Shit," she says.

"You have a gorgeous mouth." *Did I just say that out loud?* Judging by the fresh frown, yes. I did just tell the Special Agent about the attractiveness of her mouth. She is special...

Slowly, I raised my gaze up to her eyes. "I'm high," I say in defense. She draws her bottom lip under her teeth, and I can't help but drop my gaze to her mouth. "That is not helping," I say. "My focus is not very good."

She stands quickly, and I close my eyes, leaning back into the pillow, trying to find a thought that isn't drifting on a bed of pain meds.

When I open my eyes again, Sanchez is back at the end of the bed. "I'm sorry that you were hurt. And I'm sorry that you're going to have to be in pain for this conversation. But it's better than high." She meets my gaze. Direct, no nonsense. She's sorry... but not *that* sorry.

I nod. "Okay."

She glances at coat hooks by the door where a briefcase hangs along with a rain jacket and umbrella—both are dry. *How long has she been here?*

"We have to do this now." Sanchez crosses to the briefcase and pulls it down, coming back to the seat next to me.

The pain starts to bleed into my reality, bringing with it some cognitive ability.

Sanchez pulls out a tablet and starts navigating. "How do you feel now?"

"I'm still high but better."

She scoots forward on the seat, and I catch a whiff of her perfume—vanilla and some kind of herb... thyme. I'm pretty sure it's thyme. Not rosemary.

"Dan?"

"Yeah." I focus on her face. "Yes." I nod. "Ouch." Nodding is a bad idea.

She holds the tablet out to me. I take it with my left hand—the free one. On it is one of my Facebook posts. It's the koala bear meme. I used a page titled "Be Compassionate." It has over two million views, and most of that organic. "This is your page," Sanchez says it like she knows. But she couldn't possibly *know*.

I shake my head. *Ow.* Nodding and shaking are both out. Looks like I'm down to hand gestures. Except one hand is chained to the bed. The one-armed hand gesturer... I'm still high.

Sanchez is frowning at me. "Sorry." I almost shake my head again but stop myself. "My head hurts, and I keep moving it." I offer her a shy smile. My *I'm just a lost boy, won't you help me?* smile.

Not going for it.

Okay.

"I'm not on Facebook," I say. "I don't do social media."

She laughs, but I don't feel victorious. Her laugh is not amused so much as confident. She's laughing *at* me. Not *with* me.

Sanchez meets my gaze, her Bourbon brown eyes bright. "Dan." My name from those lips sounds good. "I know what you've been doing. I know how you've been doing it. What I need is your help to do it to a different group."

Wait. What did she just say?

My confusion must show on my face because she scoots to the edge of the chair, getting closer to me. Her perfume floats over me again. "Your targeting and manipulation are incredibly sophisticated."

"I don't know what you're talking about." It sounds like a lie even to my own ears. I'm incredibly turned on... *Sophisticated manipulation, yes, please.*

"What you're doing is brilliant."

Brilliant, you say?

I narrow my eyes and firm my lips to keep from bursting into a grin. "I want you to work with me. With Homeland Security. I think, with your skills, we can do major damage control." She inches even closer, her brows raised, breath coming fast. She's excited about this.

"I'm on a special task force tracking the Her Prophet followers and the incels. I've discovered that there is a group fomenting the incels in the same way that you've been recruiting and positioning Joyful Justice. I need your help to change their minds—to help them see that women are not their enemies. That the end of the patriarchy is as good for men as it is for women."

A lock of hair falls free from the bun at the base of her neck and dances around her face as she finishes. Her lips are parted, her eyes holding mine. She's waiting for me to say something.

"I'm sorry, I don't know what you're talking about. I work for a start-up in Bangkok."

Her gaze shutters. "That's not true, Dan. You know it's not. Don't play with me. This is important."

I try out another one of my smiles. Confused surfer dude. "I seriously don't know what is going on. I came home to visit because my mom is sick." Always important to include some truth in every lie sandwich—it's like the mayo, keeps things stuck together. "And a bunch of cops showed up at her door."

Sanchez sits back as my voice rises. I'm tapping into the outrage of an innocent man here. The pain is helping. Because, hot damn, everything is starting to hurt. "One of the reasons I left this country—"

Sanchez cuts me off, her voice low and as hard as diamonds. "Don't lie to me, Dan Burke." *Full name now, would you look at that. I've really pissed her off.* I try to fan the flame of my false anger, but how personally she's taking my refusal to admit to my crimes is making me happy for some irrational reason.

"Your mother doesn't have cancer," Sanchez says, her voice still low but softer. "We made that up so I could find you. Because I know all about you, Dan Burke."

Bomb drops. World Explodes. Rage unleashes.

"Wait!" I sit up in the bed, dragging at the IVs in my arm. "You're saying my mother *doesn't* have cancer?" Nothing in Sanchez's expression changes. The Special Agent has no regrets. "She is going through chemo for nothing!" I'm yelling. Of course I'm yelling!

"The chemo wasn't real," Sanchez says quietly. Her calm seems that much stiller compared to the raging whoosh of sound inside my head. "And it wasn't for nothing. I needed to find you."

I flop back onto the bed and squeeze my eyes shut. My hands fist in the rough sheets. "Unbelievable," I mutter.

"I would think you'd understand."

My eyes fly open, and I focus on the woman sitting in the chair next to my bed. "Understand?" My voice is acid, and I throw it at her, hoping to burn.

"Yes, I did what I needed to do. That seems to be something you also do." Her voice is cold mist floating above a frozen pond.

Wait, what does she know?

"You spy on your friends, you track them, you worry about them. Care about the fate of the world. Dan Burke—you are not a bad man."

What is happening?

"I'm not here to arrest you, to lock you up." She shifts forward, her hand twitching in her lap. She almost reached for me. "I am here to convince you to work with me."

My brain stutters, trying to compute everything it's heard in the last sixty seconds.

My mother is not dying of cancer.

Homeland Security faked her illness to drag me out of hiding.

Special Agent Consuela Sanchez doesn't want to lock me up. She wants to... work with me.

"Through your social media posts, you are convincing people that Joyful Justice isn't a terrorist organization—"

"It's not."

She waves my point away like it's a bothersome mosquito. "You are influencing people, reshaping their views, making them identify as Joyful Justice supporters." Her eyes are wide and bright. *She admires me.* "I want you to help me shift incels' minds—to lead them away from violence and toward reconciliation."

I don't say anything. My head is still fuzzy, and if I make any salient points, I might just admit to a crime... though there is nothing illegal about social media advertising per se. "I want immunity," I say, "and a lawyer." I almost nod my head but then remember not to. "I need a lawyer before we continue this discussion."

Sanchez stands and paces away from the bed. "That's not going to happen."

"Excuse me?"

"This is war, Mr. Burke, and you're a terrorist. The regular rules don't apply. You're either going to help me, or you're going to disappear."

Cue ominous music.

"Let me get this straight," I say. Sanchez paces back to the end of the bed and meets my gaze. "Either I help you change the minds of incels—not that I'm saying I can do that." She rolls her eyes. "Or you disappear me?"

"Yes."

"Wow."

"What did you expect, Dan? Did you think that no one was going to come for you?"

"I didn't do anything." I grin, and my face aches. A tidal wave of exhaustion washes over me, and I close my eyes. "Can I have some more morphine before you transfer me to oblivion?"

"You would rather end up in a black ops prison than help me?" Her voice is hard, cold, angry.

"I don't do well with threats." I keep my eyes closed.

"Ironic coming from a man who leads an organization that is all about the threats."

"We offer immunity in exchange for..." *Shit. Did I say that out loud?* I open my eyes, and she is standing at the foot of the bed, hands braced on the rail. There is victory blazing in her eyes. I just admitted something.

"You offer immunity?" she asks quietly, not wanting to scare me off. Not realizing I've already done it to myself.

"Lawyer," I say again, "or morphine." *Give me counsel or give me pain killers.*

"I can send you to a place where you will feel much more pain than this."

"You can threaten me all day, but that won't make me want to work with you." I stare at her, and she doesn't look away. But I can see in her eyes—saw it when she first witnessed my wounds—Sanchez is not a torturer. "You don't go in for torture," I say. "You're too smart for that. You must be desperate to be trying it now. Or your bosses don't like this plan and have not given you the support that you need."

Something flashes in her eyes, but she doesn't look away. I've hit the nail on the head though. A pang of sympathy gongs in my chest. She is out on a limb here. If I balk, she's screwed. They will lock me up, but Joyful Justice has contingencies for that. We have contingencies for almost anything.

Not for having the hots for your captor though... or thinking her idea has merit.

"Let's say for a second I am the international hacker you believe me to be."

She crosses her arms and levels me with a *look*. "Okay."

"How could you expect this genius, this absolute font of knowledge and expertise to admit to anything without any protections against prosecution?"

"Because the alternative is, like I said, a black ops prison in a miserable desert where humiliation and pain await with open arms."

"Scary."

Her eyes narrow. "You should be scared."

"And you should be worried. Because you may have caught me—with what I'm going to say is one of the most underhanded, fucked-up tricks a person has ever pulled." Her face remains impassive. Really not ashamed of arranging my mother's false cancer diagnosis, complete with a dose of chemo. This woman is a fucking warrior. "But the fact is that you can't *make* me do anything. You can threaten me, harm me"—I gesture to my face—"or should I say harm me more, but I am not the guy you're looking for. I'm just not. I run a start-up in Bangkok. So I'm not worried about getting put away in a black ops prison. Because I'm not your guy."

A slow smile spreads across her face, as if she's got another trick up her satin sleeve. "You're my guy, Dan Burke. You are most certainly my guy."

Those words stir all the wrong parts of me for all the wrong reasons. She licks her lips.

"Stop it," I say before I can shut myself up. "Dammit." I close my eyes again. "I'm in too much pain right now." I hit the call button for Richard Fern the Nern, hoping he will pump me full of morphine so I can forget about this siren of a woman and get back to floating on a placid sea of amusing wordplay.

"This isn't over," Sanchez says.

"Get me a lawyer, and we can talk."

CHAPTER ELEVEN

Lenox

Location D is a warehouse building near the Bosporus. A wet wind whips down the empty street, carrying the salty scent of the sea with it. Petra's heels click on the cobblestone as we approach the entrance. The door opens when we reach it—the darkness inside even more complete than the night. The moon can't reach in there.

Sophia's pale face appears, and she ushers us in the side door, closing it behind us. Petra's fingers squeeze my arm. I'm like a hanged man, the rope cutting off my oxygen as my feet grapple for a purchase that will never come.

Lights flare on, flooding the storage space. Shelves stretch toward the towering height of the ceiling. Stacked with pallets of goods, the shelving creates narrow aisles. Sophia leads us down the first, her boots soft against the cement as Petra's continue to clack.

The aisle opens to a central space where our two captives are tied to chairs. The lights are high above us, casting a diffused light over the scene.

A forklift sits in the middle of the space—bright yellow with fat tires. Hans leans against it, a cigarette drooping from his lip, the smoke twirling into nothingness above his head, scenting the air with its familiar scent. Ramona, a small Uzi hanging from her shoulder, leans against one of the large shelves behind the prisoners. "Thank you," Petra says to both of them. "You saved my life."

Conner, the larger of the two goons, huffs a laugh. "Traitorous bitch," he mumbles under his breath.

"Why is it," Petra asks, taking a step toward him, "that when a woman uses deceit to protect herself, she is a traitorous bitch, but when a man does it, he is considered clever?"

Conner shakes his head, as if the question is beneath him. Petra closes the distance between them, and he looks up at her. "You'd rather be here than dead, yes?" He still doesn't answer. "But are you a traitor?"

"You can't betray a dead man," Conner answers.

Hans, Sophia, and Ramona watch the show with the bored air of professional mercenaries. But they are freedom fighters, not paid killers. I'm not even sure where the line is anymore, let alone which side I'm standing on.

"You were friends with the McCain boys for years," Petra goes on, "and you gave yourself up so easily, didn't want to fight your way out."

Conner's eyes flick past her to me for a moment. There is something in his gaze I don't have time to read before he drops his eyes to the ground.

"You won't answer?" she asks.

Liam sits next to his friend, also in silence, eyes trained on his feet.

"You thought I'd let you live?" I say.

Conner's eyes dart back to me again.

He probably isn't sure if that truth makes me strong or weak. If it makes me strong, then his entire view of how the world works may be wrong. It's possible he'd rather I kill him so that he doesn't have to change his thinking.

Hans drops his cigarette and crunches it under his boot before crossing to me. His walk is brassy, bold—a man who kills and climbs mountains with similar levels of ease. The silver in his hair glints even in the diffused light. "What do you want to do?" he asks me.

"I'm not going to kill unarmed prisoners," I say.

He nods his agreement. "Could be dangerous to let them go, though.

We assume they have no loyalty but to themselves, but it is impossible to tell."

Everyone wants to be a part of something larger than themselves—if it can't be a loving family, it can be a violent gang. "Do you want to work for us?" I ask Conner and Liam.

They both look at me as if I've sprouted a second head. Petra glances over her shoulder at me, blinking her surprise. "We need bodyguards, Petra."

"They can hardly be trusted." She smiles. "They think I'm a traitorous bitch, remember? We killed their friends."

"We killed their employers."

"I can't trust them," she declares.

"You won't have to."

Petra bows her head, letting me win the argument. Trusting me with her safety.

Which one of us is the bigger fool?

I cross to stand in front of Liam. He looks up at me, and our gazes lock. His eyes are a muddy brown—there is a feral intelligence in them. He is a survivor, not an alpha. My gaze moves over to Conner; he blinks rapidly.

Watching them with Ian, I saw their loyalty—blind, dumb, unquestioning. These are the type of men running the sex trade. Really running it. Doing the actual labor of moving women, subjugating them, following orders.

We can cut off the heads. Or we can take over the limbs...

"What is your mother's name?" I ask Liam.

He shakes his head. "No way."

"You love her."

"'Course I do," he practically spits at me.

"If I killed her, would you die avenging her?"

His cheeks flush. "'Course I would."

"Yet you follow a man who treats women like objects to be bought, sold, and abused."

He shakes his head, the cognitive dissonance too much for him. *This is normal.* A man who respects his mother like a goddess but treats other females not related to him as products.

I look past him to where Ramona still leans casually against the shelves, her attention focused on the drama unfolding. She meets my gaze and gives a small shrug. She's not surprised.

"What about you, Conner? Would you have given up if it was your mother who lost her brains in the kitchen?"

He growls, that feral intelligence rumbling. Pure animal.

How do you train an animal? Reward the behaviors you want and ignore the ones you want to curb.

"I will let you live, as you guessed. In fact, I will have you work for me."

Conner's eyes narrow. He doesn't trust it. But he also banked on it. "Let them go," I say, turning my back on them. "We need to head out. I want to rest. It's late."

Petra follows me, pulling me down an aisle. "How can we trust them?" she asks.

"I don't, Petra." She glances back to where Sophia is cutting them loose. "I don't trust anyone."

Her mouth opens a little but then closes. She nods slowly. "I see."

"Come," I say. "We need to call Yusuf."

"We do?"

"Yes, we need to arrange a time to meet."

"Why?"

I give her a slow smile and lean close, brushing her ear with my lips. "Trust me," I suggest.

She shivers and nods her agreement.

Which one of us is the bigger fool?

EK

"Yusuf," Petra purrs into the phone.

"Petra, you have my money."

"Yes, let's meet."

"You can drop it at the hotel front desk. We do not need to see each other again."

"Please, I want to speak with you."

"There is nothing more to discuss." He hangs up. Petra returns the phone to its cradle before lying back onto the hotel room bed and biting into her lip. "We have to kill him."

I lean against the wall, looking at her small form on the large bed. "It will solve nothing."

She shrugs. "It will solve immediate problems for us." Her eyes narrow. "You started this fight, Lenox." She lifts her chin. "Won't you finish it?" She sits forward, her right knee bent close to her, left leg hanging off the bed. "You wish there was another way, something gentler." She shakes her head. "This will be bloody, Lenox. You know that."

I take in a short breath and expel it, turning away. "I know."

"We will have to go after anyone who stands in our way and then take over their territory. You must recognize that now that you've taken on Conner and Liam."

Though I put them in a different hotel.

I turn back to her. "Adding his territory will do nothing for us."

She frowns. "What more do you want, Lenox? Our profit margin is already so low. The amount we spend on rehabilitation"—her eyes go round—"we are practically a charity. A nonprofit running brothels." She laughs, throaty and sexy. "The things I do for love."

A deep, dark anger ignites in me. It's lurked there most my life, but I could always shove it down where it could fuel me but not burn out of control. Now it rages, refusing to be contained, refusing to be useful. Instead, it scorches my insides. "Do not say you love me." The words are tight, my voice deep.

Petra's lips lift into a half smile. She likes this rage. I clench my fists. "You don't want me to love you?"

I don't answer. What can I say? I don't want *anyone* to love me. And I don't want to love anyone. All that lies on that path is pain. "Keep those words away from me. I will not stand for them."

Her smile hitches higher, and one brow joins its ascent. "I've saved your life. You must have known then, when I could have let you die and taken all this for myself. Why else would I keep you alive?" When we killed the McCain brothers, I was shot with a powerful tranquilizer. It would have been simple for Petra to end me. But she chose to care for me instead.

"There are many reasons to keep men alive. You can use my connection to Joyful Justice to destroy it."

"Can I?" She stands slowly. "Is that what I'm doing?"

My breath is coming too fast. My head is getting light. "I'm going for a walk." I turn to leave, but she leaps to grab my arm. I look down at her, my body aimed for the door. I need to escape. "Let go of me."

"Only if you promise to come back."

"I will make you no promises, Petra. I never have, and I never will."

"Liar." The word comes out like a slap. "You promised we would do this together. You knew what it would take."

I shake my head and try to pull away, but she grips me harder. "I need space," I tell the wall.

"You need to recognize that you are hiding!" Her voice rises to a yell. Her heightened emotion calms me. I turn cold eyes on her.

"I owe you nothing."

Her eyes widen, and I shake her free. She stands in the middle of the room, her hands still out but holding nothing now.

She can't hold me. No one can. I won't be tethered by love. My loyalty to any person or cause is not tied to emotion. It can't be.

I open the door, walk into the hall, stride to the elevator, and wait patiently for it to arrive. The doors open. A woman in a short dress stands in the corner, her eyes red-rimmed, the sequined purse in her hand glinting in the light.

Her eyes meet mine and fear blooms there. "I'll catch the next one," I tell her.

She doesn't understand.

I step back, holding up my hands, offering space.

She drops the purse and raises her arm. A gun barrel sucks my attention. Her hand shakes. She is not a professional.

But she is here to kill me.

Yusuf, you fool.

I dive to the side, out of her range. The gun does not track me. The elevator doors close.

I race back to the room and use my key card to unlock the door. Petra steps out of the bathroom, a tissue pressed to her eyes. She's been crying, or wants me to think she has.

"Yusuf knows we're here," I say.

Her expression shifts into that cold, calculating mask. This I can trust.

CHAPTER TWELVE

Sydney

I still fly commercial, changing my midday flight for an early evening departure.

First class buys fewer raised brows about my giant dog. Combined with my puffy eyes, and scruffy clothing, it keeps the glares of indignation to a minimum. Clearly, I need all the emotional support I can get.

We land in Barcelona as the rising sun hits the city's haze, turning everything in the world into a soft, coppery peach with a tint of blue at the edges. A taxi takes me to the center of the city, first racing on straight, smooth highways, then winding through Medieval streets so narrow that pedestrians have to press against buildings as we pass.

The boutique hotel Anita recommended is tucked into a corner of a courtyard where pigeons coo and a cathedral towers. As the attendant checks me in, I get a text from Mulberry. *Dan taken into custody. Lenox in trouble.*

My heart thuds as I write back. *What?*

Call me.

"Are you okay, miss?" the woman checking me in asks.

"Yes, just tired." I force a smile onto my face. She shows me to a small room overlooking the cobblestone square. I dial Mulberry as soon as she leaves.

"What's going on?" I ask as I rifle through my bag, looking for Blue's travel bowl.

"Dan's Mom is sick—breast cancer stage 3."

"Oh, that's terrible." I find one of Blue's bowls and unfold it.

"It gets worse. He went to see her in New Jersey. I'm suspecting it was a setup because he wasn't there an hour before the cops came for him."

I crack open one of the complementary bottles of water. "What agency has custody?" I take a sip of the water before pouring the rest into Blue's bowl and putting it on the floor for him.

"Not sure yet. He's in the hospital, and no charges have been filed. They beat the crap out of him, Syd." Mulberry's voice vibrates with anger.

"How bad?" I ask, sitting on the bed.

"Not sure yet. We've got our lawyers on it, but you know how these things go."

We have to help without giving them any evidence of Dan's ties to Joyful Justice.

"Do you think we'll need to take extreme measures?" I ask. Will we need to send in a team to get him out?

"Not sure. Waiting to hear from the attorney. But he's safe in the hospital for now. We have surveillance, so they're not getting him out of the country without us knowing."

"Good. What's going on with Lenox?"

Blue comes over and rests his wet jaw on my thigh, dampening my jeans.

Mulberry sighs before answering. "It's complicated."

"Isn't everything?" I try a joke. It lands on its face in a big old pile of silence. "Sorry."

"No, don't apologize. I think we all had reservations about Lenox moving into this role, especially with Petra by his side. It's not in the mission of Joyful Justice to take over illegal activity—to get into the prostitution business as a way of better protecting the women involved."

"No, but Lenox was in it and on the council before this. Is it Ian?"
"It was. He's dead."
"Not a tragedy."
"No, but he had two men with him. Lenox is keeping them."
"Keeping them?"
"I don't get it exactly. I have not spoken with him. But the head of the extraction team sent a report."
"Wait." I rub at the bridge of my nose. "Extraction team?"
"Ian took Petra hostage. Lenox went in after her."
"Gotcha."
"Ian was killed, and the two men he had with him gave themselves up—threw away their weapons. So Lenox couldn't kill them."
"He chose not to."
Silence. My cold-bloodedness landing as well as the joke. *Robert would get it.* The thought at once comforts and upsets me. I stand, needing to move.

"Anita said not to tell you," Mulberry says, breaking the silence and ignoring my comment about Lenox's choices. "I figured you'd want to know. You never said you were giving up your seat on the council."

"No, I'm not." My voice is quiet... tired.

"How are you feeling?" he asks, his deep voice brimming with worry.

"I'm fine."

"Please, tell me where you are." I look out the window, down onto the square below. Mulberry sighs again. "I can find you, you know. I am a detective."

"Yes, I know."

"Is that what you want?"

"I don't know what I want, Mulberry. That's the whole point of this."

"You can't figure it out if I know your location?"

"I'm not saying that. I just—"

"If you tell me, I won't show up."

Blue's nose taps my hip. I'm standing at the edge of a cliff. "Barcelona," I say.

"Thank you."

"Don't show up here."

"I won't."

It all feels suddenly hopeless and useless and *heavy*. I lean into Blue and swallow the lump in my throat. "I don't know why I have to do this. I really don't. It's a dream... I had a dream."

"A dream?" His voice is quiet, as if he's frightened of making me run further away.

"Yes." Tears push at the back of my eyes. "James. He came to me in a dream."

"Came to you?"

Right, that makes it sound like he's a ghost. I can't really believe in ghosts. If I did, they'd haunt me. I've taken too many lives. How can I possibly create one? How can the scales of justice allow me that?

"I have to go," I say, clearing my throat.

"Okay." He sounds resigned, and it breaks my heart more than any of his blustering. *Don't give up on me.* I'm so broken, he should run. But what would I do without him?

EK

The rental agent, Catrina Bonet, whom Anita recommended, pushes open the tall, thick door, and a light turns on automatically in the vestibule. The ceilings are sixteen feet high, and the floor is patterned tile—classic Barcelona. "It is partially furnished," she says, her accent slight and lyrical, as she steps into the space. Her heels echo in the empty front room.

There are two doorways, one leading toward the front of the building and another toward the back. "It's large for one person."

She turns to me, her eyes searching for why a single woman and her dog need a four-bedroom, partially furnished apartment. Her curiosity may be a problem.

"My family is coming over soon," I say. "My husband and daughter along with—" I roll my eyes toward the ceiling in a gesture of exasperation"—my in-laws."

She smiles and nods. Now she gets it. "The children will love it here. I have four."

"Four?" It's my turn to scan her.

She laughs and starts walking toward the front of the building, flicking a light as she steps into the hall. "Yes, in Spain this is not so unusual. We love children. The smallest bedroom is here." She pushes open a door, and I peek in to see a single bed. The ceiling is taller than any of the walls are long. A narrow window lets pale light in through frosted glass.

She continues down the hall. "Will you need a cot?"

"A cot?"

"A crib?"

"Yes," I say, the word popping out because... I will.

She opens another door. "This is the master." She steps into the room, and I follow. A king-sized bed faces a wall of glass that opens to the kitchen and balcony beyond. "An en suite bathroom." She walks toward the bathroom, but I just keep staring at the kitchen. Sunlight pours in, making the surfaces gleam. There is a single stool at the breakfast bar and room for a long table and chairs. For the family I don't have.

"I'll take it," I say.

She laughs, passing me to open the doors to the kitchen. "You have not seen it all."

"I love it," I say.

"Mama!" A child's voice reaches us from the front entrance, and Catrina grins.

"In here," she calls.

Small, fast footfalls run down the hall toward us. A young boy bursts into the room, his dark hair a shiny mop on his little head. He's wearing jeans and a T-shirt scuffed with dirt. He is talking before he gets fully into the room—speaking so quickly I'm not sure I could understand him even if I did speak the same language.

Catrina nods and responds. He turns to race out and almost falls over when he spots Blue. His eyes widen, and he lets out an awe-filled breath. I laugh at the cartoonish reaction.

"Hi," I say. He brings his gaze up to meet mine and says something in a low whisper.

Catrina laughs. "This is my son, Jorge. He asks if your dog is a wolf."

"Part wolf, I guess." I smile at the boy as his mother translates. His eyes widen further. "Do you want to pet him?"

Jorge nods and takes a tentative step toward Blue, putting out a closed fist. Blue moves closer and sniffs Jorge. They are almost the same height. The little boy opens his palm, and Blue leans into Jorge's touch. A brilliant smile blooms across the boy's face.

My chest tightens and tears prick my eyes. *Damn pregnancy hormones.*

"How long will your family be in Barcelona?" Catrina asks, pulling my attention.

"Not long," I say. "My husband has work here, but I'm not sure how long it will take." The lies roll off my tongue.

"Maybe something fully furnished is better than—"

"I like this place," I say, scanning it again.

She shrugs. "Whatever you like."

"I can move in immediately?"

"Of course," she says, starting out of the room again. "We can do the paperwork now." Jorge races after her, pulling at her hand and speaking quickly. I take a moment to stare at the kitchen before following her. "If you need a doctor," she calls back to me, "my father is an excellent OBGYN."

I catch up with her in the hall; she is holding the door open for me. "How did you know?" I ask.

She smiles. "I can always tell." She leans closer. "You have a glow, you know? The glow of creation."

Okay...

CHAPTER THIRTEEN

Dan

It's Consuela Sanchez's voice, low and gentle, that wakes me. "Dan?"

A smile tugs at my lips, and I ease my eyes open. She leans over me, her hair a curtain of caramel and oak. I reach up and touch it. She glances at my fingers where they wave between the thick strands. "So soft," I say.

"You're high."

"You're pretty."

She stands up, and I frown, following her with my eyes. That's when I see the guy next to her. "Oh," I say. "Who are you?"

He holds out a business card. "Jack Wagner."

I focus on the card—it's a nice thick stock. It has his name on it. *Jack Wagner Esq.* "You brought me a lawyer," I say.

Sanchez nods.

I refocus on Mr. Wagner. "No offense, but I'd like to hire my own attorney. I don't know you."

"I hear that, Mr. Burke," Wagner says. *Nice to know the guy's ears are functioning.* "I was hired by your associate." He glances at Sanchez. "I can promise you that, as an officer of the court, I will do all I can to get you the best deal available."

"You sound like a lawyer."

He smiles. "That's my job." He turns to Sanchez. "Please give me some time alone with my client."

"I'll be outside."

"Bye." I wave with my chained hand, and it jingles. I flop the hand back down. "Can we get this taken off?" I ask Jack. "Clearly, I'm not going anywhere. I'm high as a kite and in a ton of pain. Quite the combo." *Mambo.*

Jack sits down in the big, comfy visitor's chair and pulls a legal pad out of his briefcase. He's in his fifties, I guess, with a shock of silver hair, round black-rimmed glasses, beeswax yellow skin, and a suit that says his hourly is probably similar to the cost of one of my mom's fake cancer treatments. "We can work on getting the cuff removed," Jack says, making a note on his pad. "But I think we've got bigger fish to fry."

"We have whales to fry, my friend. Whales."

Jack smiles indulgently. I sound about as stoned as I am, which is very stoned. "Sanchez has not arrested you. She says it's because you have not been cognizant enough to have your rights read, but I'd guess it has more to do with her not wanting your name showing up in any systems. They've done a good job of isolating you. You're listed in the computer system here as John Doe." *Mo Fo... low.*

"She told you what they want?"

"Yes, your help with some communications. Can you give it to them?"

"Not without possibly incriminating myself."

"Gotcha." He makes a note on his pad. "So what we need is full immunity for anything that comes up during the course of your tenure with Homeland Security."

"And an exit strategy."

He nods. "Obviously, we want you free to go once you've helped. So we need an end point. What seems right to you?"

I close my eyes to think, but all I find are clouds of pain killer. "I don't know. What she's asking for is not black and white." *What she needs is data... people who are persuadable.* "I can give them a target audience of persuadable incels in about a month if I'm given my head and a handful of decent coders. I'd like to use my own people. Obviously, they are not going to go for that, so I may need to do it alone. That's assuming I'm starting from scratch. I'd say two months if I'm solo."

Jack nods and scribbles with his pen. "So full immunity for any past crimes that you may expose during the course of helping with—" He checks his pad. "—this data set you'll build for them."

"Yes. I may need to admit to some things…" *Humblebrag about some pretty big accomplishments.* Anita is the only other person who understands what I've been up to, and she's only seen the tip of the iceberg. The icy depths of data scraping are difficult to comprehend, and the ethics get murky when you dive that deep.

Sanchez might not be a data scientist, but she's interested. I can explain this to her, and it would be good if someone in the US government was taking the threat of weapons-grade communication seriously. From the internal memos I've looked at, a couple of peons have tried to raise alarms, only to be snuffed out by old men who can't comprehend the science behind using social media for persuasion.

We all live in our own reality now, which means it's that much easier to twist. You don't have to convince an entire community, just one person at a time. Just one feed at a time.

"Okay," Jack says, standing. "I'll get negotiations started. In the meantime, don't say anything."

"Got it, coach." Jack grins again before turning away. "One more thing," I say. He turns back. "Tell my associate…" He nods slowly. "That I'm cool as a cucumber in a pitcher of ice water. You may want to write that down. It needs to be exact."

Jack takes the note and leaves.

No one will come for me… yet. Not unless this cucumber gets toasted. I laugh out loud. *Toasted. Oh, I'm toasted. Super high…*

CHAPTER FOURTEEN

Lenox

"There is one thing a man like Yusuf understands," Petra says, as she caresses the pistol in her lap. "Violence." She stands, her black leather pants moving with her like liquid—all fluidity and grace. She strides to the window. "He will come at us again, and I don't expect him to send another amateur."

Dusk's light flows into the room between the drawn curtains. We've waited in this hotel room for eighteen hours, taking turns resting. Hans and his team wait in the shadows on the street below, also on shifts. But we are still exposed. Yusuf's resources are vast and we are just five people.

Liam and Conner are free… ish. Rachel installed tracking devices on their phones so we can theoretically monitor their movements. However, they could ditch the phones and flee. But where would they go? Back to Ireland to take over Ian's remaining interests there? All he had left when he died was his anger and a few flophouses in the city of his birth.

They can run, and I will not chase them. But eventually this revolution in the sex trade will reach them. There is no escaping. If they stay though, if they can be turned to our side, then we have a path forward.

Cutting off heads won't stop anything. We must change minds. But for now they are not working to protect us.

"Violence," I say. "Yes, Yusf understands violence. It is easy to comprehend. But we will not change anything using the same methods of the men we want to replace."

Petra looks over her shoulder at me. "You have a good heart. But isn't this what Joyful Justice does? Don't you threaten violence to change behavior?"

"As a last resort, yes."

"I think we have arrived at that last resort."

I smile at her words. Why am I not at a resort or sunning myself in the final rays of day on the bow of a yacht?

Because too many people I love have died at the altar of violence. My mother and then Malina—the woman who introduced me to Joyful Justice. She worked the border between Mexico and America, sold herself to generate the resources to flee that horrid place.

After her childhood friend was raped and murdered, she met Sydney Rye and her course changed. Sydney handed her a wad of cash and asked her to live a life she wanted instead of one she felt forced into.

Malina started brothels where woman had control. We met because our business practices aligned. While I only traded in men at the time, we talked shop and shared our passion for a future where our industry put power into the hands of the product—the women and men selling—rather than the brokers and buyers. *Us*.

Slavery still haunts this world. Humans like to pretend we've evolved beyond it, but all we've done is hidden it. Sweeping dust under the rug does not make a house clean.

Malina offered me an opportunity to put my philosophical musings into practice. So, now I sit here in this hotel room, surrounded by luxury but also hunted. Hunted for my beliefs. For my ideas. But mostly for my actions.

I kill.

I fight.

I use what power I have to empower others.

Men like Yusuf understand violence, yes, but that is because they understand power. *Real power.* It often manifests as violence. But there have been movements in this world, in our shared human history, that used a people's willingness to reject violence, to sacrifice their bodies for a shared vision of a better future.

Has violence ever given us that better future?

The United States freed itself from British rule through violence, fought a bloody civil war to end slavery—only to morph it into institutionalized racism and oppression. The allies liberated Europe from Hitler through violence. Senegal, the land of my birth, was freed from colonialism by a poet warrior—who spent two years in a Nazi war camp—through peaceful negotiations. But the central government fought with rebels to maintain control of the Casamance region for decades.

Violence is often necessary and sometimes even just, but can it transform humanity in the way we need to?

"Lenox?" Petra's voice is sharp, as if she's said my name more than once. I blink and focus on her. "What are you thinking about?" Her head cocks to the side.

I shake my head. "Nothing."

"Tell me," she insists, even as she glances out the window again.

"I was thinking about the history of violence in my own life and that of humanity as a whole."

She turns back to me, a half smile cresting her lips. "Oh really, and what conclusions did you draw?"

I stand, crossing to her. Placing a hand on her hip, Petra moves into me, closing the distance between our bodies, melting into me. We fit together—all bodies can mold, but ours *fit*. As if it were planned that way.

"I have reached no conclusion."

Her chin is tilted, as she looks up at me. Her size camouflages her power. "What's the alternative? What's *our* alternative with a man who wants us dead?"

"I have no answers, only questions."

"Okay, let's not give up violence quite yet, then. We may need it to survive." She is teasing but truthful.

Staring down into her eyes a new question forms in my mind. *Why does she love me?* My chest tightens. My mouth opens and I try to cut off the words but they begin to form. "Why...?" I fight harder, stilling my tongue.

"Why do I love you?" she guesses. I shake my head, I don't want to know. "Then what were you going to ask?"

I try to step away, but she uses a hand on my waist to hold me. It's a gentle, persistent touch. More effective than a slap to get what she wants from me. "I love your philosophical musings for one." She smiles, teasing truth again.

I close my eyes, my heart hammering. Why can't I stand to hear her telling me these things? Why do I believe myself so unworthy of the love she offers? Or is it that I don't trust it?

"Stop," I say. The word comes out edged with sadness rather than the anger I hoped to find there.

Her hand comes to my cheek. "Lenox, open your eyes."

I follow her command, the softness of her touch compels me. It crumbles the iron bars I had placed between us—or were they prison bars? The only difference is who holds the key.

Is that what love is? Handing over the keys from our cages to another person? Or is it destroying the bars between you altogether? Either way, I fear the loss of their protection.

"Lenox." Tears well in Petra's gaze. "You must know me by now. You must see how deeply I love you." I try to pull away, but her hands stay on my cheek, forcing me with the gentlest of pressure to maintain eye contact. "You are brave. So brave. And good. So good. Lenox Gold, you are what every man should be."

I swallow, staring into the bright green depths of her—of the woman I love despite her duplicity—no, because of it. Her strength, her unbelievable resourcefulness. My lips crush hers, and my hands at her back close into fists. The kiss is violent—desperate. Starving. I can never taste enough of her.

She meets my violence with softness. Petra yields to me, and it makes me hunger more. I want more. More. More. I need to destroy all boundaries between us. She can have my mind, my life. She is the ultimate thief, and I love her for it. "You see, Lenox." Petra's breath is a pant. "Sometimes we must take what we want."

"Only if the other person wants it taken," I say, pushing her back toward the bed.

A throaty laugh escapes her before my mouth covers hers again.

Sharp pain in my side steals my breath. Petra moves out of my arms so quickly I am left holding empty air. She kicks my feet out from under me, and I drop to the ground. My breath won't come yet.

Her gun cocks, the sound louder than her hurried steps back to the window. She pulls the curtain shut, cutting off the shooter's vision. Then she rushes back to me. "Lenox..." Her face is over mine—eyes sharp, scanning.

Hans is trying to reach us over the radio—it crackles and pops with his voice.

Petra's gaze lands on my side where the white-hot pain sears. Breath comes again. She eases my hands away and rips open my shirt. Warm blood meets cold skin, and I shudder.

Petra rolls me to the side, so she can see the back. "It passed through," she says with the calmness of a surgeon. *A warrior.* She reaches up and grabs a pillow off the bed, ripping off the pillowcase and shoving it onto the wound. I groan.

She grabs the radio off my belt and pressing the comm button while holding it up to my mouth. "Tell Hans," she says.

"Shooter across the way," I say.

"Yes," Hans answers. "We're on it. You've got incoming."

Petra nods, her eyes hard as emeralds. She is so beautiful. She hauls me up so that I'm sitting against the side of the bed—it's between me and the door. There are spots of light in my vision. "Here." She takes one of my hands away from the wound, pressing a pistol into it. "Be my backup," she tells me. I nod.

The door flies open. Petra's slim body coils before she springs up, her elbows landing on the mattress, gun firing in two quick pops. A spray of bullets shreds the curtains behind Petra, blasting out what was left of the window. The noise assaults my ears. Adrenaline thunders into my system, shaking off the shock that cloaked me.

The assassin's heavy footfalls enter the room. Petra fires twice more.

The thunk of a body hits the wall—the slippery slide to the ground sends shivers of disgust up my spine. Petra drops next to me. There is blood seeping from her cheek. Her mouth is a thin red line.

The bed shakes as bullets pound into it.

She flattens herself, pressing her face to the carpet, and slides her gun arm under the bed. Her shoulder jerks when she fires. A scream and footfalls retreat beyond the door.

Petra rises slowly, her eyes meeting mine for a moment as she shifts position. There is nothing there but pure intent. She will win. Protect what is hers and take what is theirs. She drops the magazine out of her gun and, pulling another from the small of her back, slams it home before flashing me a grin. She will have fun doing it all.

Petra sidles to the end of the king-size bed and, gripping her pistol with both hands, takes a breath before rolling out from behind the protection. She stops, her arms extended, body pressed to the floor, aiming at the door. But she does not fire.

I tip to the side, getting onto my knees and craning around the side of the bed. A body is slumped in the doorway, but there is no one living, no one aiming, no one to shoot.

Gunfire in the hall and a gurgling sound indicate there is a secondary battle happening beyond our room. Must be Hans.

Petra rises to stand and moves carefully toward the door, picking her way over the broken pieces of doorway that blew into the room, her arms extended, the gun aimed at the door. "Lenox?" a man's voice calls into the room.

Robert Maxim?

Petra presses up against the wall by the ruined door, gun up and ready.

"Robert?" I yell back.

His laugh reaches us. "Don't shoot," he says.

I nod to Petra. "It's okay..."

Robert Maxim, wearing one of his well-tailored gray suits, steps over the dead body in the doorway. He wears dark glasses. A black beard glinting with copper and silver covers the bottom half of his face. The skin I can see is a ravaged, angry red. Anita said he fell into a toxic canal — I guess it didn't kill him after all.

He smiles when he sees Petra. "I'm Robert Maxim," he says, holding out a gloved hand.

Petra cocks her head and narrows her eyes. "I thought you were dead."

He grins as she accepts his offered hand and they shake. "Not yet." He shifts his focus to me. His smile turns to a frown. "You're hurt?"

"I'll be fine."

"He needs a doctor," Petra says.

Robert pulls a phone from his suit jacket pocket and speaks rapidly in Turkish as he moves toward me. He crouches, keeping his pants from touching the blood-spattered carpeting. "I have a safe house we can use."

"We can provide our own safe house," Petra responds.

Hans appears at the doorway. "Who are you?" he asks, his gun trained on Robert's back.

Robert raises his hands and smiles. "An old friend of Lenox's. Let's move to the safe house, and we can discuss in more detail there."

I nod to Hans, but he does not lower his weapon. *Smart man.*

I struggle to stand; Petra helps. She moves under my arm on my uninjured side, and we head toward the door. We have to maneuver over several dead bodies to make it out of the building and into the waiting van.

"May I ride with you?" Robert asks. "I'll have my men follow."

"Your men?" Hans asks.

"We can trust him," I say. Robert is a snake but one I know. He is not here to kill me. More likely he will offer me a poisoned fruit. Hopefully the scent will not be so delicious that I bite into it.

CHAPTER FIFTEEN

Sydney

Catrina's father's practice is in a beautiful old building not far from my apartment. His office is warm and inviting, nothing like the cold, sterile hospitals where most of my prenatal care has happened until this point.

There are bookshelves and a big desk. When he takes me for my ultrasound, he performs it himself, accompanied by a nurse, in a well-appointed room that, if you removed the equipment, could be used for a houseguest.

That's what I feel like: a guest. Not a patient. A friend they are welcoming. The nurse excuses herself to greet the next patient while Dr. Bonet looks through the images from the ultrasound, his glasses perched on the tip of his nose and his white eyebrows drawn together in concentration.

"A very healthy little boy." He smiles.

"A boy," I parrot back.

"Yes." Dr. Bonet looks up from his computer screen. "Congratulations." He points to the screen, angling it toward me. "See."

A giant head curls into a round little body. He is starting to look like a person, not just a bundle of cells. My eyes prickle. *A boy*. I'll name him

James. Tears blot my vision, and a smile spreads across my face. It's not a smile I've felt before—this is a kind of happiness I've never known.

Blue nuzzles my hand, and I reach out to run my fingers through his fur. Fear trickles up my throat. If anything... *when* something happens to this child... I don't know...

The doctor smiles back at me. "He looks great. About fourteen weeks, as you said."

I stare at the tiny, curled creature on the screen. Last time I saw him, he was just a bouncing bean. And now... now he has—I lean forward—he's got little tiny hands and legs tucked into his belly. My smile widens into a face-eating grin.

"My daughter says this is your second. You have a daughter."

"Yes." I clear my throat, remembering my lies. "My family will be here soon."

"It is not good for a pregnant woman to be alone. Now is a time to be cherished, yes? You and your family must revel in this moment."

Mulberry would like this guy.

I don't respond because there is nothing to say.

He sends me home with a clean bill of health—no hemorrhages in sight.

The main drag is thick with pedestrians. Blue and I duck down into one of the narrow side streets, the buildings rising up high on either side, the sky a slice of perfect blue above us. Ferns and other ornamental plants burst from the balconies, along with drying laundry.

In front of me, a man pushes a metal cylinder on a cart, clinking a stick against it, the sound ricocheting around the narrow street. A woman pops her head over a balcony and yells to him. He waves back, and she ducks inside while he heads to her door.

I pass him as the door opens. What is he selling? I can't tell.

Blue's nose taps my hip twice, and he lets out a low growl. My focus sharpens, and I casually glance behind us. A man strides down the street ten lengths back. He's wearing a dark suit, a ball cap pulled low over his brow, and a camera suspended around his neck.

I take the next left, weaving my way through the maze of streets toward my new apartment. Camera Man follows.

114

I get out the fistful of keys Catrina gave me—one for the front door, one the back, one the mail box, one the bike room, and one for the apartment. Which is which, I have no idea yet. I take long strides down the block. Hopefully, I can get into my apartment before Camera Man catches up with me. If he breaks in, then I have every right to defend myself. But I need to avoid this fight if at all possible.

Maybe I'm just paranoid.

I glance over my shoulder. He's still there, just a few lengths behind me. *Better paranoid and alive, than relaxed and dead.* I should needlepoint that onto a pillow for the nursery.

The door to my building opens as I step up to it, saving me from having to figure out which key I need. An elderly woman smiles at me as I hold the door so she can maneuver her grocery cart out.

Camera Man is crossing the street toward us, walking leisurely, like he's a tourist, his attention on a cafe next door. I pull the large front door shut behind me, the heavy deadbolt automatically clicking into place.

Blue and I take the stairs, running into another neighbor on the way out. We smile at each other and nod—the international language of *hi, how are you, fine, and yourself, good, thank you.*

Blue and I continue up the marble stairs. My neighbor's voice echoes up the stairwell as she greets someone at the front door. I pause, listening.

It's a man's voice. *Shit.* Is it Camera Man?

Hard-soled shoes start up the steps behind us.

I hurry upward, grabbing at the railing to propel myself toward the second floor. I need to get in my apartment now.

Reaching the front door, I try the first key. It doesn't fit.

Shit, shit, shit. Which key is it?

Running from a fight is not my bag. *Not my bag.* The footfalls echo, so it's impossible to judge how close, but they can't be far. Icy fingers of fear trail up my spine. My hand shakes as I shift to the next key, the others jangle, the sound echoing off the tile, and combine with the footsteps, turning the fingers of fear into claws.

The keys fall. I dive after them. *Oh, fuck this.*

A calm washes over me, cleansing the anxiety, leaving behind the clarity of impending battle. Life or death. Fate decides.

Instead of grabbing the keys, I remove my knife from its ankle holster and step back, moving silently up into the shadows of the next stairwell. Blue stays close by my side, warmth radiating off him.

The footsteps stop. They must be at the landing below my apartment, able to see the door and the discarded keys.

Cloth slips against cloth. *Getting out a gun?*

An errant bead of sweat slides down my nose. My breath is slow, even, almost silent. But you cannot be alive without creating sound. Life doesn't work that way. It's loud, it's messy... and it ends.

But not for me, not today.

Hard-soled shoes tap on the marble step. But they are moving away. I strain to hear. *Another step.*

They are retreating. Speeding up now, jogging down the narrow staircase.

I move out of the shadows and approach the hall window. Pulling back the shutter, I use it to shield my body as I peer out. A man exits the building, pulling his phone from the interior pocket of his suit jacket. The stark black of Camera Man's suit stands out in the muted colors of the street.

A ray of sunlight hits him, and the suit practically sparkles. He turns toward the building, and I step back, hidden from the street. His eyes are shielded by sunglasses so black they seem to absorb the light. A shiver of fear tingles over my skin again. He's a professional. Anita and Mulberry were right: people are trying to kill me.

CHAPTER SIXTEEN

Dan

"Tell me about this one." Sanchez turns the tablet to me. On the screen is one of my memes: a gorgeous blonde woman smiles out at the viewer. Her conservative white blouse is unbuttoned one button too far. She looks almost like a yoga mom, except for that extra swatch of skin. On the top it says: *Sex work is honest work.* And on the bottom it reads: *Like and share if you agree we should have control over our own bodies.*

I look up at Sanchez. "I'm pretty sure it's self-explanatory."

Her lips tighten, and her nostril's flare as she breathes in through her nose. "It went viral."

I glance at the tablet, to the statistics below the images. It was shared over 50,000 times and reached several million people. "Appears so," I agree.

"That's all you have to say?"

"You didn't ask me anything." I raise my brows, all innocent prisoner trying to be useful.

She narrows her gaze... so not going for the act. "How did you come up with it?"

I shrug. "The way I come up with anything." I smile. "I just keep trying until I get the results I want." *Us in bed, whispering sweet nothings to each other.*

Her jaw ticks with annoyance, as if she's read my mind and doesn't appreciate the sexual innuendo while at work. "Look," I relent, "I get that you're trying to pick apart how I did this, but it's not going to work that way."

"What do you mean?"

"I didn't do anything complicated. I just kept trying different things until I hit on stuff that worked. The more I threw at the wall, the more things stuck, and once I learned what stuck, it was easier to make new ones."

"Okay, so what sticks?"

"People feeling like their rights are being taken away. That life is unfair. I start with stuff anyone would agree with—so not this." I wave at the image. "Things like, 'Dogs are a man's best friend. Like and share if you think all dogs should be protected from harm.'"

"Okay..."

"Once I get them to like the page and begin to trust it, then I start to lean a little more in my direction. I'm not going after people who are pro-life with this meme. This is the language of pro-choice—women controlling their own bodies, whatever the purpose. And I target accordingly.

So, for what you want to do with the incels, we have to start with what they think is unfair. For example, 'Women get custody of children 98 percent of the time in custody battles. Like and share if you agree men and women should have equal rights.'"

Sanchez sits back in her seat, nodding. "That is one of their complaints."

"Yeah, they think women are the ones with the advantage. They like the idea of things being 'fair.'" I use air quotes around fair. "But the thing is, the real key is targeting." Conseula nods. "Do you have an app for that?"

Her lips twitch into a small smile. "Maybe."

Our deal has been finalized—I get immunity, and she gets a

campaign targeted to incels whose minds can be changed—but she is still holding back. "Let me take a look at it," I prod.

"When we get to our secure location."

"Where is that?"

"You'll find out once you're all healed up."

As if on cue, Dr. Travis walks in. Sanchez stands as though the headmaster just entered the classroom. *I bet she went to Catholic school.* I curse myself for the hundredth time for not researching her thoroughly—stupid. When she started the task force, I should have done a deep dive.

"Mr. Burke," Dr. Travis says, smiling, his gaze quickly shifting to the monitor on the far wall. He taps in his password and reads through the latest notes. "Looks like you're doing a lot better. Less meds today."

"That's right."

"Where is your pain at?"

"A five."

He nods, narrowing his eyes at the screen. "Okay, well, I know Ms. Sanchez wants you out of here as soon as possible."

"Yes," she agrees, crossing her arms over her chest.

"All your scans look good." He turns to me then. "You're lucky there wasn't more permanent damage."

"Yes," I agree, "but unlucky that I got beat up in the first place." I smile at him. Dr. Travis shrugs. *Criminals get what criminals get, I guess.*

He excuses himself to complete his rounds, and Sanchez sits back down, pulling the tablet close. "What are you going to do once I give you all my secrets?" I ask, a teasing tone to my voice. Even though we have a legal document between us, I want to know she will stand by it. That *she* will fight to make sure the US government doesn't try to just throw me in a hole when this is all over.

Her gaze flicks to mine. "That's in our agreement."

"So, you'll just let me walk away?"

She meets my gaze. "You're my asset, Dan. I take care of what's mine."

A shiver runs down my spine. I like that answer more than I should.

CHAPTER SEVENTEEN

Sydney

I leave a message for Catrina. "Our plans have changed, and I'll be returning to America. Thanks for all your help. I've left the keys in the apartment. I don't expect any of my money back."

I call Anita as Blue and I head out of the city in a rented car, having made my way to the rental agency without further sight of the Camera Man. "How is Dan doing?" I ask when she picks up.

"Cops beat the shit out of him." Anita's voice is hard—she's pissed. "I got him a lawyer, and we are negotiating. They want him to help with some social media stuff—convincing incels to not hate women."

"Well, if anyone can do it, Dan can."

"Yes, and it won't hurt us to have done something useful for the US government."

"How severe are his injuries?"

"He'll be fine. On a lot of pain killers still but snarky as ever apparently."

"That's good to hear."

"He's going to be working with a Special Agent named Consuela Sanchez. She was on the same task force as Declan Doyle—tracking the Her Prophet followers and incel members. Used to run it but got demoted. Declan left around the same time to work on an international organized crime task force. We don't have much in our files about her, but Rachel is working on building a profile."

"Sounds good. Keep me informed, will you? I'm not giving up my seat on the council."

Anita doesn't answer for a long moment. "Okay," she says finally.

I'm driving north, up the coast of Spain toward the French border with no destination in mind and no plan. Am I nuts? No. I need a break, with no strange men following me.

"How are things there?" Anita asks.

Do I mention Camera Man?

"Sydney?" Anita prods me.

"I had an… incident in Barcelona."

"What kind?"

"Well, I was followed by a man who looked… professional. I might have been being paranoid, but I don't think so."

"That doesn't sound good." She sighs. "I'd be more comfortable if you'd go to a secure location. Really, it would be so much easier if we didn't need to worry about you."

I grit my teeth, annoyance raising my hackles. "You don't need to worry about me," I snap with more vehemence than I mean. Blue whines softly and shifts to rest his head on my thigh. The warm weight of him grounds me.

"Oh, really?" Anita's attitude rises to meet mine. "That's so nice of you to offer. I thought we were friends. I thought we cared about each other, but if you don't want—"

"Anita," I cut her off. "I'm sorry. You're right. That was dumb of me to say." She doesn't answer. I'm not known for my reasonableness or apologies, so she's probably stunned into silence. "I promise, if anything else happens, I will go to a secure location."

"Okay." Her voice is unsure, as if I've surprised her. Look at me, growing and shit.

EK

I sip an espresso, savoring the bitter sweetness. The plaza of this medieval village two hours north of Barcelona is mostly empty, just sunshine reflecting off sand-colored, foot-smoothed stone and pigeons. I stopped to pee but stayed for coffee and to enjoy the emptiness. It probably gets packed on the weekends, but in the middle of the week, it's just me, Blue, and a few locals on the sun-filled square.

Blue watches the birds with his ears swiveled forward and front paws crossed in front of him—a combination of alert attentiveness and restful anticipation, like an audience enjoying an entertaining show. The waiter returns, and I wave him away, just wanting the coffee today. My stomach can't quite stand the scent of food at this moment, though I may be ravenous in thirty minutes... and I'll probably have to pee again.

I leave a few coins on the table next to the empty cup. It's not customary to tip but leaving nothing makes my skin itch. Too many years spent in the service industry, my wages decided by the mood of my guests, or my own, have made me a fastidious tipper.

Blue and I wander out of the square and down one of the twisting stone streets. It's colder here amongst the residential buildings than in the open square. The sun slants, hitting drying laundry fluttering above the sidewalk. I crouch further into my thin down jacket.

We pass shops closed for siesta, their gates pulled down and windows darkened. It's nice to be in a place so relaxed; there is no hustle and bustle here. *They take three hours for a nice lunch, followed by a nap.*

We come out into the parking area where I left the car, just beyond what was once probably the village wall. I turn back to look at the centuries-old village. Built on a hill in the bend of a river, it is constructed of pale gold stone—a few bars over on the color wheel from the rich red earth of the farm fields that spread out to the distant mountains.

The buildings seem to pile up on themselves, each layer building upon the next, all climbing toward the substantial cathedral at its top. *Beautiful.* Peaceful.

No one would look for me here.

"Would you like to live here?" I ask Blue. He taps his nose to my hip. "I guess anywhere you are is home." His wet nose brushes my fingers.

Blue and I reach the car, and as I settle into the driver's seat, I look at the church in front of me, one of the smaller ones, not as grand as the cathedral. "Why not live here? Why not stay in this small place and join this community? All I'm looking for is a break, a respite. Why not here?"

Blue doesn't respond. I climb out of the car, grab my duffle from the back seat, and we head back into the village.

EK

"I'm looking for an apartment to rent," I say in English to the elderly woman sweeping the sidewalk. I know a little Spanish from my time in Costa Rica, but that wouldn't be much help here. The independent-minded people in the region around Barcelona speak Catalan and have no love for the dominant Spanish.

She squints at me through her glasses. I point to the sign in three languages above her door. *Tourist apartments*. Her gaze drops to Blue, then returns to me. "No pets," she says, her voice heavily accented.

Ms. Friendly returns to her sweeping. A fine mist of construction dust dirties her sidewalk from the renovation happening in the building next door.

"I will pay extra," I offer.

She looks up at me again, raising one brow. "You pay double."

Would paying double buy me her silence or start her mouth running? "Not double," I say. "But I'll give you an extra deposit."

She shakes her head. "Double or nothing."

I glance up the block. We are the only two people out. "I'll pay two weeks in advance. And an extra third."

She leans on her broom, the apron tied around her thick waist clean but worn. A strand of the white hair pinned at the nape of her neck curls free and floats around her face, lifted by a light breeze. Ms. Friendly nods once and turns to the door, beckoning me to follow.

It's dark in the building, and she doesn't turn on a light as she starts up the narrow stairwell. Two flights up, she leads me to a door and pulls a wad of keys from inside the folds of her skirts. For all the darkness of the hall, the apartment is the opposite. Facing the street but high enough that sunlight storms in through the tall windows, it looks out onto the rooftops of the village, the fields beyond, and opaque white-tipped mountains in the far distance. It has a living room, a nice-sized bedroom and a minimal kitchen—all that I need.

I count out the Euros Ms. Friendly requires, and she leaves.

The bed is as hard as a rock, but the room is airy and bright. I open the windows, and a sun-warmed breeze carries the scent of orange blossoms. Exhaustion overwhelms me—in the way it has since my pregnancy began—and I curl up on the bed. Blue leaps up next to me, lying so that our spines align, each of us watching the other's back.

I wake to a darkened room and the reverberating chime of a church bell. Sitting on the edge of the bed, I look out over the rooftops. At the end of the sixth ring, I stand and make my way back to the kitchen sitting area with its tall windows and narrow balcony. As I rifle through my bag, looking for a bottle of water, banging starts up next door.

Construction. Heading out to my balcony, I discover equipment and tools piled up on the neighboring balcony. *Ms. Friendly totally played me.* I can't help the smile that twists my lips. *Tough old bird.*

Blue and I hit the street, quickly finding a butcher where I get him some bones and fresh meat. I drop it off at the apartment and then head back out to try and find some dinner. I'm not one to cook at the best of times, and the apartment's kitchen is barely serviceable for a cup of tea.

But I'm filled with a sense of optimism. This is going to work out…

CHAPTER EIGHTEEN

Lenox

The safe house is a renovated mansion on the Bosporus, the narrow body of water that separates Europe from Asia, with Istanbul straddling the two continents. The view is spectacular, the position fortified, the architecture Mediterranean. Hans called in more Joyful Justice members, and we now have ten guards on the property, including the three men Robert brought with him. We are at war with Yusuf now—all out. It will be a bloodbath. And I still don't know what Robert wants or why he faked his death.

"You can't tell Joyful Justice about this yet," Robert says, referencing his resurrection.

I shift on the couch, reaching forward for my glass of water, my wound sending shivers of pain over me and breaking sweat along my hairline. The numbing agent the doctor used is fading. The few hours of sleep I caught were not enough. "I will not betray Joyful Justice," I say.

Robert nods, agreeing with me. He's removed the dark glasses—his eyes, a strange blue green, are even brighter when surrounded by the red skin. He may have faked getting shot, but that canal water really was toxic. That is what convinced me he really died. A calculated risk on his part to take that plunge. The skin is blistered in some places but looks as if it's healing. It shines in the low light, as if he's recently applied ointment.

"Of course I don't expect you to betray Joyful Justice," Robert says. I suspect we have different definitions of betrayal. "It is not a breach of faith to keep some of your own business private though. Just for a time."

"You are a man of faith?" Petra asks. She is at the bar, pouring scotch over a large cube of ice. Her black leather pants, a black turtleneck and sports coat make her pale skin and red lips that much more dramatic. The lump under her jacket shows how close she is keeping her gun now.

Robert shifts his attention to her. "In my way."

She moves to join us, taking a place at the far end of the couch and crossing her legs, resting the glass on her knee, her eyes watching Robert the whole time—waiting to catch him at something.

"You are a slippery man, Robert Maxim," I say. He smiles as though that is a compliment. "I will hear you out, and if I think it's important for the council to know, I will inform them. If secrecy is for the greater good, then so it shall be."

Robert nods, a gentle smile playing over his lips. "Fair and reasonable. Sydney Rye could learn from you."

I grimace as I sip the water. "She does quite well on her own."

Robert shrugs. "She is in Spain. I don't understand why."

I suppress a laugh—the look on his face is almost comical. As if Robert Maxim not understanding something means the matter in question makes no sense. It must be hard to be so smart and sure of oneself and run up against a woman like Sydney Rye.

Running up against someone you can't understand and who makes you unsure of yourself and your world view can do... things. I feel Petra watching me as I ease back into the couch cushions. I meet her gaze. There is so much in her eyes that I want. It makes my chest ache as much as the wound in my side.

"I don't know why Sydney is in Spain either," I say, returning my attention to Robert, "but I assume she has good reasons".

He shakes himself, as if throwing off the worries and thoughts of her, though I doubt he can let them go for long. "As you know, I recently found out I'm a father," Robert says.

"Yes, it was supposedly your son who had you killed and who plans on assassinating as many members of the Joyful Justice council as he and his co-conspirators can identify, while simultaneously working to destroy our reputation." I wave a hand at Robert. "Clearly, there is a misunderstanding on some of the basic facts."

Past Robert, the French doors leading to the terrace are shut. A guard, his Uzi hanging from his shoulder as casually as a purse swings from a rich woman's arm, protects the entryway. Beyond the elegant white iron furniture and stone parapet, the Bosporus glimmers in the moonlight.

"My son—" Robert clears his throat. "—and his mother are heads of a powerful criminal organization. They are a part of a Columbia-based cartel that is intent on destroying Joyful Justice." His gaze flicks to Petra. "I believe you are aware of this."

She nods. "Yes, Lenox knows all that I know."

"I understand you took over the McCain brothers' brothels and trading routes."

"They were my routes," Petra reminds him. "We partnered for a long time."

"But you did not know they were dealing in war slaves?"

"No." Petra meets Robert's gaze. She shows no shame.

He nods and returns his attention to me. "Now you're in a turf war with Yusuf."

"You know a lot for a dead man," Petra says.

Robert smiles. "I have my ways."

"What do you want?" I ask. My side is hurting, and I want to rest.

"I want to help you take over my son's enterprise, to dismantle the cartel and bring it all under your umbrella." He pauses, watching me. I keep my face impassive. "A new criminal king for a new era. You'll promise—as you've proven you can provide—fair wages and a stable, voluntary work environment where all can prosper."

What a shiny, lovely apple he offers. "You want me to kill all the men and women who are fighting against Joyful Justice, take over their networks, and profit from them."

Robert shakes his head, leaning forward and resting his elbows on his knees. A lock of his dark hair falls over his brow. "I don't plan to kill them all. That would be far too difficult and attract the wrong kind of attention." A smile plays over his lips. "I'm going to have them all taken into custody, tried for their crimes, found guilty, and sentenced appropriately."

Petra laughs. "You want to take down *all* of them. Some of the most powerful heads of organized crime on the planet?"

"Yes." Robert nods. "I do. And I will." The confidence in his voice is absolute. "That is why I faked my death. I am the only person who can pull this off, and no one will see it coming if they think I'm gone."

"You're working with law enforcement?" I ask.

Robert nods. "A special task force that works across several agencies and in coalition with Interpol. This is all in an effort to keep my son out of my way, but not dead."

"You're a wonderful father," Petra quips.

Robert ignores her. "I need your help to avoid a power vacuum. If we don't have a powerful organization ready to step in and take over operations, then I believe we will see a bloodbath amongst subordinates as they clash to be king."

"Why not let them fight it out?" Petra asks. "It will cull the herd."

Robert shrugs. Sydney would not like it. But will she like this plan any better? "Obviously, drugs will continue to move across borders, and sex work will never stop. The question is, do we want the most exploitive and bloodthirsty in charge or you?"

Petra raises both brows. "Me?"

"As Lenox's partner, of course," Robert says.

"What are you asking for exactly?" Petra asks, pinning him with a hard stare.

"I will take out all your competition, even people you never competed with. You will use the manpower you already have, and the inside information I will share with you, to rule them all. We will use your reputation to seize power when the vacuum opens." He sits back in his chair. "Like Genghis Khan, you will use the existing power structures within the organizations to rule effectively from a distance."

My head pounds. "Genghis Khan used rape, mass murder, *and*

existing power structures. He used threats of extinction to gain obedience. He also had an army."

"Khan never tried to enforce cultural or religious changes—that is important—but he did have a set of laws that reached across his entire empire. More than anything, he kept things peaceful. He, to put it in modern parlance, made the trains run on time. If you can show that everyone can still make money, with peace and good practices—" Robert smiles, his eyes brightening. "—you'll change the world, Lenox Gold."

The burns on his face give him an air of horror that makes his words more powerful. Only Robert Maxim could use gruesome facial burns to his advantage. "I believe that you can convince criminals to stop the most abhorrent of their practices."

"No one has ever successfully run an international criminal organization the size and breadth of which you describe," I say. "Also, Petra and I don't have an army."

"Don't you?" he asks, gesturing to the gunman by the door.

"Members of Joyful Justice are not going to fight for us if we become an improved version of the criminals we rally against," I point out.

"People want to be a part of something larger than themselves," Robert says. "They are willing to kill to end the practices that we are talking about ending—but they are not willing to be the standing army that keeps the peace? I think you underestimate them."

"You can't expect me to agree to any of this without speaking with the council. You're talking about using Joyful Justice as an army to destroy your enemies."

"They are Joyful Justice's enemies, Lenox. I'm just caught in the middle, really."

Petra snorts. "You are something else, Mr. Robert Maxim."

He grins at her, his white teeth stark in the dark beard. "Let me show you what I can do. I want to prove myself."

"How?" she asks.

"Let me solve your Yusuf problem."

"Solve it?" Petra asks. "You mean have him arrested?"

"Yes."

"But why would anyone in the city decide to do as we say if we are not the ones who take him down?" Petra says, pointing out the dog-eat-dog reality of life and how pack animals work.

"This will be the testing ground for my theory. If I'm right," he says it with more humility than I suspect he truly has, "then, Lenox, you can speak with the council and we can move forward."

Silence descends as he lays the proverbial apple on the table. Petra looks at me and raises a brow.

"Okay," I say.

"Good." Robert nods. "I ask one more thing."

"Yes?" My voice is weary, and Robert smiles congenially—the friendly doctor who just has to run one more test.

"Let me tell Sydney I'm alive. I don't want her to find out from someone else."

"I will not promise you that."

"Fair enough for now. But if I prove myself and my theory, will you grant me that request?"

"Yes," I say, biting into the sweet juice of the apple, not tasting the poison yet but suspecting it's there.

CHAPTER NINETEEN

Dan

"A private jet," I say as Sanchez and I move across the tarmac toward a small plane complete with Homeland Security seal. "I must be important."

"Or I am," she points out.

"Touché. Are you?" I know the answer: no. If she were, I'd know more about her—I keep track of important figures in Homeland Security. From what I can remember of her file, she's the daughter of a New York City cop. The task force she started is now headed by a man, and she was demoted to his deputy... hence me starting to ignore her. Something I won't ever do again.

"Very." She says it like she's joking, but when I glance down at her, she isn't smiling. Well, I can't see her eyes—they are hidden behind dark tortoiseshell sunglasses—but her lips are a straight line.

A wind tugs at her hair, pulling a few strands loose as we start up the gangway.

Inside the small aircraft, Sanchez takes a seat at one of the four tops, gesturing for me to sit across from her. My guards, Tweedledee and Tweedledum, sit by the entrance. They look like what you'd expect federal agents to look like—suits and ties, mirrored aviators, and strong, clean-shaven jaws. *Don't worry, boys, I'm not going to make a run for it.*

And no one will come for me as long as everyone sticks to the agreement. My being in Homeland Security custody is not the end of Joyful Justice—everyone knows that. Rachel is perfectly prepared to take over. In fact, she was already performing most of my duties since I took a leave of absence to be with my mom.

My *not* dying mom. "I'd like to call my mother when we land, if that's possible."

Sanchez looks up from her phone. The sunglasses sit on the table between us now, so I can see those gorgeous eyes again. Sunlight hits them from the side, bringing out the sparks of golden sunset hidden in the dark amber depths. "That can be arranged."

"What did you tell her about my arrest?"

"I have not spoken to your mother," she says it like I'm some kind of an idiot for thinking she had.

"Okay, not you *personally*, but what is the story you're using? What's the cover? What are you telling my mom and that poor, frightened neighbor who saw me get my ass kicked about why a cadre of cops showed up, chased me down, and beat the ever-loving shit out of me?" *Still a little bitter about that? Yup.* "Oh, and how she doesn't actually have cancer."

Sanchez frowns. "You were suspected of violating the Computer Crimes Act."

"That's not a violent crime. Why beat me up?"

"You resisted arrest, remember? Snuck out through a tunnel and then made a run for it through the yards of your mother's neighbors. Or should I say, *your* neighbors." My eyes narrow. *Where is this going?* "You own the house your mother lives in. Paid off the mortgage and now it's in both your names." *A subtle threat...*

A smile sneaks across my lips. She looks up at me from under her lashes. "You want me to work with you," I say. "I've agreed to help. I'm not going to piss you off, Consuela." She stiffens a little at the use of her first name. Wonder if she likes to hear me say it the same way I adore hearing her say mine. "I'm going to be perfectly behaved. I promise." Her frown deepens. "You don't believe me?" It's my turn to raise my brows, all innocent, confused prisoner.

"Just seems a little too easy."

I grin. "Easy is my middle name." I glance at the briefcase sitting next to her. "That's not in your files?"

She huffs what could be a laugh, and my grin widens. "I think you've got a good plan," I say with a shrug. "I'm always happy to help try to convince zealots to lay down their weapons."

"You don't consider yourself a zealot?"

"You do?"

"Fanatical and uncompromising in your ideals. I think that sums up you and the rest of the Joyful Justice membership."

"We're not uncompromising," I say with a smile. "We are always looking for solutions."

"Solutions that lead to *your* outcome."

"Solutions that lead to the *best* outcome."

"How do you decide what's best?"

I point to the sky as the plane begins to rumble across the tarmac. "From the big man upstairs." She cocks her head, not believing me. I touch my finger to my temple. She shakes her head and rolls her eyes.

"You refer to your brain as God?"

Better than referring to my other head as such. Her eyes narrow as though she's read that thought off my face. "What about you?" I ask. "How do you decide what's right?"

"I don't worry so much about right and wrong. I stick to legal and illegal."

"But that's not what this is about. It's not illegal to be a misogynist rabble-rouser."

"Rabble-rouser? What are you, an eighty-year-old woman?" She's smiling... she's teasing.

The plane speeds up, and the engines whine. "No, I'm just a man," I say as we lift into the air.

She shakes her head. "Well, Dan—"

"The man," I interrupt her.

She has to bite her cheek not to laugh. I'm almost sure of it. *We are getting very close to victory.*

"I'm not calling you Dan the man."

I shrug. "Your loss."

She clears her throat and sits up straighter. "I'm glad you want to help. I think we can make a real difference." She's earnest now, all teasing gone. We hit a patch of rough air, and the plane jerks. She doesn't flinch. *Oh, I like her. Brave, bold, and trying to make the world a better place.* I might be in serious trouble here. I may be a frog, enjoying a warming bath, unaware it is going to slowly rise to a deadly boil.

Sanchez pulls out her laptop and opens it. "Okay," she says, "tell me what you're thinking."

"Frogs in big cooking pots."

"Excuse me? What do frogs in cooking pots have to do with changing incels' minds about women?"

"It's the slow boil. Everyone wants to be a part of something larger than themselves," I say. "We all want to connect. The irony of social media is that it does the opposite of what it *feels* like it is doing. You think, I have all these friends, all these connections. But what you actually have is a reality constructed for you by artificial intelligence that is manipulating you in a million different ways. Using *your* data to change *your* behavior. These platforms are designed to be addictive. They take all the most potent aspects of casino gambling and propaganda and put it in a device in your pocket. The drinks are not free, but your feed is."

Sanchez nods. "I get all that. I get the power, Dan." She leans forward. "What I want to figure out is how to use it for good."

I can't help the smile that crosses my lips. "You picked the wrong organization to work for, Sanchez." She shakes her head, brushing me off. "The job of Homeland Security isn't to do good; it's to protect the American people at all cost. That's noble in some ways and evil in others." I have a few philosophers I could pull out at this moment, but I won't.

She frowns now. "Let's not have a moral discussion about the role of the US government in world politics please."

"Why? Because you'll lose?"

"Hardly. Because our realities are just too different." Her eyes twinkle with humor, and I can't help but feel a tug in my chest. I clear my throat and sit forward, pulling the laptop closer. "Right, so you want to get to incels and the Her Prophet—"

She interrupts me. "Just the incels."

I look at her and cock an eyebrow. "You don't want to stop the Her Prophet from getting a foothold in young women's minds?" She gives me a dead-eyed stare. "Really? Interesting."

"So how do we reach these young men?" she pushes on.

"First we have to find the ones that are reachable. We have to get in their phones, in their lives. And to do that, we need a quiz, an app, and a game. A game they will like."

"This sounds illegal."

"Read your terms of service closer. It's perfectly legal for my app—which I write the terms of service for—to do whatever the fuck I want."

"You're not serious."

"You came to me for a reason. It is totally illegal to hack into a business and steal their customers' information, but it is perfectly legal to put anything we want in our terms of service. I'm not going to tell you what I use to scrape data for my own purposes, but I will build something for us to use in this project."

"So that's how you target?"

"It's simple data science. When building an algorithm, you need to create a training set. Before we can sway behavior, we need to get people to answer a 120-question personality quiz."

"How do you get people to do that?"

"I pay them."

"Pay them?"

"Yes, a few dollars. To get paid, they have to download an app and accept the terms of service. That's when we scrape their profiles and those of all their friends. I'll then use the scraped data from the app to target specific users I think can be persuaded. I can see the profiles of every single person who downloads my apps, as well as all their friends. It's compound math. Combine that with the personality test, and we can start to predict behavior better than most people's mothers."

"I can't believe that's legal."

"Talk to your congressperson." She does a weird half laugh. "What?" Her cheeks brighten in an embarrassed flush. "No, seriously, what?"

She rolls her eyes. "None of your business, Dan. We're not friends. You're an asset."

Gut punch. But that's okay, I'm tough.

"So, once you have their personality tests and profiles, what's next?"

"We will have our 'training set,' that's the data in its entirety: the Facebook likes and the personality tests. We can use that data to train my algorithm to look for persuadables—people whose minds we can change. Then we can target them with messages we want by creating Facebook pages and profiles to manipulate them. We can slowly change the nature of their feed and, therefore, change the way they see the world around them."

"Slowly boil the frog," she says. I nod. "That's amazing… the possibilities."

"Yes, this is weapons-grade communication." *Which is why I will be building self-destruct codes into all my work.* "In order to build this for you, I'm going to need access to a computer day and night, as well as a superfast internet connection." I hold my hand up to halt her protests. "You can watch everything I'm doing. But the way I work, it's all hours and it cannot be throttled. Feel free to check all the logs in the morning. But if you want this done, you'll have to let me work. You came to me for a reason."

She chews on her lip for a moment. "I guess… I'll see what I can do," she promises.

EK

We land at a small airport just outside Washington DC, and Sanchez leaves in a black town car with Tweedledum for some kind of official business, while Tweedledee escorts me to my new living quarters. It's corporate housing at its best with a view of a generic courtyard, the kind of kitchenette one needs if their diet is 90 percent takeout, and carpeting that would probably be as comfortable outside as in.

I flop onto the bed of the studio apartment and throw an arm across my eyes, letting out a deep, pathetic sigh. It's only been a few days—and several of those I was high as a kite—but not having a computer to work on in the evenings will drive me insane if I don't get one soon.

I'm like an addict going through withdrawal. How did people live before the internet? I stand up and pace to the window, pulling the curtains aside. The courtyard is empty at this hour. The building is in walking distance to the Pentagon, so most of the people staying here are probably on assignment there—a fun bunch.

Exercise is the only answer.

I start with pushups, taking in air as I lower my nose almost to the scratchy carpeting before expelling my breath and forcing the floor away. "One," I huff out. "Two." *Her eyes are really marvelous.* "Three." *Intelligent and fierce.* "Four." *Stop thinking about her.* "Five." *How am I supposed to do that without any distractions?* "Six." *Just shut up.* "Seven." *You shut up.* "Eight." *Now you're talking to yourself.* "Nine." *I told you no internet would make you crazy.* "Ten." *Concentrate on the burn.* "Eleven." *It's not burning enough.* "Twelve." *We need more weight.* "Thirteen." *Don't worry, just keep going. It will start to hurt.* "Fourteen." *See, now you're feeling it in your triceps.* "Fifteen." *Shift your hands to diamond position.* "Sixteen." I jump my hands together and start over. "One." *This is going to be a long-ass assignment.*

A knock at the door saves me from my internal dialogue. I check the peephole. Consuela Sanchez stands on the other side; her face is in profile as she chats with Tweedledee.

I open the door, grinning. "Couldn't stay away," I say.

She turns to me, her eyes rolling. "I brought you a book." She holds up a paperback.

"How thoughtful. Won't you come in." I step back, pacing to the kitchen bar.

"I have a dinner, so here." She stands just inside the door, the book outstretched.

"A dinner?" I ask, coming back to her. "Sounds serious. Who's it with?"

"None of your business."

"Okay. Is it business or pleasure?" I waggle my eyebrows, and she rolls her eyes again. If eye rolls were laughs, I'd be killing it over here.

"Seriously, none of your business."

"Fine." I hold up my hands, still not taking the book from her. "But I'd like to make a plea."

"A plea?"

"For a computer and an internet connection."

"We discussed this earlier. I'm going to work on it." She holds the book out, and I glance down at it.

"*One Hundred Years of Solitude*? Is this a subtle threat?" I smile at her.

"It's one of my favorites." The thick volume is worn at the edges. It's her copy. She clears her throat. "Do you want it?" Sanchez starts to pull it back.

"Yes." I reach out, taking hold of my side and raising my eyes to meet hers. She blinks once, long and slow, before releasing the book.

"Good night," she says, her voice edged with *something*... or my imagination is putting something there.

"Good night," I say.

She clears her throat and turns away. "We start work tomorrow, first thing."

"Looking forward to it," I say as she closes the door. *And I am.*

CHAPTER TWENTY

Sydney

Blue and I get home from our walk, and the tall French doors in my living room are open, the long curtains shifting in the breeze.

I did not leave them open.

We stop in the entryway, and I lay my keys quietly down on the pier table—where I've placed them every time we've come home from our walk for the past two months. We've lived an idyllic life in this small village but it appears to be coming to an end.

Blue sniffs the air. His hackles rise, but he does not growl. We don't want them to realize we know they're here. Adrenaline slowly seeps into my veins. *I've missed this.* Calm washes over me as I follow Blue's gaze toward the bedroom.

Should I just leave? My hand finds my stomach—bulged with new life. A small movement inside me pulls my attention, but I quickly refocus on the problem at hand.

They may expect me to leave and have a second operative in the hall.

I let the front door close behind us and walk casually to the balcony, as an attacker might anticipate I'd do. Otherwise, why leave the doors open? It's either to scare me away or tempt me in.

I step through the curtains. A long, metal pole sticks out from the next balcony over, a part of the construction project. Reaching out, I take hold of it, pulling it to my side.

It's about six inches shorter than me, the circumference just wide enough for my hand to close around it. It is heavier than my normal fighting staff with ragged, sharp ends, but will do just fine. Blue sits by my side as I take a deep breath. A movement in the living room behind the curtains draws me forward.

I step into the space, the pole held lightly in my right hand.

A man wearing a black balaclava aims his gun at my head. The pistol is silenced, the barrel elongated. He holds it with both hands. His bulky sweatshirt is tight across the bulging muscles of his arms but loose at his stomach. The opening of his mask frames a dark beard and full lips. Balaclava's shoulders are wide, his waist narrow, his worn denim jeans hug his legs all the way down to running shoes. *Should have run when he had the chance.*

Balaclava's lips begin to tilt up into a smile. I drop low, swing the pole out, and let it slip through my fingers. The long, thin weapon sails through the air inches from the floor.

Blue coils his body, a growl rumbling his chest.

The pole strikes Balaclava's ankle, letting out a soft ring. A church bell outside begins its mid-day tolling as he cries out and begins to fall. He fires on the way down, and the light on the ceiling explodes, raining glass. Blue uncoils, thrusting with his back legs, aiming for Balaclava's gun arm, his jaw wide. As they meet midair, Blue latches onto Balaclava's arm and speeds his descent.

The bell tolls a second time.

Balaclava hits the floor with enough force to shake the building. I follow the pole, snatching it up, twirling it around my waist and over my shoulder, using the momentum to strike hard onto Balaclava's gun wrist, close to where Blue's teeth dig into his forearm but a safe distance from the dog's face.

The bell tolls.

Balaclava's hand goes limp, and the gun slips free. I kick it away, so that it skitters toward the curtains, which are still dancing in the wind.

A knife glints in Balaclava's free hand. "Off," I command Blue, who leaps back as the man strikes out, hitting empty air instead of Blue's flank.

The bell tolls.

I drag the tip of the pole across the floor, scratching a line in the wood with the sharp edge. It's now well positioned to strike again, well before he could reach me with his knife. Balaclava's eyes rise to meet mine. "Who sent you?" I ask.

The bell tolls.

His breath comes in deep, heavy pants as he lays on his side, his wounded arm outstretched, the wrist swelling, blood seeping from the holes in his dark sweatshirt. His good arm—the one with the knife—stays tense and ready. Balaclava shifts, as if to stand. I shake my head. He stills.

The bell tolls.

Blue circles to his back, putting himself between the front door and Balaclava. My back is to the French doors leading to the balcony. "Is there someone in the hall?" I ask quietly. Balaclava doesn't answer. The skin around his eyes is tight—probably from the pain of his injured arm.

The bell tolls.

Balaclava drops the knife; it clatters next to him. He opens his palm, raising his hand, giving up. What should I do with him? "Lie on your stomach, both arms out."

The bell tolls.

Blood smears across the floor as Balaclava retracts his injured arm. His shoulder tenses as his hand disappears under him and he begins to shift his hips to lay on his stomach.

Blue growls a warning. When Balaclava' hurt hand comes out the other side, he's got a new gun—must have been under his sweatshirt. One quick step and my foot connects with his stomach hard enough to flip him back, so that he lies on his injured arm, trapping the new weapon under him.

The bell tolls.

I step over him, straddling his waist, holding the staff like a tightrope walker. Balaclava struggles, his eyes wild now; he's trying to get his arm out from under his own weight, but between the bites and the swollen wrist, he's struggling.

On my exhale, I use my shoulders and the strength in my abdominals to spin the staff tip into the side of his head. His lights go out.

The bell tolls.

I reach down and drag his arm out, capturing the small pistol, then step back, my balance faltering as I slip in a slick of blood. I stumble and reach out, finding the wall for support.

The bell tolls.

I press my back up against it and drop the pole. It clatters on the floor and rolls a foot away. I bring my hand up to cradle the small bulge at my belly. My gaze focuses on the still-open balcony doors. Broken glass litters the floor, glinting in the bright sun pouring into the room.

My breath comes in deep drags. Blue touches his nose to my hip. "Careful of the glass, boy," I say, laying a hand on his head and looking down at him. My fingers leave smears of blood on the white fur at the crown of his head.

The final bell tolls. It's noon.

"We better get cleaned up." My eyes land on the broom, leaning where I left it by the balcony door this morning. The apartment gets dusty from the construction.

Footfalls on the stairs pull a new low growl from Blue's throat and send a fresh wave of adrenaline through me. No time for cleanup.

Blue nudges my hip again. I click the safety on the small pistol and shove it into the waistband of my jeans. Kicking the glass aside, I walk out onto the balcony; Blue follows in my wake. I blink in the sunshine, then look down on the dark street below, shaded by the medieval houses —narrow and quiet.

Pressing my lips together, I release the sweet, brief dream of normalcy. Violence always wakes me from this fantasy.

I'm not normal. I never will be.

My hand swipes briefly at my belly before gripping the edge of the balcony. I vault over it, dropping to a narrow roof ledge below. Blue launches himself after me, his claws scrambling for purchase. I grip his collar, steadying him. We move along the roof until we are over another neighbor's balcony.

Crouching, turning and gripping the edge, I lower myself down and drop the last six inches onto the balcony. Blue lands lightly next to me.

A scream from above. Ah, must have been the landlady on the stairs, not another assassin. *Sorry, Ms. Friendly...*

The French doors leading into the neighbor's apartment stand open, the interior shielded by flowing curtains and shadow. I don't hear any noise inside. Sirens wail in the distance.

Pushing through the curtains, Blue and I enter a living room. Two couches face each other. A TV is mounted on the wall. Kids' toys litter the floor. A wet diaper lies on the coffee table. The front door is to my right.

Blue's ears twitch in the direction of the hallway to the left. I listen. A woman is singing, probably putting her baby down for a nap. We move quietly toward the front door. I open it slowly, easing it on well-oiled hinges. My eyes catch on the low table by the door. Next to a sippy cup and a half-eaten sandwich are a set of car keys.

Blue nudges me to keep moving. I swipe the keys and step into the hallway, shutting the door quietly behind us and releasing a breath.

The apartment building hallway smells like a mix of roast chicken and coffee—staples for any well-lived life. We make it to the front door, and I ease the thick door open, peering out onto the street. The sirens are closer but not here yet. There are no vehicles parked on the street. *Where does she keep her car?* The sirens' increasing volume urges me out the door.

Blue and I move onto the sidewalk and jog quickly down the block. I take the first turn I can—a right—and climb the narrow steps. My sneakers make hardly any noise on the ancient stone. Above us, laundry flaps outside windows bracketed by wooden shutters. So picturesque.

I take a left and move down a side street too narrow for cars. The sky above is bright blue, but the lane is shaded and cool. The sirens closer still.

We are headed up the hill that the village is built on, toward the cathedral. A door opens and a middle-aged woman with dark hair, carrying empty grocery bags steps out, calling back into the apartment before dashing into the street, almost knocking into us. She apologizes and smiles. I shrug and act like I'm not spattered with blood.

The shopper's eyes catch on it, and her face pales. I put both hands up in a *shit happens* gesture. "I'm okay," I say.

Shopper's eyebrows bunch. "Do you need help?" she asks in accented English.

Yes. "No," I say.

Her eyes narrow. "Come." She takes my arm, and before I can protest, Blue and I are in her living room. A clock on the mantel ticks. Dust motes dance in spears of sunlight. An elderly woman, a blanket over her shoulders, smiles at us from the couch. A film over her eyes suggests her vision is impaired.

"Your man?" the woman asks as she tugs me through to a kitchen. It's narrow and runs the length of the back of the house. It has worn Formica countertops and the Lilliputian appliances of Europe—it's cute and homey and tugs at my heart. I shouldn't be here. I'm not good like this woman. She thinks I'm a victim... I'm the monster who goes bump in the night.

Shopper wets a cloth under the tap and glances up at me, raising a brow. "A man," I answer her question honestly. The woman clicks her tongue against her teeth and nods. She knows about the violence of men.

"I am Maria," she says, turning off the tap and wringing out the cloth.

Maria is about my height with a thickness that suggests health and strength. Her woolen waist-high slacks look well made. The blouse she's wearing has a bow at the neck, the peachy color a beautiful shade against her coppery skin.

She steps up to me, her eyes focusing on my face. Maria holds up the dish cloth as if to question if she can wipe at my face. I nod. Her eyes narrow as she dabs my cheek. I suck in a breath when she touches a gash I didn't even realize was there. Must have been from the light fixture shattering.

I close my eyes, fighting back tears. Not from the pain. From the tenderness. Her finger brushes my nose, and I open my eyes to find her smiling at me.

"You are good," she says.

The tears escape, rushing free as I shake my head. "I'm not." The words tumble out on a sob that bows my body. Suddenly I'm in this stranger's arms. She holds me tight, rocking. Maria rubs my back. I curl into her, desperate for the comfort. For the tenderness.

When the storm passes, I pull away and let out a choked laugh. "I'm sorry," I say, brushing at my eyes. "I can't believe I just did that."

Damn pregnancy hormones. But the thought doesn't have any power behind it. I'm broken right now but lighter.

Maria smiles at me, as if she's been standing where I stand now. As if we have a shared past, a shared experience. But this woman is not a killer. She is a survivor.

"You are good," she says again. It makes my chin wobble. Maria turns to the sink, rewetting the cloth before focusing on me again. She cleans my face. Then her eyes drop to my clothing, and she does the tongue-clicking sound. "Come," she says. "I give you clothing."

I open my mouth to protest, but she is already moving. I look down at Blue. He meets my gaze; then his attention turns to Maria, already through to the living room.

I follow.

She dresses me in a pair of wool pants and a blouse; they are loose but fit well enough. I keep my sneakers and the small pistol. Before we leave I text Anita and Lenox. They give me the address of a safe house in Paris. Maria loops her arm through mine as we step out onto the street.

Tires squeal and a police car slides to a stop at the bottom of the street. Pulling free from Maria, I break into a sprint, Blue at my heel, racing up the hill. But another police car appears at the top of the road, officers pouring out the door, yelling for me to freeze.

I turn back, catching Maria's gaze. Her eyes are wide, her mouth forming a small O of surprise. I'm not the victim she thought I was.

But it *was* self-defense. I raise my hands slowly. I'm a tourist who was attacked in her apartment. Nothing more and nothing less.

CHAPTER TWENTY-ONE

Dan

Sanchez drops a paperback on my desk as she heads to her own. "Did you like it?" I ask, picking up the copy of *Harry Potter and the Sorcerer's Stone*. She sits down and pulls out her laptop, avoiding eye contact. "You did," I accuse, sitting back in my chair. "You liked the kids' book." I'm grinning.

She opens her computer and meets my eyes. "Yes," she acknowledges, then quickly looks away.

"Wait." I lean forward. Our desks face each other, the back edges touching, so that the printout of Facebook profiles and other papers we pass back and forth throughout the day can slide across the expanse of our desks easily. She doesn't look at me. "You downloaded the next one, didn't you?"

Her cheeks brighten, and an embarrassed smile tugs at her lips. Consuela had insisted she did not need to read the Harry Potter series because she was an *adult*. "Ha!" I point at her. "You loved it."

She rolls her eyes. "It was good. I already said it was good."

"You *loved* it."

"Shut up."

I laugh and settle back into my chair. "You're in trouble now," I say.

"That series is addictive. Hope you didn't have plans for this weekend, because you're going to be reading all day and night." She just shakes her head. "Next I'll have you reading *His Dark Materials*. That series is awesome."

"It's my turn to pick a book," she points out.

"True. Do you have one in mind yet?" We've been trading book recommendations back and forth for the last two months, ever since she gave me *One Hundred Years of Solitude*. It's been fun to escape into fiction. While I still spend most of my evenings working on our project, I've carved out time for reading.

It's just one of the many ways Consuela has affected me.

"Not yet," she says. "Now get back to work."

I smile, returning my attention to the computer.

Hours fly by as I type, absorbed in writing code. Consuela sits across from me, equally engrossed in her own work—she is going through the data I've scraped, looking for targets to put under surveillance in the hopes of stopping another mass shooting or attack.

She stands and stretches, pulling my focus. I blink, my eyes catching on the time. It's early evening. "Want to see something cool?" I ask her.

She nods and circles to my side of the desk. Consuela's hair brushes my shoulder as she leans over me to get closer to my screen, and I take in a lungful of her scent. She turns her face at the sound. Because I just inhaled her.

Our lips are close. She realizes how close when our eyes meet. Consuela's pupils widen, but she doesn't back away.

I can feel every inch of my skin, and it is all desperate to touch her. But I don't move. I'm frozen to this spot, stuck between a desperation for contact and terror that reaching out will destroy the connection we've built over the last eight weeks—discussing books and plotting how to best effect change.

She is not going to kiss her asset no matter how much I want her to. She's a true professional, practically a zealot for good procedure. That's become clear in her words and actions. Though her reading tastes do lean toward the underdog, and even occasionally the vigilante, Consuela Sanchez is a die-hard believer in the rule of law.

She still hasn't moved though. My breath is shallow. I don't want to frighten her away. "This can't happen," she says.

Just stay very still. Don't spook her.

She swallows, her throat bobbing. Then her tongue comes out and wets her lips. *She just wet her fucking lips. What is she trying to do, melt my brain?* My vision is swirling, and she is at the center of it. Her scent is all around me—sweet vanilla, the heart of an orchid plant, mixed with the earthy metallic edge of thyme. I groan. *Shit.*

She raises a brow. "Did you just groan?"

I make an affirmative grunt. Words make the best shovels.

My focus is drawn to her lips again when her tongue peeks out. She pulls it back in as soon as I'm looking at it. She straightens, standing tall and creating distance between us. I flex my fingers over the keyboard, stretching them, giving them something to do besides haul her close to me.

She clears her throat. "This data is impressive. You've made incredible headway."

I give another affirmative grunt. She laughs, and I turn to look at her. I did it! I made her laugh. Consuela's cheeks are pink, and she's smiling down at me. I bite my lip to keep from telling her how beautiful she is, that she makes me happy.

If this is Stockholm syndrome, then I don't ever want to leave Sweden.

She shakes her head and walks to the far side of the office, leaning against the wall. "Don't look at me like that."

A smile curls my lips as I give her that same grunt. She laughs again, and I beam. Consuela shakes her head.

"I can't help it," I say. *Shut up, Dan!*

She clears her throat, and the shutters drop again. She's rebuilding her defenses. "It's been a long day. Let's call it." She starts gathering up her things and pushing them into her briefcase. "Jones"—*that's what she calls Tweedledee*—"will escort you back to your room."

I stand slowly. She'll have to pass me to leave. Maybe if I manage to just shut up, she won't be able to escape me so easily. Maybe she wants me as badly as I want her.

But she has everything to lose.

I'm her prisoner, her asset. Why does *that* turn me on. Because everything about this woman drives me crazy. I'd never have built such a beautiful algorithm for anyone else. She is my muse.

A weight lands in my stomach. Maybe she knows that. Maybe she is using her wiles to manipulate me. Maybe I'm a total fool, and she feels nothing for me but the professional interest she puts on when anyone else is in the room.

Consuela, her briefcase full, looks up at me. She wets her lips again… because she is trying to kill me. It's the only explanation at this point. No one's lips are that dry. If I buy her Chapstick, will she get the joke?

If she can walk by me, then I'll know it's all an act. She takes a deep breath, her peach silk blouse shimmering and slithering over her skin. Consuela leans forward, picks up the phone, and presses a single digit. "You can come and take him now. We're done for the evening."

The door opens and Tweedledee enters. "Come on," he says to me.

"Sure." I turn to my computer and stroke a few keys before closing the laptop and slipping it into the case. I've had plenty of time in the evenings to work on my algo but have not risked researching Consuela further. In part because I know she checks the logs, and I don't want to come off as a creeper. But also because the thrill of getting to know her in real life is so tantalizing and delicious.

Tweedledee hovers behind me. Consuela busies herself with something on her desk. "Good night," I say.

She glances up. "Good night." Her eyes catch mine for a moment longer than is professional, then drop to her work again. I lead Tweedledee out the door, willing myself not to look back.

CHAPTER TWENTY-TWO

Lenox

"It's time to tell the council," I say, passing Petra a glass of champagne.

She smiles at me as she accepts it. The emerald choker that hugs her throat sparkles in the powerful rays of the sun reflecting off the sea. We bought it from a jeweler named Muhammad. He laundered money for Yusuf, and now launders it for us.

Light pours in the large windows of the yacht's salon. Outside it's cold, but in here we only see the beauty of the day and can't feel the harshness of the wind or feel the frigid spray of the sea.

We're on a yacht off the coast of Bulgaria, en route to a meeting in Romania. I turn back to Liam, accepting the scotch and soda he offers. Robert takes the Scotch neat off Liam's tray before settling back into the booth next to Petra. His skin has largely healed, but he has kept the well-trimmed beard.

I remain standing, watching Liam leave before turning back to them. Ian's former enforcer has chosen to take on a role of steward—he has a passion for wine and food that his humble upbringing never allowed him to explore. Now he and Petra pore over tasting notes, enjoying the challenge of ordering just the right bottles for her cellar.

Robert turns to Petra. "You're pleased with how this turned out then?"

Petra sips her champagne, meeting my gaze, keeping her expression neutral. But we all know that Robert's plan came together as beautifully as the moon rises over a calm sea. Yusuf awaits trial in Istanbul; his closest allies are either in prison, dead, or working with us.

With a very minimal amount of bloodshed, not only are Petra and I the new leaders of the most powerful crime syndicate in the city of Istanbul but for hundreds of miles in all directions. Our influence spans out east and west. It is a small portion of the globe but vital.

Combining Yusuf's markets with Petra's existing structures in Romania and her trade routes around the globe... well, we are off to a very good start. I've kept the council informed of our operations without mentioning Robert's name.

I glance down at my phone, waiting for the text that tells me Sydney has reached our safe house in Paris. The recent assassination attempt is evidence it's time to bring Robert out of the shadows and share his larger strategy with the council. It won't work on the scale that we hope to achieve without their consent.

There is a message from Rachel. I open it using my retinas as my code. "Sydney has been captured by local authorities in Spain," I say, my gaze rising to meet Robert's.

He nods. "I see. We can certainly tell the rest of the council of my continued existence and involvement in Yusuf's demise, but as I requested, I'd like to tell Sydney myself."

"You want a chance to explain," Petra says, her voice laced with humor. She's come to understand and, dare I say, admire Robert Maxim over the last months. They are similar creatures, I'm afraid to admit.

"I will go to Spain, arrange her freedom and explain my position. I have a meeting with Declan anyway." He waves off the possible difficulty of removing Sydney from police custody after fleeing a murder scene.

"Fine." I agree because the fight is not worth the prize.

We drop anchor for the night in a quiet cove in Bulgaria's Burgas Bay, the large yacht rocking gently in the protected waters. Robert takes the helicopter to the Burgas airport, where he will fly on to Barcelona, then head north to retrieve Sydney. She never seemed to fully believe he died. A smile tugs at my lips as I imagine her reaction at finding him alive. Will she hug or punch him?

Petra comes out of the bathroom, steam from her shower filling the stateroom with fragrance. I lay my book on my chest and watch her as she sits in front of the mirrored dressing table. She meets my gaze in the reflection.

"You are worried the council will be angry?"

"No." I shake my head.

"Then what?" she asks, unwinding the towel from her wet hair, sending thin rivulets of water down her bare back. I sigh, and she smiles. "Lenox, you worry so much." Petra picks up her brush and pulls it through her hair. "This is all working out beautifully."

"That does not concern you?"

Her hand stills, and she turns on the padded stool to face me.

"I think Robert is a dangerous man. But I can see how all this"—she uses the brush to indicate the sphere we live in—"works to his favor."

"He is plotting something beyond what we can see."

She raises a brow. "I'm sure you are right. But I think he will follow through on the promises he had made us."

"I agree." I fall silent, unable to express the concern that keeps me restless. Perhaps, once I've spoken fully with the council, it will become clearer to me. Dan will be done with Homeland Security soon, and then I'll have his advice to turn to as well. While I trust Rachel, she doesn't have the same deep background knowledge that Dan does.

"What is it?" Petra asks, beginning to braid her hair. The towel covering her slips down to her waist, and my eyes run over her body as her hands work. There is no shyness between us now—our relationship has deepened, aged like a fine cognac. Sweet and strong, yet still sharp. I am wary not to let it become numbing. It would be easy to drift away into dreams with this creature.

When our eyes meet again, she is smiling. "Lenox," she purrs, standing, leaving the towel behind, and coming to the bed. She removes my book from my chest, placing it on the bedside table.

She puts a delicate hand on either side of my face. "Together we can accomplish anything. Whatever Robert Maxim is trying to do, he is not so foolish as to think we are not watching him closely."

I tug her down to me. She lays her wet head against my naked chest and toys with the gold chain around my neck as she butterflies warm kisses across my collarbones. "I know," I say. "But I worry about more than just the two of us."

She angles her head so that she can see my face. "You worry what he plans around Sydney."

"Yes." I nod. "He left her the bulk of his fortune."

"She would never have believed he was dead otherwise."

"I'm not so sure she does. But what I wonder is why he wanted her to think that he was gone?"

She sits up and cocks her head. "The more people who don't know he's alive, the better, you must see that."

"Of course I do. But..." I shake my head. "He is going to pull something."

"Pull something?" she teases me with a soft smile. "Sydney can take care of herself. Maybe he did it to try to force out her feelings for him." I don't answer. "Perhaps losing him makes her realize how much she cares for him. Maybe she will miss him."

"Maybe." I don't want to go down this road... talking about feelings.

Petra reaches for my lips, kissing me. "Let's not talk anymore," she whispers. Once again, she's read my mind.

CHAPTER TWENTY-THREE

Sydney

The door opens, and a man in a navy-blue suit enters. Gray salts his dark hair, and bags drape beneath his brown eyes. His eyebrows stretch from one temple to the other. His olive skin is splotched with red.

The detective sits across from me and smiles, deep lines bracketing his mouth. He's trying for good cop. *Okay, I'll play.* I smile back. They let me keep my dog, so seem to be buying the poor, frightened tourist bit.

Blue rests his head on my thigh. I glance down at him. He blinks, the black of his eyelashes stark against the white fur circling his eyes. I bring my attention back to the detective. His suit is wrinkled like he's at the end of a long day. *Me too, fella.*

Shifting in my seat, I try to ease the ache in my back. Why are we just sitting here? "I'd like a lawyer," I say, my voice even.

He clears his throat. "We are waiting for Homeland Security." His accent is thick but understandable.

"Homeland Security?" I ask. *Shit, do they know who I am?*

He nods, then glances around the room. I follow his gaze. There is a camera in each corner and a two-way mirror. We are not alone.

His gaze returns to mine. There is something in there... Is he a Joyful Justice sympathizer?

My heart thumps a little faster, and Blue shifts, sensing the change in me. I lay my hand on his head again.

I'm not in cuffs. Maybe they call in Homeland Security for every American in custody? It's possible they don't know who I am.

"You are here on holiday?" the detective asks. I nod. "And this man, he breaks into your rental?"

"Yes. It was horrible."

"So you are forced to defend yourself."

Uh-huh. "Yes." I let my voice hitch like I might cry.

"Very unfortunate. I am sorry this happened to you in my country. We do not have so much violent crime here, you know. Not so many guns like you have at home in America."

"He had a gun."

The detective nods. "But you have a pole and a good dog, so you win." He raises those impressive brows of his in question.

"I want a lawyer," I say again.

He shakes his head. "No need. No need." He waves his hand. "Obviously self-defense. It's no problem."

"No problem?" Me killing a person is no problem? Is a pig about to fly by?

"Come, I take you for fingerprinting."

Okay...

We step back out to the main room; there are several empty desks in the open space. He leads me past them to a processing room where he shuffles around, looking for the tools he needs. *A real professional this guy.* A knock at the door interrupts him just as he finds the ink pad.

The female officer who greeted us at reception speaks to him. "Ah," he says, turning to me. "Homeland Security is here for you, I think."

"You think it, do you?"

He smiles—all affable, friendly, tired fool. "Come." He waves me back into the mostly empty room.

Mulberry stands by the door, wearing a fedora pulled low and covered in droplets of water. The shoulders of his raincoat are darkened. *A freaking fedora.* Where is my apron when I need it? How will I be Mrs. Cleaver without it?

He looks up at our approach, his eyes peeking from beneath the rim of the hat, and looks at the detective. I don't say anything, just clench my fists, holding myself very still.

"Good evening," Mulberry says in his deep baritone. Once a cop, always a cop. "Thank you for bringing her in. I can take it from here." He shows the man a badge and they shake hands like old friends. *The detective must be one of ours.*

The female officer blinks several times and goes to speak, but the detective silences her with a look. Mulberry steps forward and takes me by the bicep. "Good evening Ma'am," he says.

As we walk away, the female officer whispers madly to her superior.

Mulberry leads me back through reception, pulling a soaked umbrella from the stand and passing it to me.

"Thank you," I say.

He meets my eye for the first time. "You're welcome."

When he opens the door, a gust of chilly, wet wind blows in, pulling at his hat but not unseating it. I step out into the night, opening the umbrella against the deluge, Blue close to my side, his nose tapping at my hip—*I am here. You are not alone.*

No, I'm not.

EK

We drive in wet, dog-scented silence. The car is petite, making Mulberry look that much more like a hulking figure behind the wheel. Like a troll taking over an elf's car.

I smile.

His eyes dart to me. "How are you?" he asks, his voice gruff.

"Tired."

"You led them on quite the chase."

"Don't worry, I didn't run that much. Thanks for coming to get me."

"Of course. I had planned to meet you in Paris."

"How have you been?" We'd texted over the last few months but not spoken. Mulberry had given me the space I asked for. What did he expect in return?

"We have a hotel suite reserved." He clears his throat. "There are two bedrooms."

I don't answer him, just look out the window. The landscape is cloaked in night and thick rain clouds. Fat drops of water slap the glass, then are swept back in what looks like a hostile dragging—as if the droplets don't want to go but the wind and wiper blades are forcing them.

Mulberry exits the highway, pulling onto a roundabout. He changes gears, downshifting, the subtle movements sexy in their own special way. Blue sits up from where he's been laying in the back seat and puts his massive head between us to watch our passage through the narrow streets. His tongue lolls out. I reach out and scratch his chest. One of his back legs starts thumping in appreciation. A smile pulls at my mouth. He's so cute.

Mulberry parks in front of a small hotel, its lights a beacon in the rainy night. The lobby is small. The woman behind the desk coos over Blue and offers to bring up dog bowls and kibble for him. Mulberry orders some food for us too. I'm so tired I barely hear him.

When we get to the suite, I pause in the doorway. The living room is all plush purples and deep blues. The floor-to-ceiling doors leading to the narrow balcony are bracketed by shutters painted matte black. A small wood stove sits between the doors. In front of it, a silk carpet in dove and charcoal shimmers. The room is stylish and elegant, if a little worn around the edges.

There are bedrooms to the right and left. "I need a shower," I announce.

"I brought you some clothing," Mulberry says, his voice low. I turn back to him. He's taken off the coat and hat; his hair is flattened from wearing it so long. "Give me a minute and I'll get it out of my bag."

Mulberry runs a hand through his hair, standing it up on end as he moves toward the other bedroom, carrying his small suitcase. He comes back a minute later with a small satchel. I open it up and find a new T-shirt, a pair of leggings, and clean underwear.

"Thanks."

He shrugs.

My throat tightens when he raises his gaze to meet mine. "It's good to see you," he says, all quiet and sweet.

"You too."

He breaks into a smile that lights up his eyes and releases something in my chest.

I shower, and when I come back out to the living room in the big T-shirt and leggings, Mulberry is closing the stove door on a roaring fire. He turns to me, the pride of a fire well-built shining in his eyes.

He pushes up to stand and points to the table where two domed dishes wait. Blue is already eating out of a bowl on the floor.

"Thanks for feeding him," I say.

Mulberry shrugs as he makes his way over to the table. I realize how hungry I am when I sit down and Mulberry reveals my plate of pasta with red sauce. We eat in near silence, both of us ravenous.

When we're done, Mulberry gets up to tend his fire.

I move around the couch and join him on the rug in front of the stove. Blue follows but hops onto one of the couches. I let out a tired laugh. Mulberry looks over at Blue and smiles before settling on the rug, his gaze on the fire. Its crackling is the only sound for a long moment.

"I've never thought of you as just brave," Mulberry says, his voice low, big body still.

I let out a snort of a laugh, and Mulberry turns away from the fire, looking at me with those eyes of his—summer grass green with rays of yellow spanning out from the pupil, like the sun reflected in an algae-rich pond with a black hole at its center. Something eternal and universal and not at all real.

I look down at myself, unable to maintain eye contact. My shoulders are hunched forward; the T-shirt I'm wearing drapes like a smock.

"You are courageous more than brave," Mulberry says.

I blink and give my head a small shake—infinitesimal but necessary. "What?" I glance up at him.

Mulberry lowers his lashes, looking down at his hands, intertwined in front of his chest. His left elbow supports the weight of his upper body, and it arches to the floor, his legs relaxed and crossed. His remaining foot is inches from my knee. The prosthetic foot on the other leg extends neatly from his remaining calf... natural now. He's grown used to the loss.

So have I.

"The origin of the word courage is cor. The Latin word for heart. And the original meaning conveyed a person's willingness to bare their whole heart." His eyes rise to meet mine once more, the depths sparkling. "That's why you'll be such a great mom. Because you'll show our child who you really are, a woman of courage."

My hands spread on the rug, running over the fine silk, the thick weave. I stare down at them. My hands. Out of all the parts of my body, I see them the most, but the changes in them seem to strike me at the oddest moments.

A flash of my hand wrapped around a silver pole on the New York City subway crosses my mind. I'd painted my nails burgundy, and I thought it looked so *adult*. My pale, unlined hand gripping that pole—my first moment as a free adult, paying my own rent, living my own life. The hands in front of me now, with their short, bare nails and scarred, wrinkled skin... they are as much me as those hands years ago were. *The things right in front of us become invisible.*

Rising onto my knees, I crawl toward the father of my child, waiting to lift my gaze until my hand brushes his knuckles, so we're close when our eyes meet again.

I don't know what to say. How do I respond to words so sweet, so fucking gentle and yet... tough? Words I can lean into when I need a strong wind at my back.

"Thank you."

He touches the tip of my hair, squeezing it between his thumb and forefinger, then wraps the strand around his finger and gives a gentle tug. An invitation and a request. An offer and a plea.

Be mine.

"*You* are enough, I know you always want to do more, be more. But," he clears his throat. "You are enough." It comes out rough—as rough as the stubble on his jaw, as the gravel-rutted road of our past. It comes out rough but perfect.

I follow the pull of him. Inhale his warm, heartening scent. Our lips meet, and we open to each other. The palm of his hand cups the back of my head, pulling me with him as he lies back onto the rug, pulling me into so much more than this one kiss. Pulling me into a promise I never thought I could make and now can't imagine living without.

I move with him like we are dancers, fighters, in sync and *alive*. Living in this moment alone, knowing that our fate lies in this breath, this heartbeat. All is now. Now is all. And yet in this impermanence is a promise... this moment won't last, but it will always be here. Waiting for us to claim it. To remember it. *This* can never be taken, given away, or destroyed. It is us. *Us*. One plus one makes more than two. It is infinite.

CHAPTER TWENTY-FOUR

Dan

I turn my computer toward Consuela. "Look." I point to the Facebook profile up on my screen. "Billy Ray Titus." His profile picture shows him at a lectern, one hand in the air, his mouth open, as if he is making a rousing speech.

He'd look like a politician except for the lack of polish. His thinning, lanky hair is pulled into a ponytail. He wears a wrinkled button-down shirt over his narrow shoulders and round belly. Billy Ray Titus looks like a dweeb, but he is a dangerously effective hate monger. Funny how looks can be so deceiving.

"I know who he is." Consuela circles the desk and leans next to me to get closer to the screen as I turn the laptop back toward me. "He downloaded your app?" She turns her face toward me but is careful to keep distance between us.

I look up at her and grin. "Not exactly."

Billy Ray Titus is smart enough not to take a personality quiz, sign a petition to remove women's right to vote, download a game where he goes on mass shootings, or any of the other traps I've laid for his followers. But he can't protect himself from data harvesting. Financial information from credit agencies, public records about homeownership and voter registration and many other bits of data that define us as individuals can all be bought and sold.

With me targeting so many of Billy Ray Titus's "friends," he was bound to churn up in the chum of Facebook profiles. And with enough data points, it is easy to deanonymize anyone. There are no laws in much of the world that protect an individual's data. No one needs to consent to being bought and sold on the web. My mind wanders to Lenox and his arm of Joyful Justice that fights with such vehemence to keep people's bodies from being traded in the same way I use data to target... to manipulate.

Consuela reaches out and scrolls down Billy Ray's profile. "He is one of the loudest voices, gets the highest speaking rates, and is definitely a big reason that so many men are moving from Men's Rights Activists into more extreme groups like incels. He's also suspected of trafficking in Isis war slaves," she says.

"Yes. All that." She looks over at me again as I tap his picture. "He is a big part of the problem. Anytime one of my persuadables stops commenting, begins to bow out, or even says anything more tempered, Billy Ray is all over it."

"I've suspected him of financing several attacks, including the attempted murder of April Madden."

He financed the attack on Sydney's mother.

"If he was out of the way, things would be simpler."

"I know," she sighs. "He's careful though. I've never found any hard evidence of criminality. But trust me, I'm still looking."

She is a huntress.

"There are other ways to take care of problems like Billy Ray Titus." I blink at her.

"Dan." Consuela's voice edges into annoyance. "Homeland Security does not *assassinate* US Citizens."

"Doesn't it?" I ask.

She frowns. "You're a conspiracy theorist."

"I'd say I'm data driven."

Her lips quirk into a half smile as she steps back from me.

She takes in a deep breath and lets out another sigh, and I wonder what's going on with her today. Consuela has seemed down all morning. She stretches toward the ceiling, fuzzing my brain out for a minute as I watch her. The shirt she's wearing rides up to the waistband of her slacks and then slips over smooth skin, exposing a line of flesh.

Dear God in heaven, have mercy on my soul.

When I tune back in, she is in the middle of a sentence.

"—so, I guess you're done."

"What?" I shake myself, trying to catch up while my eyes are still stuck on her stomach, even though the brief flash of skin is gone.

"Dan."

I drag my eyes up to meet hers, passing by her frowning lips en route. "I said," she enunciates as if speaking to someone with a processing problem, "that your work here is done."

"It is?"

Her eyes flick to the screen, then back to me. "You gathered the data you promised and built the pages. We can take it from here. You did it within your timeline." She cocks her head, looking at me like I'm the crazy one.

I glance at my calendar. She's right, my deadline is in a few days—but I've never worked in Newtonian time, preferring Einstein's. *It's all relative.* I did do everything I promised...

"Wait." I lean back in my chair, swiveling to fully face her. "You can take it from here?" *What does that mean?*

"Yes. You're free to go." She doesn't sound happy about it.

"So, I'm no longer an asset?"

"You'll always be an asset, Dan." She smiles down at me.

"Does that mean our relationship"—I wave a hand between the two of us just so she is totally clear who the "our" in that sentence refers to —"is no longer a professional one?"

She rolls her eyes. I stand up slowly. Consuela braces, her eyes narrowing.

"Since it's my last day, consider buying me lunch?" Her head cocks. "Off campus."

"Okay…"

It's cold outside, and I hunch into my down jacket. Consuela pulls her scarf tighter as we cross the courtyard, headed to the city street. A spark of insight ignites in my mind. I can't believe I missed this. Love *does* make you blind.

"It was you in Sydney's phone," I say. Consuela's eyes dart to meet mine, but she keeps walking. She doesn't answer. "I found a bug in Sydney Rye's phone; it wasn't classic Homeland Security though. You didn't code it. Who did?"

"I'm not going to share information with you."

"No way was it your team," I say, working through the problem out loud. "It had hints of Fortress Global to it. Their department has a real slickness I've always admired. Leaves a trail of slime though."

"What are you talking about?"

"Are you working with some of Robert Maxim's coders?" I hold up a hand to stop another canned response. "I'm not actually asking. I'm thinking out loud."

"Far be it for me to interrupt a genius at work," she grumbles as we enter the park.

"Did you bring any of Robert's guys in? Would they work with you?"

She doesn't look over at me, just keeps walking. I stare at her hard. Consuela stops walking and turns to me, her breath blooming white in front of her face. Her eyes are almost accusatory. *You don't know me well enough to read me, asshole.* Or do I?

I face her fully, putting my hands on my hips and really *look* at her. She straightens her shoulders and raises her chin, letting me look, daring me to see her.

"Robert Maxim is alive," I guess. She doesn't flinch. Gives nothing away. "He's working with you." Same cold, unflinching stare. It dawns on me. "Not you. He's working with Declan Doyle... on the international organized crime task force." Her eyes narrow. I've guessed right. It was all right in front of me this whole time. "I'm right."

Her nostrils flare, and spots of color flash on her cheeks. "No, you are not."

I shrug and turn to keep walking, all casual stroll with a friend. "If you say so. Makes sense though. Robert is obsessed with Sydney. Of course he'd want access to her phone." *But what is that snake up to?*

Consuela falls into step with me. "And you're not obsessed with her?" she grumbles.

"No, I'm not," I say it quietly, hoping she'll hear the words I'm *not* saying... hoping she can read me. The way I just read her. She stops and looks up at me, anger filling her gaze. What's she pissed about?

"It's cold out here," she says. "Let's go back inside. I'm not hungry anymore." She turns back to the office, not waiting for my reply. I follow, my mind sifting through this new information. Robert Maxim faked his own death to then join Declan Doyle on the international organized crime task force. Is he trying to protect Sydney... or destroy Joyful Justice? Maybe both.

Consuela pushes in through our office door and starts taking off her coat, her movements jerky, like she's really pissed. It draws my focus from the Robert Maxim problem. "I should have watched you closer," I mutter. *Shit, I wasn't supposed to speak that out loud.* She won't figure out I meant surveillance, right? *Yeah, Dan, she's a real idiot; that's why you're so into her. You love dumb broads.*

Crap.

Her breathing is still heavy, but some of the fire in her eyes cools at my words. I hang up my coat, and when I turn back to face Consuela, a smile broadens her mouth—that one she gets when she's hunting. Sly, skillful, foxy as all fuck.

"I hid, Dan." I don't get it, so she goes on. "I knew you were watching us. I didn't know how, or I'd have stopped you. So I got myself demoted. I *made* you stop looking at me."

My mouth gapes a little. I don't ever want to stop looking at her again. She's so brilliant. "I'm in love with you." The words pop out before they've even formed in my mind. They just jump right out of my heart and into the air bypassing all protocols meant to hold them in place. Like an electron that quantum leaps from one location to another, skipping all space and time in between. Scientist don't know how it happens. They just know it does.

She blinks and steps back. Blinks again.

Well, now that the truth is out there... I take a step forward. She backs up and hits my desk. Consuela puts up a hand, and I stop. We stare at each other. She fumbles behind her for the phone.

"Don't."

She shakes her head. "This can't happen."

"It already has."

"You're an asset."

"I'm yours."

"Stop it!" Consuela takes her hand off the phone and points a finger at me. "I will not let you ruin me."

"Ruin you?" It's my turn to shake my head. "I'm not ruining you! You've chosen to be blind to your reality." *Oh, the irony.* "I know you, Consuela Sanchez. You want to do good, make the world a better, safer place—"

"Within the confines of the law," she cuts me off.

"When the laws are created to oppress some and lift up others, then you're working at cross purposes, can't you see that?" My frustration is gurgling inside of me, crawling up my throat, tightening my fists, and beating my heart like a drum.

"The law is an evolving system. We have to have a system, Dan. Otherwise it is just anarchy. That's why we'd never work; you're a freaking revolutionary, and I'm an officer of the law."

"So you'll admit you've thought about us working?" Her lips tighten and eyes widen. *Caught ya.* "At least admit you've thought about it."

"Of course I have!" Her outburst feels so good I can hardly stay on my feet. "But just because I think you have a hot body doesn't mean I'm going to throw my whole life away to touch it."

Ouch. "You cowardly liar." I say it low, so quiet that she actually leans a little forward to catch it. "You know it's not just physical." Her nostrils flair, and she goes to reach for the phone again. I huff out a sound of disgust, and she turns back to me.

"Fuck you," she says.

"It would be making love, and you know it."

She takes in a stuttering breath. I take a step forward. My hands are shaking, but I keep walking toward her. Consuela shakes her head. I stop. She wets her lips. *Again.* I walk forward.

Tears fill her gaze, and I rush to close the distance between us. My arm finds her waist, pulling her against me. We stare at each other, so close now, closer than we've ever been. Her chin is tilted up, her watery eyes holding my gaze.

I brush my fingers across her cheek, and she closes her eyes. A tear trembles free and slides down her cheek. "I love you," I whisper, this time on purpose. This time because I want her to know, to really know that *I love her.*

She opens her eyes. My heart beats even harder, pounding at my rib cage. Hers pounds back. Dipping my fingers into the hair at the base of Consuela's neck, luxuriating in the silky depths I have dreamt of, I lean down, my eyes sliding closed as she lifts up to meet me.

The door opens behind me, the hinges creaking as loud as a thunderclap. Consuela tries to rip free of me, but the desk is behind her and we are tangled. It's not that I'm holding her so tight—it's that we have crossed a bridge too far.

"Freeze, asshole!" It's Tweedledum. *Fantastic. Just awesome.* "Hands in the air."

I unravel from Consuela and begin to lift my hands. "That's unnecessary," she says, stepping around me to face Tweedledum. "We're fine here."

Consuela's voice is even, but her hair bun is loosening, and one long strand hangs over her shoulder. There is color in her cheeks—a bright pink flush of excitement.

What will she do now? Send me away? Or send my guard out of the room? "Are you sure," Dum asks.

"Yes." She clears her throat and straightens her shoulders. "Leave us."

My heart gives a leap, and I bow my head to keep from doing anything crazy... like grabbing her in front of Dum.

He leaves, the door clicking quietly into place. I stay very still, my hands by my sides, fingers twitching, head bowed, gaze on my feet. Consuela isn't moving either.

"Your contract is fulfilled," she says. "You should go."

"I—"

"I'm engaged." She drops the bomb. It explodes inside my chest.

"What?" I choke out, looking up at her. Hard eyes meet mine.

"I am getting married."

"Who?" I'm incredulous.

"None of your business."

"But—"

"That was a mistake," she says, referencing the best moment of my life. The one that happened seconds ago. "I'm sorry."

"Me too," I say. "Me too." I slam my laptop closed and sweep it off the desk and under my arm before whirling toward the door.

"Dan..." I turn back to her. "The computer stays."

I snarl at her. Not on purpose, it just pops out. Striding back to the desk, I lay the laptop down. She isn't looking at me. I'm choking.

I whip my coat off the hook. My hand on the knob, I turn back to look at Consuela. She stands behind her desk now, eyes focused on her computer screen—as if she is so unaffected that she is just reading her email.

Liar. Coward.

I rip the door open, filled with self-loathing and frustration. Tweedledum waits for me. He blinks when he sees the expression on my face. I need to get out of here immediately.

CHAPTER TWENTY-FIVE

Sydney

"I hate leaving you here," Mulberry says, his breath warm on my forehead as I burrow into his chest.

"I'm right behind you," I promise, looking up at him. "I'll see you in the jungle." I smile, my heart tugging at that idea... We will be together in the sunshine soon.

Mulberry sighs. "I know." He kisses my forehead, his warm lips lingering. "I love you," he says against my skin.

Last night broke something in me, knocked down a wall. He got in, and I don't think I'll ever be able to get him out. Maybe I never could.

Mulberry leaves, and I turn back into the hotel suite. Blue taps his nose to my hip as I move into the bedroom, the only one of the two we ended up using. I pull Robert's letter from my duffle—Mulberry had someone pack it up and bring it from my apartment and to the hotel. The paper's softer now, the creases threatening to split. I don't open it, just hold the paper, my heart aching.

Robert is really dead.

I feel at once relief and deep fear. I trusted him in a way I've never trusted another man. I *knew* he could keep me safe. I was wrong. No one can keep me safe. There is no such thing.

Blue lets out a growl and races into the other room. *Shit.* I left the gun Mulberry gave me in the fucking living room. That's one way to *not* be safe. I race after Blue.

The hotel suite's door opens as I enter the living room. The gun is on the high table behind the couch, mere feet away. I'll make it.

Robert Maxim steps into the room, stealing my breath and stilling my forward momentum. Emotions pour through me—relief, anger, confusion… and then back to relief. Back to anger. *He's not dead.*

Blue taps his nose to my hip, asking permission to go say hello, but I stop him with a light touch.

I have to ball my hands into fists to keep from reaching for Robert. I will not run to him. The motherfucker tried to make me think he was dead… for my own good I'm *so* sure.

Anger and relief are now neck and neck, tightening my jaw and swirling up my throat, making it impossible to speak.

He smiles at me, his eyes sparkling with humor. "Good to see you, Sydney."

His suit is classic Robert Maxim, tailored to perfection, gray with subtle pinstripes running through it. The material looks like pure money. He hasn't bothered with a tie. The top button of his cream shirt is open, exposing the notch between his collarbones. He's grown a beard, the same black and silver as his hair but with glints of copper too.

Even in this spiffy a suit, most men couldn't look as rich. Robert oozes wealth and power the way a slug leaves a trail of slime. It makes me grit my teeth.

"You think this is funny?" I snap.

He cocks one brow in that way he does—all arrogant, controlled monster. *Takes one to know one.* "I thought you'd be happy to see me."

"Did you?" Something moves behind his eyes—a shadow of doubt. I should make him suffer. "I figured you'd show up somewhere. You're like a cockroach, you always survive."

"I'll take that as a compliment coming from you," Robert says, breaking eye contact to glance around the sitting room.

The door stands ajar behind him, and Blue lets out another low growl right before the sound of the elevator doors opening reaches me. I close the distance between me and my gun, gripping it with both hands as I move toward Robert to shut the door.

He intercepts me in a fluid motion, fast enough to stop me but slow enough not to spook me. Oh, he knows me too fucking well.

Robert's body blocks the door, and his hand rests on my forearm, keeping the gun down and his touch light. "I'm expecting someone," he says, his face way too close to mine. But I don't shy away from his gaze.

His blue-green eyes—the warmth of the Caribbean and the ice of the arctic—wait for me. He always waits for me. How can one man be so patient and yet move so fast. Hot, cold, fast, slow... all the contradictions. Yes, Robert Maxim is *all* of the contradictions.

My gaze flicks behind him, and Declan Doyle walks into the room. Robert steps into me, forcing me to either press against him or move back. I let our bodies meet for a brief moment before sliding away, getting enough distance to aim the gun if I need to but keeping it down.

"Declan," I say. He nods at me. "You two together is quite the conspiracy. What's up?"

"We need to talk, Sydney," Declan says, moving past Robert toward the windows. Declan glances over his shoulder at me as he pulls a shutter aside, his gaze roaming the street. Dust motes twirl in the beam of sun around Declan. He's wearing a black sweater, cashmere judging by the way it absorbs the light. The gold watch on his wrist sparkles—as hard as his sweater is soft. Dark indigo jeans and scuffed-up boots complete the look of handsome, wealthy, white tourist. The bulge at his right ankle gives the only indication that he might be something more.

He turns, his eyes meeting mine—the sun makes them glow a warm brandy brown. He closes the shutters again and turns into the room. "Sit." He gestures to the couch.

"I like standing."

"I heard you were supposed to be on bed rest."

My jaw tightens again. If one more man tries to make me lie the fuck down, I'm going to start shooting.

"She's fine," Robert says. "Bed rest isn't proven to be effective, you know? It's antiquated really." I meet his gaze, finding it placid. Just the facts. Sound obstetrical advice from Robert Maxim. "Sydney does a very fine job of taking care of herself," he continues. "I'm sure she knows what's best for her and the baby."

Hearing those words shouldn't feel this good.

"Fine." Declan shrugs. "We can do this standing. We need to talk about Joyful Justice."

"I don't think it's necessary for us to talk," I say.

Declan's eyes drop to my stomach. "I'm assuming you're on some kind of leave."

"You know what they say about assumptions?" I smile.

Declan rolls his eyes. *Oh, what? I'm not mature enough for you?*

I'm still holding the gun with both hands, ready to raise it if I need to. Declan lets his gaze rest on it. "There is no way you have a permit for that." He moves toward the leather chair across from the couch and takes a seat.

"You're making yourself at home," I say, ignoring his comment about the permit. He's not taking me in over an illegal weapon. We all know that. I feel Robert's gaze on me. When I turn to him, he's smiling. "You're in too good a mood," I say, narrowing my eyes at him.

His grin widens. "I'm happy to see you, even if you won't admit the same."

"I don't trust you."

He starts toward me. Blue lets out a warning growl. Robert stops, meeting my dog's gaze. Blue's growl deepens, and his hackles slowly rise.

"What are you doing, Robert?"

"Saying hello to Blue, reminding him that I mean you no harm. Ever."

Blue's growl fades, and I look down at my dog. He glances up at me, licking his lips, ears flat. Submissive to Robert Maxim. *Ugh.*

"Now, as you were saying," Robert says. "You don't trust me. But the thing is, you do." I meet his eyes and shake my head. He takes another step toward me. "You know me—what motivates me. So you can trust me to act in certain ways."

"Selfish ways."

"Yes, selfish..." That same something slides behind his eyes again. "I protect what is mine."

"I'm not yours," I am quick to point out.

"Well," Declan interrupts us, "he's still trying to protect you."

"I thought I knew what was best for me and the baby," I say to Robert.

"Don't you want to know what we've been up to?" Robert asks, his head cocking slightly, as if he is genuinely curious.

"No. I'm on leave. All I want is peace and quiet."

Robert laughs out loud. Declan chuckles. "A leopard can't change its spots, Sydney. And you can't stand peace and quiet," Declan says, grinning.

"We are taking down a powerful criminal organization that Joyful Justice also wants a piece of. I think you'll like this." Robert smiles.

"Do you know what I am really, truly sick of?" I ask the two grinning idiots in front of me.

They both shrug. I take a step forward, Blue close, sensing the shift in my mood. The grin on Robert's face falters, slipping slightly. He is almost as perceptive as Blue. Declan is still toothy—thinks of himself as untouchable. Rich, powerful, white man. I want to hurt him just to prove it's possible. "People telling me what I want or need."

Declan sighs. "We are offering you something here."

"Really, because it looks like you lied to me." I stare daggers at Robert. "Letting me think you were dead for months."

"Did you mourn me?" he asks.

"Shut up." He grins again, and I turn my attention to Declan. "And you, you're here on official business. With a dead man. You two are plotting some kind of extra-legal action against a criminal organization, and you want Joyful Justice's help. This is just rich."

"No." Declan shakes his head. "I'm here to make you an offer, one you should not refuse."

"The way you all made Dan an offer?"

Declan meets my gaze, his eyes bland. "He has done good work. His country appreciates it."

"Fine." I jut out my chin. "What do you want from me?"

Declan gestures to the couch. "Sit," he says. "Let's talk."

"Please," Robert says.

I round the couch and sit, resting the gun on the cushion next to me but keeping my hand close. Blue sits by my side, his focus on Declan. Robert perches on the far arm of the couch, offering me plenty of space. "We need you to act as bait," Robert says.

"Bait?" I ask. "What a lovely offer."

"We want to let the organization we've been hunting know about Robert's resurrection," Declan continues. "We know they've been tracking you."

Sure, yeah, tracking. Trying to kill me.

"So we will have dinner," Robert says.

I laugh. "Only you could turn a game of cat and mouse with murderous criminals into a dinner date." He winks at me and another laugh escapes. "You are too much."

"Many have said the same of you," Declan points out.

"Why do you want to reveal Robert's return at this moment?" I ask. Neither man answers. "You don't want to tell me?"

"We have laid a trap," Robert says. Declan shifts his focus, his eyes narrowing. Cluing me in was a part of their original plan maybe. "My death gave them a false sense of security."

"Who is them?" I ask.

"My son, his mother, other parties. As you know, a cartel of criminal organizations has joined forces in an unprecedented effort to take down Joyful Justice."

"They are still trying," I say. In the past few months, the attempts at ruining our reputation have continued to ramp up. They want to turn us into criminals in the minds of the public.

"Yes," Declan says. "They are trying to prevent you from gaining new members while at the same time killing key members of your organization. The price on your head is high." *An honor I'm sure.* "But if they discover Robert is still alive—and it looks like he does not want them to know—the flurry of communication will help us pinpoint certain individuals, allowing us to move in partnership with other law enforcement organizations to take down the entire network."

"Wow," I say, because it is an impressive plan.

"So," Robert says, "dinner tonight?"

I turn to Declan. "Will I be free to go afterwards, or do you plan to try to arrest me?"

Before he can answer, Robert interrupts. "I will personally escort you to the airport. Where"—he raises a brow—"your plane will be waiting to take you anywhere you want."

I roll my eyes. "You don't want your plane back?"

Robert shrugs. "Not yet."

A shiver runs over me—familiar and yet always exhilarating. What is he planning now?

EK

"Will you join me?" Robert asks as the waiter pours his wine. I shake my head. He shrugs. "In Europe, they recognize it's safe for a woman to have a glass of wine while pregnant. It is not frowned upon like in the States."

"The smell grosses me out." The waiter leaves the bottle on the table and departs. The umbrella heater glows coal red next to us, pumping off heat that keeps the evening chill at bay. Beyond the warm bubble of our table, pedestrians huddled in their coats walk arm in arm. Holiday lights twirl around the palm trees fronting the cathedral dominating the village plaza.

"I'm surprised Mulberry didn't tell you. I didn't realize he had such duplicity in him."

"What didn't Mulberry tell me?" I ask, feeling like a fish chomping onto a hook—but the worm just looks so freaking tasty.

"That I was alive. That he helped fake my death." I don't respond. Just stare at Robert. A slow, roughish smile teases his lips into a crescent moon. He picks up his wine and takes a sip. I watch him swallow, watch his Adam's apple bob and resist the urge to punch him in it. "He is the one who shot me." *Lucky guy.*

Strains of accordion music start up. Robert glances past me to where the melancholy music is coming from. I don't turn around. I can always trust Robert to have my back. The music moves closer, and Robert reaches into his jacket pocket, pulling out a ten Euro note.

The accordion player steps up to our table—a middle-aged man wearing a fedora, dark overcoat, and resting his instrument on an ample stomach.

He plays a few bars, smiling. Robert extends the bill, and the musician dips to accept it. He moves on to the next couple at a wave of Robert's hand. "I'm sure Mulberry had his reasons," Robert says, casual, unconcerned.

"You both always do," I say, my focus still on the accordion player. Blue lets out a low growl, and I nod, agreeing with him.

Robert doesn't stiffen, but there is a subtle shift in his demeanor. He listens to Blue almost as closely as I do.

His hand dips back into his jacket, but this time instead of pulling out a bill, he flashes the matte black barrel of a pistol briefly before lowering it to his lap.

Tension thickens the air. The smattering of other couples at the tables don't notice, but Robert and I have snapped into survival mode. Where a moment ago we were cruising down a calm, winding river, now a waterfall looms.

"Did I tell you about the assassin in Barcelona?" I ask, just as casually as he assured me of Mulberry's intentions.

Robert raises a brow as I reach for my water glass. "Assassin in Barcelona? This is different than the one who met the wrong end of your curtain rod."

I shrug. "It was a length of pipe. They were doing construction on the building next door." Robert lifts the fingers of his free hand off the table and tilts his head in a silent, teasing apology. "Maybe assassin is the wrong term for the man in Barcelona. He didn't try to kill me, just followed me. That's what made me move out of the city. I wanted to get away from the city. From prying eyes."

Robert flashes a smile. "Small places are always harder to blend into, Sydney, you know that."

"That goes both ways though. This is a touristy area, and I can look like a tourist," I say. "But an assassin would stand out more—at least this guy would have. Dark suit, glasses, you know the type."

"Yes," Robert agrees, giving nothing away.

Was my Barcelona stalker one of his men watching me?

The accordion player turns away from the restaurant toward the center of the plaza. "Also," I continue, "an assassination attempt in a small community is riskier. You can't pretend it was a random mugging or attack. That kind of thing doesn't happen. And if it did, the investigation would be easier. They could narrow down the culprit."

"Culprit." Robert smiles. "I like that. Culprit," he says it again, rolling it around in his mouth.

To the outside world, he appears totally relaxed, but he is focused on the accordion player, on the space behind me—the dark alley that leads down through narrow streets to the river. He's watching the group of men sitting on a bench not far away who at first glance might be waiting for a friend but could also be here to harm us. They could also just be watching... waiting to report back to their bosses the way that Robert and Declan plan.

"You can only love someone as much as you love yourself. And Mulberry doesn't love himself enough to be the one for you," Robert says, his eyes locking onto mine. "I love myself a lot. And I love you just as much."

My heart roars—a wild stallion set free from its pen galloping to the horizon. I stand. Blue is already on his feet, anticipating my every move. My chair tips over behind me. The other diners startle, and gazes dart our way.

Why am I standing? Robert smiles, as if he knows the answer.

"Fuck you," I hiss.

His smile becomes an invitation. "Any time. Any place." He leans back in his chair, creating room to look up at me more fully.

I turn, righteous indignation ringing my ears and clenching my neck. Blue's nose taps my hip, a gentle brush. *I am beside you. You are not alone.*

My hand lands on his head as I walk away from the table, my peripheral vision tracking the group of men and the accordion player as I step into the darkness of the alley... luring my prey into the hunt.

They don't follow, though. Instead, I wind my way alone down to the river where Declan waits in a boat. I climb aboard, and we sit together in silence under the bright moon. He keeps his focus on his phone—waiting for confirmation that our plan worked. I focus on keeping my breath even and my mind empty.

Mulberry knew. He lied. Motherfucker.

CHAPTER TWENTY-SIX

Dan

"Good to have you back, boss." Rachel grins at me, her eyes making a quick run over my form. "You look like crap." She laughs. "Guess being a prisoner will do that to a man."

"I was an asset."

"Oh, hello grumpy. Miss captivity, do you?"

"Something like that." I am grumbling, which is super attractive *and* productive.

"Okay, grouchy. I was thinking we'd go over what's been going on in your absence, but you need a paddle."

I rub my eyes, knowing she's right. It's my rule. We are not allowed to just live underground in the hollowed-out mountain that is Joyful Justice's Pacific base. When we feel pressured or upset, we go out into the sun. What's the point of living in a tropical paradise if we spend all our time in the bunker? I've been traveling for almost thirty hours. I need to use my body.

"You're right."

"Oh, say it again," Rachel coos. "I just *love* those words." I can't help but smile. "Get changed," she says. "I'll meet you at the beach."

"I see you got comfortable giving orders while I was gone."

"Sure did." Rachel strides out of my apartment, and the door swings closed behind her.

I look around the sterile space, and my chest aches. I miss Consuela. Closing my eyes, I see her face. She's smiling at me the way she did when I showed her data she liked... when she saw the way we were subtly shifting minds. I groan.

There is a knock at my door, and Rachel yells from the far side. "Get changed!"

I can't help but let out a short laugh before heading to my bedroom and doing as my subordinate commands.

Fifteen minutes later, we are fighting the breakers to get out to the swells. My arms burn, salt spray mists my skin, and the powerful waves absorb my attention. I need this.

A wave crests in front of me. I take a deep breath before pushing my board down, letting the ocean roar over me, pulling the stiffness from my limbs and the painful thoughts from my mind.

I emerge back in the shallows, water sluicing off me, and gasp, tasting the ocean on my lips and tongue. "Come on," Rachel yells at me. I glance up to see her already standing on her board, beyond the breakers, paddling out toward the horizon. "You're getting slow in your old age."

I laugh as I set off again, this time clearing them, then hop to stand and begin paddling. We move in silent synchronicity, our arms rising and falling along with the swells as we move parallel to the shore. The sun blazes down on us, making me squint even under the brim of my floppy hat.

Consuela would like it here. I push the thought aside, forcing my mind to focus on my movements, the burn in my muscles, and the gentle undulation of the ocean.

Hours later, Rachel offers me a beer from the fridge in her apartment. I take it and follow her to where she's set up chairs in front of the large picture window. She's got it propped open, the salty breeze blowing into the small sitting room. The sun is setting and throwing off bright oranges and pinks that the ocean reflects.

"So," she says, settling into her chair and opening her can of beer, "let's talk business now that you've had a chance to unwind."

"Thanks for covering everything here."

"You read the files, I'm assuming." Rachel sent a laptop and phone along with the plane that picked me up. I nod. "We have a lot going on between the Sydney situation and what Lenox has been up to—which is a whole can of worms."

"I know. I read Merl, Lenox, and Mulberry's memos on the flight. Robert Maxim is alive and taking down our enemies for us. Lenox has known about it and didn't share. We have a meeting tomorrow to discuss in detail Lenox's outlined plan."

"What do you think about it?" Rachel asks, her voice quiet, unsure. Not like her at all.

I turn to look at her. She's changed out of her swimsuit into a pair of cutoff jean shorts and a T-shirt. Her short hair is still wet from the shower she took down at the beach. She watches me with wary brown eyes.

"I'm worried about it," I admit. "I get the theory. We take over the sex trafficking, brothels, and the drug running, so that we can do it the right way and use the funds to continue our operations."

"We have plenty of money," Rachel points out.

"I know." I'm the one who's managed our finances since the beginning. "But let's not forget Joyful Justice started with a crime. Sydney stole the gold bullion from a long-sunken ship that served as the seed of our endowment."

"When a man is denied the right to live the life he believes in, he has no choice but to become an outlaw," Rachel quotes Nelson Mandela.

I smile. "I don't think taking over the brothels of the world and buying up Isis sex slaves to free them is exactly what Mandela had in mind." I sigh. "The thing is, I always thought it was important that the change come from within. So if a sex worker came to us and said, 'I was held prisoner, come and help me free my fellow prisoners,' we would supply training and expertise to get the job done. But we were not going out and finding trouble. Now we are putting ourselves in the line of fire."

"Inviting Fire," Rachel says. "That is the name of Merl's martial art."

"Yes," I agree. The martial art he developed invites attack so that the opponent's energy can be used against them. Similar to Aikido, except that with Inviting Fire, you search out the attack to draw fire from those less equipped to handle it.

"The cartels we are opposing are not just made up of the criminal class," I say. "The governments of sovereign nations are involved. If we destabilize those governments without inspiring grassroots resistance to replace them, we risk creating anarchy. That goes way beyond our original intent."

"Why can't we find leaders, more honest politicians to take their place?" Rachel asks.

"I guess we can. It's just not how we've ever operated. We are supposed to be from the ground up, not the top down." I sigh. "That's what's supposed to keep us honest. But at the same time, I can see how we got here. We are under attack. So what can we do?"

"Absolute power corrupts absolutely," Rachel says.

I take a long drag off the cold beer, staring out to the Pacific Ocean. There is nothing beyond the horizon but thousands of miles of water. "I guess we will find out," I finally say.

"So you'll go along with it?"

"I don't see how I can argue against it, really. As much as it is a power grab, it is also defending ourselves. We tried to shift the way these organizations behaved based on the complaints we received from those they abuse. We threatened them. But instead of doing as we proposed, they came at us. Now we are using the US government and its international partners to take them all down. I think it will save lives and change others for the better. Declan Doyle will get one hell of a promotion."

"What about Consuela Sanchez?" Rachel asks.

"Our work together will probably help her career."

"If she keeps working after the marriage," Rachel says casually, as if she assumes I know all about it.

I turn to look at her. She cocks her head. "You didn't look at my research on her?"

"What research?"

"I left it in our shared file."

"I didn't have time to check that yet." *Was too busy reading Joyful Justice business.* "Who is she marrying?" I fight to keep my voice even, to hide how much the answer matters.

"I guess you two didn't talk much."

"Not about her personal life."

Rachel snorts. "They announced the engagement just yesterday, but they've been dating for years. She's marrying Senator Richard Chiles, the head of the Intelligence Committee. Word is he is going to run for president." My head starts to spin. "I bet they looked at your algorithms on how to persuade the unpersuadables and figured they could use them for his campaign."

Holy shit. That's what she meant. "We can take it from here."

"I put a self-destruct code in them all," I say, my mouth numb.

"Of course you did," Rachel says. "Obviously. You'd never trust the US government with that kind of power."

"No." *I hardly trust myself.*

Later, alone in my room, I pull my computer close and navigate to the file Rachel created.

It starts with public records. Consuela Sanchez is the only person on her apartment deed, so they are probably not living together. Waiting for marriage possibly? I try to fit that with what I know of Consuela. Would she commit to spending a lifetime with a man she'd never shared living space with? She was raised Catholic, could be for her mother...

My mind wanders back to how she vibrated in my arms. I have to shut it down, lock that away. It will haunt me into madness if I let it.

Special Agent Sanchez's record is impeccable—her demotion in her own task force the only mark against her, but I know why that happened... hiding from me, the sly fox. My lips curl into an admiring smile.

She keeps her phone clean, but I am able to scroll through messages between her and friends. One from a few days ago—right after our near kiss and my leaving—has her sister asking if she is okay.

I'm fine, Consuela responded.

Mom said you seemed really upset.
Just work stuff.
She thought it was a matter of the heart.
Leave it alone.
*Fine, tell your diary about it. But I'm here if you need me. *Kissing face emoji**

Consuela didn't reply. My own heart gives a little thump. What I wouldn't give to see that diary.

I keep digging. She keeps her personal inbox mostly empty. Rachel hacked her work email and downloaded thousands, but the password changed again, so I can't get anything new. I save the emails for another time, hoping to find something more personal.

Two hours later, my eyes are burning. It's time to sleep. I'm willing to bet her diary is paper. I'd have to break into her apartment to find it.

I close the computer and push it away, but then drag it back to me almost immediately. I don't know if I can give up on her. I just don't know if I can leave it alone. I don't think she wants me to.

CHAPTER TWENTY-SEVEN

Sydney

"We have your house ready." My escort, Felicity, is young and eager. Her curly hair is shoved under a brimmed cap but escaping in bouncing tendrils that shudder with each bump on the road. Blue pushes his head between us, watching out the front window. I turn back to look at Nila and Frank in the back seat with him and grin. It's good to have them all together again.

As I face forward, Felicity's hands tighten on the wheel. Oh no, she's going to say something gushing.

Just don't call me a hero.

Please, anything but that.

"I have to tell you something," she says. *Here we go.* "You're an inspiration to me."

Ugh, inspiration may actually be worse than hero.

"Thank you," I mutter, having learned that arguing with zealots is like arguing with fish. We aren't even breathing the same stuff, which makes it impossible to communicate.

"You're a hero."

"I'm not." *Bubble, bubble.*

Felicity's head whips around so she can look at me. I meet her gaze. "I'm just a pissed-off asshole who's spent a lot of years not caring if she lives or dies." Felicity's mouth opens a little in surprise. "Keep your eyes on the road. I'm hoping to live now."

She jerks her attention forward. "Sorry."

I sigh because, while I want to live now, I don't seem to have shed the being an asshole thing. What kind of a mom does an asshole make? According to Mulberry, as long as I tell my truth, it will be all good... As if I can believe a word that lying sack of shit says. Still a pissed-off asshole. That's my truth. "Look," I say, hoping to maybe not be such an unrelenting douche of a human being, "I appreciate that you're inspired by the Joyful Justice cause. I really am."

She steals a quick glance my way, her blue eyes wary now that I've shown her my true colors.

"I think our organization does important work," I go on. "All I'm saying is, if you're looking for someone to admire, look in the mirror." Felicity takes in a sharp breath but keeps her eyes on the road. "It's really brave to be here, fighting for what you believe in."

We ride in silence for a while, bouncing over the rough roads that lead to the secluded Central American training compound of Joyful Justice. "I don't think so," Felicity says.

"Don't think what?" I ask, having forgotten where our conversation left off.

"That I'm brave. I think I'm... hurt."

Wow.

She pushes at her hair, forcing it behind her ear before continuing. "I lost someone important." There is a catch in her voice, and my throat tightens, echoing her pain. "I had to do something." She glances at me.

I nod. I get it. "If you didn't, you'd explode."

"Yeah," she agrees quickly. "I'd fucking implode."

"So you had to let it out."

"Lash out."

My hand lands on my stomach. Losing my brother led me to this road. Felicity slows to navigate around a gaping puddle. The golden-brown surface shimmers in the bright sunlight. A cow munches at grass on the far side of a fence, its ears flicking at flies.

"It feels good to be here. Lots of ways to do something," Felicity continues.

"That's all anyone wants," I say, watching the cow swish its tail as our front wheels start to climb up a steep grade to avoid the puddle. "To do something. Be a part of something bigger than themselves."

The Jeep grips the surface of the road—uneven, steep, dangerous—and climbs. "Yes," she agrees. "I'm glad you started this. It saved my life."

"You saved yourself," I say as we crest the hill and start down.

"Thanks," she says quietly. I nod, holding my tongue. See, that wasn't so hard.

EK

I reach across James and grab the shot of tequila, spilling some onto my hand as I sit back in my seat. "To motherhood." I hold the glass aloft.

James grins at me and clinks his cup against mine. We both drink. I wince at the harsh liquor as I rush a lime to my lips. The tart juice is a fresh assault.

I shudder as I toss the rind into my shot glass.

James hooks an arm over the back of his chair. "So," he says, "what are you going to do about Mulberry?"

I shake my head, searching the backyard for answers. Lights twinkle in the tree above. Four-story townhouses rise up on all sides. The sky is opaque with light pollution. "I don't know. He's not reliable."

"Isn't he?"

"What do you mean?" I return my focus to James. He sits forward. There are lines around his eyes that didn't used to be there. He's aged. How does a dead man age?

He looks like our father. I swallow the thought.

"You can depend on him to always do what he thinks is best for you."

"Right, what *he* thinks is best."

"Like you're any better?"

"Excuse me?"

James laughs, the sound washing over me like a warm wave. I've missed him so much. "You are so high-handed it's a joke. Little miss *the justice system isn't good enough for me. I'll do what's right no matter what.*"

I open my mouth to defend myself, but he's right... as usual.

"You can't depend on Mulberry to do what *you* want. What *you* think is best. But he is dependable. He has a code. Just like Robert."

"That's true."

"I know, I'm always right." James grins at me, and I can't help but return the expression.

The scent of coffee breaches the dream, and the backyard fades as I come to consciousness. As I blink my eyes open, grief and joy fight for space in my chest. Dreaming about James in such vivid detail is a gift and a curse. The pain of missing him is sharpened by these visits.

Blue whines by the door. "Who is it, boy?" He looks over his shoulder at me, his tongue hanging out, and thumps his tail. "Merl," I guess.

Blue's tail thumps harder. Frank prances behind him, absolutely overcome with excitement. Nila sits quietly by the door, waiting patiently. On the other side of the door, dog nails click on the tile floor. Blue backs up, pressing his nose to the crack and sniffing. His tail wags wide.

I pull on a robe before opening the door. One of Merl's Dobermans, Michael, waits patiently, his nub of a tail thunking against the tile floor the only indication that he is happy to see us. Chula, the youngest of Merl's three dogs, sits just behind Michael. His tail beats the same rhythm, but he also controls himself. He's grown up so much.

"Go ahead," I say. Blue streaks past me to the open door, and the Dobermans give chase. Frank follows, losing purchase on the tiles and sliding into the couch in a jumble of long legs and giant paws. He shakes himself and leaps out the door. The dogs disappear into the brush, the shrubbery shaking violently as they thrash around in the bushes.

Merl stands in my kitchen, holding a steaming mug. His tight black curls are pulled back into a bun, and he's wearing a black tank top that exposes the corded muscles of his shoulders. He smiles at me, showing the charming gap between his front teeth.

His female dog, Lucy, comes out from behind the counter. She scans me with her intelligent brown eyes, then casts her gaze upon Nila, who stands by my side, before disappearing back behind the breakfast bar, presumably to sit at Merl's feet.

"They are going to get covered in burrs," I say as I take one of the stools across from him. Nila settles at my feet.

Merl shrugs. "You need to shave them anyway if you're planning on staying down here."

"Ha, right. They will *love* that."

Merl turns to the coffee maker, pouring me a cup. He gets milk from the fridge and pours some in before sprinkling cinnamon on top. The man knows me well.

"Mulberry will be back this afternoon; he made a supply run," he says as he places the mug on the bar. He taps a folder on the counter. "Your evacuation information." My eyes drift to the folder. Every person staying at the training compound has an exit plan in case of a raid. In the folder, I'll find the location of my meeting point where I'll rendezvous with other members to either retake the compound or escape, depending on the situation. It will also show me where to find my survival pack—a bag with fresh water, dried food, and other survival essentials—kept in a tree on the outskirts of the camp. We are all trained to survive in the jungle for several days if necessary.

I pull the mug of coffee close, breathing in the aroma. Yum. It's strong and caramelly, and I close my eyes to better enjoy the wonderful scent.

When I open them, Merl is watching me with a smile. "You do love your coffee."

"That I do."

"How are you feeling?"

"Fine." He cocks his head, the expression so similar to his dogs it brings a smile to my face. "Really." *I'm going to kill the father of my child... but other than that, I'm good.* I smile.

He shakes his head. "No, you're not. But that's okay. You will be." He leans against the counter. "Come to tai chi today." He sips his coffee. "It starts in thirty minutes."

"I have to eat something in the mornings now or I feel like I'm gonna puke all day."

His brow furrows. "That must be hard for you."

"Eating in the morning?" I laugh. "Not the biggest obstacle I've faced, but it is annoying."

Merl shakes his head. "Not just that, but everything about your body changing. For people as grounded in our physical forms as we are, change like that can be difficult."

"Yeah." I shrug. "I haven't really thought about it. I mean, I've thought a lot about being a mom but not about how my body changing is a part of the pressure I'm feeling." I sip my coffee, feeling somehow lighter, as if I'd been sitting in a dimly lit room and someone started a small fire in the hearth.

"I'll have some toast brought over for you. Then come to Tai chi." He turns to put his now empty mug in the sink.

"I can get my own toast, Merl." My grip tightens on the mug. *Don't treat me like an invalid.*

He turns back to me, slow and steady, just like always. "You don't want to be taken care of, do you?"

"No," I bite out the word, Mulberry's betrayal roaring to the forefront of my mind. I can take care of myself.

Merl rests his hands on the counter across from me, his arms flexing as he presses into it. "Is it because James used to take care of you, and his love for you got him killed?"

I sit back as if struck. "What?" It comes out in a harsh whisper.

Merl nods, the skin around his eyes wrinkling. "Well, you're going to have to get over that once and for all."

"Excuse me?" It's my turn to cock my head. "What right—"

Merl cuts me off. "We've been friends for a long time. I've let you care for me. Hell—" He grins. "—I let you save my life." I can't help but huff a laugh. "And my fiancée's life. That's how generous a guy I am. So it's your turn now. You can't do this alone, Syd. Your lone wolf days are over."

"I have three dogs, Merl. I'm a pack leader."

"You can't lead if you're not taking care of yourself. How many ways do you have to learn that lesson before it sticks?"

I can't hold his gaze anymore; it's too filled with compassion and love. The man's eyelashes are criminally long. No one should look that sweet when they are pissing all over my defenses.

He comes around the breakfast bar and lays a heavy hand on my shoulder. "See you at tai chi in twenty-five minutes at the main pavilion. Toast will be here soon. Accept my help, Sydney. It's your turn to be generous." There is no joke in his tone. He means it. I nod, not having the guts to speak. I'd probably start crying. *Damn pregnancy hormones.*

EK

After tai chi I take a shower. Catching my reflection in the steamed bathroom mirror, I pause. The fuzzy image transfixes me. I lay a hand on my rounded stomach. You can really see it now. The baby moves, that soft butterfly feeling. A love so deep it feels almost like pain wells up in me, set off by that slight motion.

When I come out, there is a message on my phone. Mulberry is here and wants to know where I am.

The love and joy that overwhelmed me in the bathroom morphs into a protective rage. I pull on shorts and a T-shirt and pick up my phone to respond. *Meet me at the training circles.*

Can't wait, he writes back.

Dark clouds are advancing, a storm brewing as I head down the jungle path toward the open field painted with fighting circles where recruits practice. It's lunch hour now, so we'll have the place to ourselves. The better to kick his ass...

Mulberry is there when I arrive. The grin he gives me fuels my rage. *Don't you fucking dare look at me like that, you lying motherfucker. In some kind of hidden cabal with Bobby while leaving me confused and in the dark.* The smile fades quickly as I stalk toward him.

He gets his hands up when I'm two feet away, but I lunge forward and, putting a hand on each pec, thrust him back. He loses his balance and stumbles.

Blue growls, his hackles raised. He doesn't know why we're mad, but he knows we are *pissed*. Frank barks and circles us, thinking it's a new game, while Nila sits, not sure where her loyalties lie.

Mulberry manages to stay upright but just barely. He has both arms out, knees bent, those eyes of his watching me with a new wariness. He knows I know.

"How could you?" I scream. The wind picks up, echoing my anger.

"What?"

"Don't you dare!" My hands fist. I will punch him so hard if he even pretends for one fucking second.

"I'm sorry." But he doesn't sound sorry.

I shake my head and take a step back, my anger morphing into disgust. "You idiot." Tears are choking me. *Fuck pregnancy hormones. Fuck them right to hell and back.*

Mulberry straightens as I take another step back. "I *am* sorry." That sounds better but still not nearly good enough. "I'd do anything to protect you." Now he's starting to sound righteous. "To protect our child."

I shake my head again, and my lip raises in an involuntary snarl. "Fuck you."

"I love you."

"You can't love someone you don't trust, Mulberry."

"Yes, you can."

"I can't."

"You do." His words are low, solid. Heavy. *Shit, he's right.* I don't trust him, but I do love him.

"No," I insist against all evidence.

He takes a step forward, and Blue warns him off with a snarl of his own. *We will hurt you. You hurt me.*

Mulberry stops, his hands fisting at his side. "You can trust that I will do anything to protect you and our baby. That I will be fearless for you." His jaw tightens, and he takes another step toward me. "You make me brave. Brave enough to risk everything and anything to protect you."

"I don't need your protection!"

"You don't get to decide!"

Now he's mad? Uh, no.

I move into him, and my fist is connecting with his jaw before I even realize what's happening. My anger made me do it.

He goes down hard into the grass. I stand over him, panting, legs wide, knees bent, fists balled. *I will destroy you.*

He shakes his head and looks up at me, those damn eyes seeing me. Seeing me the way that only he can see me. As the mother of his child. The love of his life.

"You lied!"

"You're right." He touches his jaw gingerly and winces.

"I don't need your protection."

He stills, his eyes meeting mine again. There is a solid determination in them. This is not the stuff of daily life. This is the stuff of a higher purpose.

"I will protect you and our child until the day I die. And if it's possible, I will continue from the other side. There are some things you don't get to decide, Sydney. Me loving you. Loving our child. Me protecting both of you. Those are mine. You can't have them. I can't give them up. Not even for you."

"Fuck you and your pretty words." I turn so quickly I stumble and go down, landing hard on my hands and knees. *Awesome exit, Syd. Super effective.*

I breathe for a second, regaining my composure. Rain starts to patter against the trees and wet the grass. Blue's nose swipes at my hair. Mulberry stands over me. Sitting back on my heels, I look up at him. He holds out his hand. I stare at it.

It's calloused and big—bigger even than his bulk would imply. His palm is open, and he wants me to take it. But I'm not done with my anger. It is spinning inside me, a tornado of hurt and fear so strong that only pure rage can contain it... keep it from destroying me.

I rise on my own and meet his eyes.

"I love you," he says, his jaw red where I hit him.

"Fuck you."

I head down the jungle path, my dogs behind me. The rain lets loose, soaking me to the bone. Mulberry doesn't follow. I don't look back, but his gaze is like a laser on my back, burning me. Always fucking burning me, that one.

EK

"I keep having to learn the same lessons over and over again."

Merl nods but doesn't turn to look at me, his eyes still staring into the hot, humid depths of the jungle. Light and dark dance together between the leaves. The storm passed as fast as it came, leaving the air heavy and the light eerie.

"That is true for all of us, I think." He leans back, the hammock seat swaying as he brings his feet up into it. "Maybe it's why we're here."

"Are you going full philosopher on me?" I tease.

Merl gives a brief smile. "Maybe."

"Mo Ping is a deep thinker, right?"

He shrugs. "In her way, but she's also light and fun." He pauses. "And tough."

"That's important." I nod.

"It is. We must be the right amount of hard though. It's important to have protection, but not so much that no one can get in."

"Does she let you in?" I ask quietly, curious. This conversation isn't about me anymore, and that's a relief. Merl meets my gaze. His long lashes curl away from the deep brown of his eyes, looking almost fake. Almost, but not quite. Because there is nothing about this man that is false. He is raw honesty in human form. "Yes," he answers, "she does."

"And you let her in?"

"Yes."

Tears spring to my eyes for the millionth time since a new life started to form inside of me, and I curse them yet again as my cheeks grow hot and my throat closes. It's just so damn wonderful that Merl is in a supportive, beautiful relationship. Makes me want to curl up in a ball and cry!

I rub my eyes hard, hoping to banish the wayward emotions. Pregnancy is like being at sea with a devil at the helm and an angel reefing the sails; my body is the boat, driven through the waves, present for it all but with no control over the heading.

That's how the world treats me too, as if I'm a vessel, not a person. How can creating a new human strip your humanity in the eyes of others? It doesn't make any sense.

"Sorry," I say, pushing at my eyes hard.

"You don't need to apologize to me for having feelings, Sydney." There is humor in his voice, and when I look over at him, he is smiling.

I can't help but laugh. "It's just—" I sniffle. "—it's really nice you and Mo found each other. It gives me hope." I offer a watery smile, and he grins back.

"Look at you."

"What?"

"You're finally getting in touch with your vulnerability."

"Oh, shut up."

"Ah, there they are, those walls we know so well."

I shake my head and sit further into the chair, staring out at the jungle again.

"Sydney," Merl's voice is quieter, a stern, loving tone I recognize.

He's about to impart some wisdom. Ugh.

"What?" I say, petulant as ever.

"I get that you're in a complicated situation."

I huff a laugh. "That's putting it mildly."

"But the thing is, Syd," he presses on, "you're never going to get what you want until you allow yourself to be vulnerable."

My body clenches at the word. I'll never be vulnerable again. It hurts. It breaks. My head shakes a no, but I don't respond.

"I get that you still experience pain from your past. But you're at a crossroads here. If you keep going at life the same way, you'll wear yourself down to a nub."

I glance over at him. "I've been dreaming of James."

He cocks his head in that way that he does, so similar to his dogs, it brings a smile to my lips. "From what I understand, pregnancy can cause intense dreams."

"Yes, they are intense." I pause. Merl waits. "We hang out." I shrug.

"As if he was alive. It makes me miss him more and also gives me a lot of comfort." My hand finds my belly. "The baby's due date is his birthday, and it's a boy."

"I'm not surprised he's on your mind then."

We sit in silence for a while. "Do you think I should forgive Mulberry?" I finally ask.

"For keeping secrets?" Merl shrugs. "We all have secrets."

"Do any of yours involve helping Robert Maxim fake his death?"

"No."

"He keeps doing the same thing, going against my wishes in what he considers my best interests. He doesn't trust me to take care of myself." I'm whining again.

"You should talk to him," Merl suggests. "You're going to have a baby together either way. So you'll need to find a path forward."

Ugh. Merl and all his correctness make me crazy sometimes.

EK

Mulberry is waiting in my living room when I get back. His jaw is swollen, and a bruise is starting to form. He stands up off the kitchen stool when I walk in, his eyes wary. Frank runs over and sits on his foot, thumping his tail. Mulberry keeps his gaze fixed on me, ignoring the giant slobbering beast leaning into his leg.

I reach for Blue's head; it's always there. My fingers brush warm fur, and the tension in my shoulder slacks slightly. *Be vulnerable.*

"Do you think we can do this?" Thickness in my throat quiets the question.

Mulberry's lips quirk to one side, and his eyes soften, practically melting. "We can do anything… together." His answer is even quieter than the question. Mulberry takes a tentative step forward.

My chin dips. He answers my subtle invitation with a rush of movement, wrapping me up in his arms, nuzzling into my hair and breathing in a giant breath.

I press my face into his chest, hiding in the dark warmth of him. His hands run up and down my back. His phone beeps, and I pull back. He lets me, slipping the phone from his pocket. "Council meeting in an hour," he says, his gaze rising back up to meet mine. "That probably leaves enough time for us to make up."

I slap his arm and laugh. He catches me up and kisses me. The world fuzzes, the truth settles. One plus one plus one is an equation I can't solve yet, but if I don't try, I'll never find out what it can add up to.

CHAPTER TWENTY-EIGHT

Lenox

Petra's heels leave round holes in the thin coating of snow as we climb the front steps of the manor house of a sprawling estate. Hans and Ramona flank us. Sophia waits by the car, her arms crossed, looking as fierce and beautiful as a mink.

"Good to see you," Boris Negayav says to Petra when we are shown into his sitting room. His rosy cheeks, receding hairline, and round belly give him a jolly aura. Boris kisses Petra's cheeks, and we shake hands. He offers us coffee, and we accept then sit on the couches facing each other.

The glass doors to our right offer a view of a snow-dusted landscape that slopes down to the sea where our yacht is anchored off the Romanian coast. Hans and Ramona wait by the doors leading back into the front hall behind us. Two men in dark suits stand on the far side of the room covering Boris's back.

Petra and Boris have worked together moving women from the former Soviet bloc out to the western world for years. We are here to make it clear that all women being moved must know what their work will be in the west.

The debt they will incur will be paid with their bodies. It is a way out; it is the road Petra followed. But it is not for everyone. And we will not allow the transport of women who believe they will work in offices or anything other than the sweaty, dangerous world of selling themselves."

Boris spreads his arms along the back of the couch, his body language blatantly obvious: *I am the king of this castle.*

"You've come to tell me your new plans. Your new rules." Boris grins.

"Yes," Petra says in one of her purrs—this one is not sexual but rather the one she uses when discussing money. "We have decided to follow the advice and rules of Joyful Justice to create a safe working environment for our employees—and to avoid Joyful Justice's intervention."

Boris laughs. "Employees. You have changed, Petra." His eyes, dark and deep set, wander to me. "Is this your doing, Lenox Gold?"

"We are partners," I say.

"You never sold women." My reputation precedes me. "And now you deal in women but only in this new—" He winds a hand into the air as if searching for a word. "—method."

"Yes, I think it's better for everyone involved."

"I am a businessman," Boris announces, leaning forward to pick up his cup of coffee from the low table between us. "And I do not think that your new methods are good for business."

"Human rights have always been difficult to weave into a business like ours, but history shows that it pays in the end to have a happy, healthy workforce," I say. "It's good for the longevity of the business."

"Longevity?" Boris raises a brow. "You speak of longevity to me?"

Petra crosses her legs, the red sole of her shoe flashing and drawing Boris's attention. "We have worked together for a long time—"

"Yes." His voice drops as he interrupts her. "Almost as long as you worked with the McCain brothers. Their business is not so good now though, is it?"

"No," Petra answers, her voice even.

A knock at the door behind Boris interrupts us. He turns, waving to his men to open it. One of them does. A man steps into the room. He wears rumpled khakis and a buttoned-down shirt. His thinning hair is pulled back into a ponytail. His eyes land on Petra and flare with anger. The hairs on the back of my neck stand.

I recognize him from the Isis slave auctions I visited while researching for Joyful Justice. His name is Billy Ray Titus, and he is a leader of what he calls the Men's Rights Activists, but he is more extreme than the average member of that group. Billy Ray is an incel—an involuntary celibate. He used the McCain brothers to purchase sex slaves and transport them to his followers in the United States and other Western nations. Now he is here.

Boris turns back to us. "Do you know Billy?"

"By reputation," Petra says, her gaze roaming over him like a farmer inspecting a heifer for sale. "You are involuntary celibate, yes?" she asks as her gaze meets his.

"That's right," he says, rounding the couch.

"Sit," Boris says, gesturing to the far end of his couch. Billy perches on the edge while Petra continues to stare at him. Her gaze is bringing out blotches of color on his face.

"You think women owe you sex," she asks. "That you should not have to pay?"

Billy Ray throws on a smile and meets her gaze. "I have no interest in discussing anything with you."

Petra laughs as he turns his attention to me. I raise a brow.

Boris sits forward. "Billy Ray," the American name sounds harsher in his accent, "is offering to provide the same services as you two."

"He does not have the networks," Petra says, her voice silky smooth.

"He says that he does," Boris says. "That he is working in a whole new way—with men who share his values."

"Yes," Billy Ray says. "They won't just work for the highest bidder. They won't cave to Joyful Justice or anyone else. They are loyal." He glances at Petra. "Loyal in a way that only men can be." Petra holds her tongue. "Women can't run businesses," Billy goes on, his confidence building at Petra's silence. He clearly doesn't understand women. "Boris will be working with me from now on."

"Is this true, Boris?" Petra asks.

Boris shrugs. "Why shouldn't I work with Billy?"

"He has no experience," I point out, "and belongs to a movement of men who don't think they should have to pay for sex." I smile. "Paying for sex is the basis of our business."

Billy Ray laughs—the sound like the braying of a donkey. He stands and paces toward the window, then turns back to us, his chest puffing out, an orator preparing for his speech. "I am a supreme gentleman," he begins. "This arrangement with Boris," he sweeps his arm out, "is necessary to provide my followers—who are all being denied sex—the opportunity to take back control."

He clenches his fist and draws his arm in tight to his body, as if grasping the submission of women he so deeply desires. "It is the perfect union. My brothers and I believe in the equality of the sexes, but that is not what is happening now. Men are being oppressed while women use their sexual prowess to subvert what is best for our society.

"Look at you, Lenox." He lifts his chin, gesturing to me. "This woman sits beside you as though she is your equal when it is clear that you don't need her to run your business."

I blink at him but do not respond. He is clearly delusional.

"She can't possibly figure out the complexities necessary to move bodies across borders. And then to suggest that we must be completely honest with them. Why? Women are all lying sluts. Why should we show them respect that they will never return? It is time for us to reclaim our dignity."

Billy sits again, smiling, his dissertation delivered. I open my mouth to respond, but Petra stands, pulling my attention.

She reaches into her blazer and draws her gun in one smooth, fast movement. Billy's eyes widen. She aims while Boris's men are fumbling to draw their own weapons—no one expected the petite bombshell to draw a gun with such speed and precision.

She fires. Billy's head snaps back, and his brains explode on the couch, spattering Boris in the process. She shifts her aim, the muzzle landing between Boris's eyes. He puts up a hand. She fires through it.

Boris flops off the couch, dead. His men have their guns out, but so do Hans and Ramona. She looks at the men, their weapons trained on her. "Do you think a woman can run a business?" she asks them in their native tongue.

They don't answer right away.

"Well?" she asks.

One shrugs and looks over at the other. They lower their weapons. "Good," Petra says. Her gaze wanders to the glass doors. "I like this view."

My brain catches up with the quickly unfolded events. Petra glances over her shoulder at me, and I recognize with a clarity as loud as a church bell. *I love her.*

CHAPTER TWENTY-NINE

Sydney

Felicity hurls one glove and then the other across the open-air dojo, sweat-sticky curls plastered to her face. "I'm such an idiot," she yells.

"What's up?" I ask.

She jumps and lets out a small screech of alarm, her hand thudding against her chest as she whirls around to face me. Color brightens her already red face. She closes her eyes and frowns deeply. She might be about to cry.

My chest tightens, and I want to turn and leave, not face this bundle of insecurities in front of me, but Blue's nose taps my hip, reminding me that I'm a leader. That I *can* do this. Felicity deserves my attention. Merl is training with Nila and Frank; the least I can do is help out one of his students.

I take a step forward even as the tightness in my chest moves up into my throat, trying to silence me. "You're not an idiot. You might have done something stupid, but that doesn't mean there is something 'wrong' with you." I put wrong into bunny quotes, feeling like a dill weed. But a dill weed who's right… and should not call herself a dill weed.

Felicity opens her eyes, and there are tears filming her gaze. "I—" She closes her mouth, dropping her focus to her bare feet on the mat.

"You trying to learn something and getting it wrong?" I ask with a smile.

She nods, still staring at the ground.

"Show me," I say. "Maybe I can help."

Her eyes jump to mine. Fear and excitement war in Felicity's expression. Her hero is offering to help. I want to tell her not to look at me that way, but I swallow the words. She will eventually realize on her own that I am just a person. Telling her won't do a damn thing except make us both feel bad. Look at me, learning. And you thought pigs couldn't fly and hell always broiled.

Felicity is working on a roll that Merl teaches. In my present condition, I can't show it to her—my belly gets in the way—but I talk her through it. Within twenty minutes, she's dropping onto her shoulder, rolling, then popping up into a high kick like a pro. I clap my hands, her success feeling like my own.

"Good job!"

She beams at me. "Thanks so—" The warning sirens whirl to life, vibrating through the air. Felicity and I both look up at the speaker mounted in the eaves of the outdoor practice space. "This is not a drill," Merl's voice comes over the loudspeaker. "Evacuate immediately. I repeat, evacuate immediately."

Felicity's eyes meet mine, sparking with a mix of fear and fascination. Movement breaks out across the compound as trainees run in choreographed, practiced, evacuation plans.

Time to go.

EK

I jog along the narrow trail through the thick, tropical foliage, weaving and dodging the larger branches, letting the thinner ones slap into my upraised arms. Wet leaves soak my shirt. Vines reach for my ankles. My breath comes in easy draws. The weight of the baby tugs at my belly.

Blue stays right behind me, moving like a silent ghost in my wake.

The sound of a helicopter drones overhead. Shouting back at the camp reaches us in quiet waves. I find my marked tree, spotting the camouflaged package up in the limbs.

Running my hand along the trunk, I feel the rope. I try to unwind it from its post, but the knot has swollen. *Shit.* Pulling my knife from my waist, I saw through the thick line. The pack falls through the leaves with a crash. I separate my bag from Blue's.

Blue barks a warning, leaping through the underbrush to my side. I scan the forest but see nothing. Blue's nose points back toward the compound. There are people hunting us. I better just keep moving. They heard that crash. Blue's chest rumbles with warning; then he goes silent. They must be close enough to hear him.

I lower to my knees, hiding amongst the foliage. Blue flattens himself to the ground. Moving ever so slowly, I lower to my hands, then my side, curling around my stomach.

"Come out," a woman's voice reaches me.

I stay motionless except for shallow sips of air.

A whisper of movement behind a tree. Sweat stings my eyes. A figure appears covered in armor and camouflage. Its helmet is plumed with leaves. Its rifle long and deadly. I don't move. It is looking down the path I abandoned to retrieve the pack.

Hard, dark eyes scan the forest. It's a woman. Her face is painted the same mix of greens and black as the jungle around us. My heart hammers in my chest. Sweat soaks my tank top. Bugs circle me, buzzing in my ear.

The baby spins, kicking out. My need to survive pulses in my throat. The soldier's eyes level on the space above me and keep scanning. She walks forward, disappearing from view.

I wait. Time slides by. My heart slows down, my breath evens, the rushing in my ears quiets. My grip on the knife's handle loosens. Blue's nose taps my ankle. I look down at him. His ears are flat. There is no one close now.

I rise up to my knees, placing my knife next to me on the ground, and then open the pack. So well organized. First, I pull out the waist holster—one side for a handgun, the other for the machete. The pistol is secured in a foam-lined case. I check the weapon before holstering it. Next, I pull out the machete, the long, wide blade is sheathed in soft leather. I stand to properly attach it to my waist, tying the string around my thigh so that it won't bump against me if I run. When the blade is out, the soft leather allows me free movement.

I holster my smaller blade again and return to the pack, pulling out the map to the meet location and the compass. There is a GPS unit as well, but it won't be useful unless the people hunting me give up—its signal is too easy to trace. I check the rest of the supplies. Where is the radio? There is supposed to be a handheld radio in here.

I open Blue's pack, but the radio isn't there either. I'll have to make do without it. Blue pushes up against my arm as I pour him some fresh water. He laps at it while I settle the pack onto his back. With two zipper compartments, one on either side of his back, I have to be careful to keep the weight even. When he is done drinking, I return the bowl to the side it came out of and eyeball the assemblage to make sure it is balanced.

I heft my own pack, pulling the water tube free and taking a long draw from the interior bladder. I clip the hip support of the bag under my belly and tighten the chest strap. The pack lies tight against me so that I can still jog with it on.

Blue nuzzles my hip, and we move back to the narrow path as I orient with the compass and map. We have a few miles to go, and I want to make it to my meet point before darkness falls, staying alert to my pursuers. I break into a light jog, moving carefully through the jungle.

Following the map leads me off the trail and slows our progress as we have to hack through the jungle. Hours later my shoulder is aching, but the avoidance of the trails seems to have achieved its purpose of evading our attackers. I pause at a fallen tree, slipping off the pack and giving Blue more water and some kibble, watching the pink hues of sunset fade into the dusty blues of dusk.

I check the map again. We are not far now, but exhaustion is tugging at me. I gnaw at a protein bar. Darkness creeps in from between the trees. I let out a pathetic sigh as I pull out the headlamp. Bugs are going to swarm my head. Blue looks up at me from where he is lying next to the tree.

Should we just stay here tonight? I check the map again. *No.* We are close. "We can do it," I tell Blue. He cocks his head, as if that is obvious. I laugh and heft the machete.

It takes another forty-five minutes before I get to the rendezvous point. It's at the bottom of a cliff, so the vegetation is not as thick. I check the map again, swatting at the bugs swarming my light, then click it off and stare at the rocky ledge. I'm the only one here.

Too tired to think anymore, I set up the small tent included in my pack and curl up with Blue before falling into a deep sleep.

EK

The howler monkeys wake me—their penetrating bellow pulling me from a dream that fades quickly, leaving me with a sense of unease. Blue sits up and presses his nose to the bottom of the zippered door of the tent. He looks back at me, his eyes glinting in the dark.

I reach for my gun, taking off the safety, and wait, straining to hear over the sounds of the jungle. Blue releases a quiet growl. There is someone out there. Could be other members of Joyful Justice who have arrived at the meet spot... or it could be someone else.

Light seeps through the tent slowly. I had slept in my clothing and now pull my boots close, tying them on quickly before picking up my gun again. Birds announce the sun cresting the horizon, their songs loud and gleeful.

The tent opens on both sides. Blue's focus remains on the south entrance, so I unzip the northern exposure. Blue tries to brush past me, but I stop him with a small gesture. If enemies are out there, I don't want them shooting Blue. I roll out of the tent, popping up in firing position—one knee down, the other leg bent, the pistol extended straight back in the direction that Blue growled in.

I'm aiming at a wall of vegetation. I scan my environment. Blue comes out of the tent and sits by my side. No one's out here. Maybe he was just growling at the monkeys.

I stand and slowly lower my weapon. But when Blue barks, I turn quickly, raising the pistol.

The woman who almost found us near the camp stands in the shadows. Her rifle is aimed at my head. But she doesn't fire. *She wants me alive.*

Our weapons trained on each other, eyes locked, we both just breathe for a moment.

Blue's growl rumbles low and deep. The insects whine and buzz, their song rising and falling. "I have to take you in," she says.

"Is it worth dying over or killing?"

"I'm not afraid of either of those outcomes."

"You should be. Have you ever killed anyone before?" She doesn't answer. "Ever killed a pregnant woman?" Her eyes flicker for just a second to my belly. "Or a dog? You'll never be the same. We will haunt you forever."

"I don't believe in ghosts."

"You should." Time stretches, my arm muscles begin to ache from holding the gun. An idea begins to form. "Why do you want me so badly?" Her brow furrows. "This isn't random. That you and I are here—and no one else. You planned this—me specifically being taken in." Something moves behind her eyes. Guilt maybe. Her jaw tenses, and her eyes drop to my belly again before she answers. "They told you not to hurt me." She still doesn't answer. "Was it Robert Maxim?" Her eyes flicker again, but she doesn't speak. "You promised to take me in personally. What do you get out of it?"

Her lips purse for a moment, and then she finally answers. "I got Dan Burke. Robert told me how to lure him back to the States."

"You're Consuela Sanchez." She nods. "Dan told me about you." I smile. "He likes you." Her eyes narrow. "So in exchange for Dan, Robert gets me."

"You're part of a larger deal."

"A deal?"

"A package."

"Like a present."

"A compensation package. We promised you'd be apprehended."

"Because he wants to save me." I almost laugh, but I'm too pissed. "He got someone to fuck with my pack. To remove my radio, change the map..." She doesn't answer. "What if...?" My voice trails off as an idea starts to crystalize.

"What?" she asks, curiosity softening her tone.

"What if I could help you? What if we worked together?"

"How?"

"Lower your weapon. I'll lower mine. We can talk." Her eyes narrow. I gesture with my chin at my pack. "I can make us coffee." She still doesn't move. "Look, reality check, Consuela. You're not going to shoot me. I'm not going with you unless I choose to; you can see that." She doesn't answer, but we both know I'm right. She might have the weight of the US government with her, but she can't hurt me. And, if necessary, I *will* hurt her.

She begins to lower her gun, and I mirror her movements. We slowly holster our weapons. "Do you have cream and sugar?" she asks.

This is going to work out just fine.

CHAPTER THIRTY

Dan

The key-code lock disengages, and I ease the door open. Consuela's apartment lies mostly in darkness—the only light a diffuse pale yellow from the street lamps outside her windows. A white cat strides out from the bedroom, its eyes flashing iridescent green in the half light. It sits and watches as I close the door quietly behind me. I tried not to come back here. To stay on the island. I really did. But I couldn't resist. *This is necessary.*

I stand at the threshold of her living room and take a deep breath. It smells like her—that sweet vanilla and metallic edge of fresh thyme. The cat moves forward and winds between my legs. I squat down and rub the top of its head with my gloved hand. I find a collar and turn over the name tag. *Fuzzy Face Franny*.

The cat purrs deeply and flops onto her back, offering a white belly for further ministrations. I smile—Fuzzy Face Franny does not belong to Consuela. She is cat sitting for her sister who is on a cruise with their mother. Consuela got back from the raid in Costa Rica two nights ago, so couldn't make the trip, but did swing by her sister's place to pick up Franny on her way home. She's a good sister.

My watch face glows softly. Consuela will be home in an hour—she's at her favorite spin class. It's time to get to work. I cross to the windows and pull the thick drapes before getting my nonlinear junction detector out of my backpack. It detects electronic semiconductor components through dense materials such as bricks, concrete, and soil. Mine is made to detect and locate hidden cameras, microphones, and other electronic devices regardless of whether the surveillance device is radiating, hard-wired, or turned off.

I extend the telescoping arm and press it to the closest wall. The touchscreen display shows nothing unusual as I scan the area. I move through the living room then round the kitchen island. Nothing in there either.

I find the router in the bedroom and unscrew the cable link even though any government device will use its own radio frequency; I like to follow best practices. Consuela's queen-sized bed is neatly made. There is a hamper with laundry in it and none on the floor. I pull the drapes closed before moving on.

Opening her bathroom door, that vanilla scent wafts out. While scanning the room, I discover the source of the smell. Her body lotion. The shampoo is herbal and explains the aroma of thyme that lingers around her.

There is nothing in the bathroom to suggest her fiancé spends time here.

I find no evidence of surveillance equipment in her apartment either. Her phone will need to be neutralized immediately upon entry. She can't keep her phone clean… I should know.

It is impossible to believe that the woman set to marry the head of the Senate Intelligence Committee is not being watched. Consuela probably does her own sweeps regularly though, and I doubt they'd waste the energy to put a unit on her. I set up a white noise machine in the living room that will block any long-range microphones just in case… best practices again.

Twenty minutes left to look for the diary. I start in her bedroom, opening the bedside table drawer. Next to a Bible is a black bound notebook. *That was easy.* She obviously doesn't expect to have her home invaded by someone searching for her most intimate thoughts.

I pick up the notebook, my heart beating furiously. Sitting on the bed, I open to the first page, recognizing her neat cursive writing. The first entry is from the time we started working together several months ago. I start to read.

Eighteen minutes later my phone alerts me that Consuela is close. I move to the couch. Fuzzy joins me, settling into my lap. Images of Dr. Evil flash through my mind as my gloved hand pets the white cat. I don't want world domination. Just a conversation… an explanation.

The door opens, and Consuela tosses her keys onto the table by the front door, continuing into the living room, her head bowed over her phone. She stops to finish typing. The cat leaps off my lap and stalks over, winding between Consuela's ankles.

I drink her in. Her hair is up in a high ponytail that is still swaying from her entry. Consuela's down jacket is unzipped. Her leggings hug her like a second skin. My eyes can't help but drift over them, setting off an ache in my chest. *Enough.*

I stand slowly.

Consuela's eyes find me in the dark, and she startles, dropping her phone and reaching for her gun before she's recognized me. I hold my finger to my lips. I've got to get her phone neutralized before she makes a sound.

Recognition blooms in her gaze, and her eyes narrow. But she doesn't speak. I hold up the Faraday box I brought with me—a black cell phone size case that distributes electrostatic charge around the exterior, acting as a shield. Nothing gets in or out. I point to the phone where she dropped it on the floor. She darts her eyes to it, keeping the barrel of her gun aimed at my chest.

I silently ask for permission. She kicks the device over to me. I pick up the phone and slip it into the box. I tip it toward her so she can see mine is in there too. I close the box.

"What are you doing here?" she asks.

"We need to talk. Can you put the gun away?"

She slowly lowers it but does not re-holster the weapon. "You spoke to Sydney about the raid in Costa Rica," she says.

"All is fair in love and war."

She tilts her chin up so she can look down her nose at me. "This isn't another declaration, is it?"

"No. I recognize that you're engaged to Senator Chiles."

"Good."

"You'd make a captivating first lady some day. Give him a lot of credibility with people of color *and* law enforcement."

"He will make an excellent president."

"Not with my algorithms he won't."

Her head shakes slightly, setting the ponytail off. "He is what is best for America. As you've pointed out so many times, Dan, there is nothing illegal about your algorithms." She holsters her weapon and puts her hands on her hips. She might get off legally if she shot a man who surprised her in her darkened living room, but days of tabloid coverage would be politically damaging.

I glance at my watch. The self-destruct sequence in my algorithm has begun. Her phone is in the Faraday box, so she won't know until I'm gone.

"You're so loyal to your nation that you'll sacrifice your own happiness?" I ask.

"I'm not sacrificing anything."

"Really? I read your diary."

Her eyes go round. "What right—" She cuts herself off.

"You have feelings for me. We both know it. Let's not pretend."

She shakes her head, setting off the ponytail again. "I'm not going to be in a relationship with a criminal, Dan." There is acid in her voice.

I meet her gaze. "A freedom fighter. A brilliant coder. A man who can love you more than your senator."

Her eyes flash in the near darkness. "Get out."

"Come with me."

"Get out." Her voice slices through the air, cutting right down my center.

"I don't think that's what you really want."

She steps to the side, almost tripping over the cat and cursing. "I—" She takes a deep breath but does not meet my eyes. "I *had* feelings for you. That happens when you're working closely with someone. But..."

Now she meets my gaze. Even in the dark I can see her determination. "I have made my choice."

"You won't be able to live with it," I warn her. "You're too passionate to subjugate yourself for anything—not even your own purposes."

"You"—she points at me—"you don't actually know me."

I laugh, harsh and short. "I know you better than your senator. Does he know how you feel about me? What you wrote in your diary? That you've never felt this before—the butterflies." I take a step toward her. She backs up, her lips pursing.

"I'm not throwing away everything I've worked for, my family, everything I believe in for butterflies!"

I want to kiss her so badly that I have to turn away from her to stop myself. "It's more than butterflies." I take a calming breath and turn back to face her. "Can't you see that we are in love?"

"It doesn't matter what I feel for you." Her voice is choked. "I can't. I won't be with you. Ever."

Pain stings my eyes. "Okay," I say. "If that's what you really want, I'll leave." My heart beats like a hammer.

"Go." The word is as heavy as a punch.

I pick up my backpack, leaving the Faraday box on the table. The phone in there is for her... so that we can communicate without others knowing.

I turn and head to the door. "Dan..." Her voice is choked. I turn back. Consuela looks so confused it almost breaks my heart all over again. She licks her lips. Before I even realize what I'm doing, I've closed the space between us and pulled her close, crashing my lips onto hers. Consuela ignites in my arms, wrapping herself around me as though she plans to never let me go.

We hit the wall hard enough to knock a painting down. My bag drops off my arm. As I pick her up, legs wrap around my waist. We are lost in each other. Totally destroyed.

CHAPTER THIRTY-ONE

Lenox

At the age of five, an octopus in a glass bottle washes up at my feet. The creature pulses a rainbow of colors, its suckers pressed against the clear glass. I stare down at where it lies between my feet, mesmerized.

The next wave rushes in a frothy white over my feet, stealing the new prize away. I go after it.

My mother calls out, but her words are lost in my excited race after the bottle into the bubbling foaming sea—it pulls me along, invites me in. The bottle rises in front of me, caught in the next cresting wave. It towers above me, a sheer gleaming wall of blue topped with white sprays. The bottle rises above my head as the water arches over me.

The wave takes me. It tumbles me. I don't know which way is up or down. Even as my cheek grates against the sand, I cannot figure out where the surface—the air—has gone.

I hit something hard, my shoulders striking twin pillars. Strong hands grip my arms and heave me up. My mother clutches me close; water streams off us both. "Don't do that again, Lenox."

I promise I won't. I believe I've learned my lesson. I never want that to happen again.

Now, more than thirty years later, I stand at the bottom of another towering wave. The same sense of misplaced time and space enveloping me. I followed the prize—justice in an unjust world—and perhaps again failing to see the danger rising in front of me, forming into a towering wall of power that can subvert my sense of direction.

My calculations, my insistence that I use weights and scales to judge rather than guts and vulnerability, has twisted a vigilante organization into a criminal one. I strove to free strangers from slavery and delivered myself and my friends in the process.

"Sydney will be fine," Petra says, rubbing my shoulders, her strong hands digging into the tight muscles. "She told you she has a plan."

"Sydney is strong," I agree. *I fear we will murder the ideals Joyful Justice set out to spread.*

The image of Petra standing over Boris and Billy's bodies, chestnut hair falling in soft waves around her face, the glittering green of her eyes, flashes in my mind. The wave of love that washed over me then—inspired by her strength and clarity—pulses inside me still, undulating with the same certainty as the sea.

Petra kisses the back of my neck and slinks her arms around to rest on my chest. "You are afraid for yourself then?" she asks. I reach up and cover her hands with mine. My voice is locked in my chest. "Speak to me, Lenox," Petra says. "I love you. I want you to share with me. Please."

I raise one of her hands to my mouth and kiss her knuckles. "I love you," I admit.

She sucks in a breath. "Oh, Lenox," she breathes out, kissing my neck, moving around so that she can sit in my lap and look up into my face. "I love you." There are tears in her lashes. She kisses me, then lets out a low, throaty laugh. "Lenox, you wait so long to tell me." She smiles. "But you know I know."

"Yes," I agree. "You know me well."

"So I also know you fear what we are doing—that you will have too much power and that power always corrupts."

"Yes." She is right again.

"But do not worry, my love," she purrs. "I will keep you in line." It's my turn to laugh. She slaps my arm. "You do not believe me?"

"We have not always shared the same values," I say.

"True," she answers. "But I am a different woman now. You have shown me how to take care of people, not just use them to take care of myself." I blink at her, surprised yet not. "You make me a better woman, Lenox Gold."

Only time will tell if she makes me a better man.

CHAPTER THIRTY-TWO

Sydney

The orange jumpsuit scratches as I walk down the hall. The chains linking my wrists to my waist clink in time with the ones that link my ankles and waist. My guards each hold an elbow.

We arrive at the visitors' corridor. I'm the only prisoner here. They are taking this solitary confinement thing seriously—wouldn't want me inspiring a revolution. I see Robert Maxim as they bring me to the booth.

Sitting in the chair provided, I turn to my guard so he can remove my wrist restraints, then pick up the phone between us. Robert already cradles his to his ear. "Sydney," he says, no smile.

"How nice of you to visit." *How nice of you to fall right into my trap.*

He ignores my sarcasm. "I have a proposal for you." I wish I could raise one brow but never did master the skill, so I just purse my lips. "Marry me."

I cough a laugh. "What?"

He scoots forward on his seat, getting closer to the glass. "You need to marry me."

"Excuse me?"

"My testimony is the most damning against you."

"Nice to know."

"If we are married, then they can't make me testify against you."

"Wow." I sit back, the clink of my chains a not-so-subtle reminder of how much this man has tied me up in binds. "You planned this. I mean, you really fucking planned this." I reach out with my free hand to touch Blue's head, but it isn't there. I swallow the panic rising up my throat. *This is not permanent.*

"I plan everything," he says.

I suppress a smile and look down at my hands to hide my eyes. *He can read me well. I must be very careful.* "You faked your own death, you set up your child, the mother of your child, and brought down a *huge* number of criminal organizations all to marry me?"

"One stone, many birds." He doesn't smile. He's still not sure if I'll do it.

"Robert, even if I marry you, if you force me to marry you, that won't make us husband and wife in the way you want," I point out.

"I will get my fortune back. You will have to be with me for a lifetime to avoid prosecution."

I laugh, letting the ridiculousness of this very serious man roll over me. I knew he wanted to save me; I didn't realize his plan involved marriage. "Do you hear yourself?"

"I am very self-aware."

I fold over myself laughing, tears wetting my lashes. "Self-aware," I say aloud, shaking my head. "You are an idiot." I raise my head to meet his gaze. "You can't force me to marry you and expect it to be a *good* relationship."

"I expect it will keep you safe. It will keep you close. And those are the two things I want most in this world."

"You're willing to risk my freedom on this gamble?"

"It's not me risking it. I can get you out within days. All you have to do is agree. You are the one risking your freedom. I am the one offering it to you. Is the idea of being with me worse than prison?"

"I'm not totally sure of the difference."

He snorts. "You are not so impractical, Sydney. You can see that living with me—something you've chosen to do in the past—will be far superior to spending the rest of your life alone behind bars. I have Blue, Nila, and Frank. We are all just waiting for you to come home. I can protect you, Sydney. You know that."

I close my eyes and take a deep breath, bringing in the stinking staleness of the prison. He put me here. This selfish bastard will taste the stink of failure soon though.

"What about Mulberry?" I ask, playing along, pretending like I don't have a plan of my own.

"He can see the child, of course. But you will be *my* wife. I expect you to live with me, to be faithful."

"Faithful." He's fucking crazy. "You think I'm going to sleep with you?" I lean closer, wishing the glass wasn't between us so I could hit him upside the head.

He smiles, this slow, teasing smile, as if he knows how to woo me. As if I'm a bunny with its leg caught in his trap. *I will gnaw my fucking leg off and beat you to death with it, asshole.*

"I guess that can all be discussed on our honeymoon," I say, sitting back.

"So, that's a yes."

"You've left me no choice, Robert. Obviously, I will marry you to get out of this hellhole."

The smile that steals over Robert's face is like a thief, lightly floating over rooftops, leaving no trail, but taking everything of value with it. It tugs at something in my chest. He is trying to get my heart, but he can't have it.

My son kicks out and spins once in my belly before settling down again. I lay my hand over him and smile at Robert, pretending I'm a bunny, pretending he has caught me but knowing that it is the other way around.

EK

Turn the page for a sneak peek of *Fatal Breach*, Sydney Rye

Mysteries book 14, or purchase it now and continue reading Sydney's next adventure: emilykimelman.com/FB

* * *

Sign up for my newsletter and stay up to date on new releases, free books, and giveaways: emilykimelman.com/News

SNEAK PEEK
FATAL BREACH, SYDNEY RYE MYSTERIES BOOK 14

Chapter One

Robert meets me at the prison gate, his smile predatory and victorious. I blank my mind. If I think about what I have planned, he will see it on my face. The man knows me well. Robert will be expecting something from me—it's part of the fun for him.

Is this fun for me, too?

His hand cups my upper arm as he bends to brush a kiss against my cheek. His beard is soft against my skin and the scent of him engulfs me: low notes of sandalwood and fine leather balanced by a sharp tang of cold metal.

"You look lovely," Robert says.

I'm wearing black cargo pants tucked into boots that lace tight at my ankles—they keep spiders out when you're in the jungle—a black tank top and the parka that Special Agent Consuela Sanchez gave me when we flew back to the States. It's cold in D.C., not so much in Costa Rica.

Robert is wearing a camel hair overcoat—it's a shade lighter than his skin, and a few shades more gold than the copper in his beard. The collar is pulled up against the chill, and his cheeks are tinged pink from the cold. A soft wind plays with his pitch black hair gone silver at the temples.

Behind Robert a black SUV with tinted windows idles. Brock, his head of personal security, climbs out of the driver's seat and comes around to open the back door. Brock is big and broad with weathered skin the color of a brushed penny. If his name was Block it wouldn't be off by much. His eyes are hidden behind mirrored sunglasses. His dark coat captures the sunlight and hides it away somewhere it will never be found.

"Good to have you back, Ms. Rye," Brock says in a rumbling baritone as I get into the back seat.

"Thanks, Brock."

Robert joins me. "Where are we going?" I ask. "To *my* apartment?"

Robert smiles. "Yes," he says.

When Robert faked his own death several months ago he really went the extra mile by leaving me most of his worldly possessions, including his apartment in Washington D.C. Now that he is forcing me to marry him to avoid prosecution—a husband can't testify against his wife—he'll be getting his wealth back.

"I may need you to sign a prenup," I say. "You realize I'm a very wealthy woman."

Robert laughs, his blue-green eyes glittering as we merge onto the highway. "Your wish is my command."

"Yeah, right," I grumble, looking out the window and watching the industrial area we're leaving slide by in a smear of speed.

Robert captures my hand, pulling it into his lap. "Sydney," his voice is serious and I turn to look at him. "I recognize this isn't what you wanted."

I huff a laugh. "You're so observant Robert. Was it the threat of giving birth in prison, or just the regular old forcing me to marry you?" I hold my chin with my free hand, pretending to be *really* thinking. "I wonder if I'm just being triggered by the fact that you're treating me like an object to obtain rather than a person with a life and heart of my own."

The skin around Robert's eyes tightens. "Sydney," his voice is lower now, a warning. The way you might talk to a child complaining about their bedtime. *As if he knows what's best for me.* I have to look away to keep the thoughts bubbling up in my mind hidden from him. *You will learn that I am not an object. Only a thinking, feeling, sentient being could ruin you the way I plan to.*

"If you don't want to marry me, you don't have to, Sydney."

"You're right," I tell the window. "I could *choose* to give birth in prison and have my son taken from me." I turn back to him, the idea bringing untapped rage to the forefront. "Do you think that is a choice I'd make?"

"No, you would rather murder me in my sleep."

I can't help the lightning grin that flashes across my face. "That *has* crossed my mind."

"But I do not think you are so heartless as that. You are angry with me now, but we are bonded."

"Ha, bonded. Is that what you call this?" I try to pull my hand free from him but he holds it tight. "Bondage is more like it." A spark ignites in his gaze and I sneer at him. "Don't even think about it."

His lips twitch into a smile and he gives a small shake of his head. "I'd never want to do anything without your consent."

"Wow, you're a big man. So generous. My consent. Lucky me." He opens his mouth to speak. "You know what?" I cut him off. "Let's just not talk for a minute. You don't want to get punched, I'm assuming." I shrug. "So we should stop speaking." I yank my hand out of his and scoot closer to my window.

"As you wish," he says.

Out of the corner of my eye I see him reach into his jacket. I lunge at him, grabbing his wrist with one hand and pinning it to his body so he can't pull a weapon. My other hand reaches into his open jacket, and slides up his abdominals searching for the gun. I don't find it.

"I keep my gun on my right side, Sydney, you know I'm left handed." His breath touches my cheek. I tilt my face to meet his gaze. He's so close our lips are practically touching. He's staying very still. I'm still pressing his right hand into his body. "Did you really think I'd pull a gun on you?" There is hurt in his voice. "I love you, I keep telling you."

I push off him, creating space between us. "This isn't love, Robert, this is obsession and possession."

He removes his hand from inside his jacket pocket, revealing a black velvet ring box. "We need to make it look real," Robert says, opening the lid.

Nestled in pale blue satin is an elegant, subtle engagement ring—a rose gold band with a round diamond set into it. The ring is not what I expected. His ex-wives wore chunks of diamonds that could drown a puppy. "It was my mother's," Robert says, taking it out of the box. "She was a music teacher, you know."

"Yes." His mom taught him to play piano.

"She used her hands, so needed a low profile ring." Something steals over his face, a memory of his mother, maybe. "She would have liked you."

"What would she have thought of you forcing me to marry you?"

Robert meets my gaze, his eyes are hard now. He's done with this line of conversation. "I offered you an escape—"

"You orchestrated it."

"Yes, that's right, Sydney, I *orchestrated* taking down your enemies, bringing you immense power and wealth. The price you have to pay is to spend the rest of my life with me as my wife. Is it too high for the destruction of the criminal cartels you fought to destroy? For the freedom of the sex slaves you fought to save? You would have given your life for the cause but won't offer me my happiness for it."

"There is freedom in death."

"There is freedom with me if you will allow it."

Silence fills the car, vibrating with unsaid words, with unspoken truths. I drop my gaze to the ring. He inches it closer to me. I take the box and settle back into the seat, resting it on my belly.

My son moves inside me, pressing against my ribs and making me arch to accommodate him. "Is he moving?" Robert asks, his voice so low I almost don't recognize it—there is something in his tone...

"Yes." I look over at Robert. He's sitting perfectly still, staring at my stomach. "You want to feel him?" I guess.

Robert's eyes jump to mine. "May I?" There is something so incredibly human about him that I'm struck speechless. I nod and he moves closer, gently laying his hand on top of my belly. My son punches out and a smile breaks over Robert's face. I've never seen his expression like this before. It's soft and…vulnerable.

When Robert looks up at me, his hand still resting on my belly, only the thin layer of my tank top between us, I can't understand what I'm seeing. He looks…*awed.*

What in the actual fuck?

EK

Continue reading *Fatal Breach*: emilykimelman.com/FB

AUTHOR'S NOTE

Dear Reader,

Thank you so much for reading *Blind Vigilance*! It means so much to me that readers enjoy my work. And the fact that you're having enough fun with my series to keep reading is a big deal to me. I'm so grateful to you.

Much of this book was inspired by the incredibly sophisticated social media manipulation by Cambridge Analytica—not just in the 2016 election but also in their propaganda campaigns around the globe. Fascinating and scary stuff. If you want to learn more about it, I suggest you read *MindF*ck* by Christopher Wiley. It breaks down how social media can be used to push us into ideological corners that we *think* we created for ourselves. It is as Wiley says *"weapons grade communication"*.

To put it simply, we are all very easy to manipulate because our lizard brains are not designed to deal with the onslaught of information the internet and social media companies feed us. Each of us is curating our reality—and advertisers are able to insinuate themselves into that stream—which gives them immense power.

We are easier to control, and sell, if we are blaming each other for our problems rather than searching for the systematic changes necessary to move into a more perfect union. Blaming "the other" is a time tested way to control a population.

I hope we can recognize that we are one people, we live on one planet, and we are all responsible for each other. If we look at power and policies, instead of each other, to find the root of our division, I believe we will discover a path forward for humanity that supports freedom, safety, and joy for all.

I'll leave you with a Stephen King quote I've always loved. *"I never opened my mouth and you never opened yours. We're not even in the same year together, let alone the same room... except we are together. We are close. We're having a meeting of the minds. [...] We've engaged in an act of telepathy."* -Stephen King, *On Writing: A Memoir of the Craft*

Thank you for reading my words and allowing me inside your head. Without you, I'm just a woman typing into the void. Together we are telepathic.

Let people know what you thought about *Blind Vigilance* on your favorite ebook retailer.

Emily

ABOUT THE AUTHOR

I write because I love to read...but I have specific tastes. I love to spend time in fictional worlds where justice is exacted with a vengeance. Give me raw stories with a protagonist who feels like a friend, heroic pets, plots that come together with a BANG, and long series so the adventure can continue. If you got this far in my book then I'm assuming you feel the same...

Sign up for my newsletter and
never miss a new release or sale:
emilykimelman.com/SRnews

I also have an exclusive Facebook group just for my readers! Join *Emily Kimelman's Insatiable Readers* to stay up to date on sales and releases, have exclusive giveaways, and hang out with your fellow book addicts: emilykimelman.com/EKIR.

If you've read my work and want to get in touch please do! I loves hearing from readers.
www.emilykimelman.com
emily@emilykimelman.com

facebook.com/EmilyKimelman
instagram.com/emilykimelman

EMILY'S BOOKSHELF

Visit www.emilykimelman.com to purchase your next adventure.

EMILY KIMELMAN
MYSTERIES & THRILLERS

Sydney Rye Mysteries

Unleashed

Death in the Dark

Insatiable

Strings of Glass

Devil's Breath

Inviting Fire

Shadow Harvest

Girl with the Gun

In Sheep's Clothing

Flock of Wolves

Betray the Lie

Savage Grace

Blind Vigilance

Fatal Breach

Undefeated

Relentless

Coming Winter 2023

Starstruck Thrillers

A Spy Is Born

EMILY REED
URBAN FANTASY

Kiss Chronicles

Lost Secret

Dark Secret

Stolen Secret

Buried Secret

Coming 2023

Lost Wolf Legends

Butterfly Bones

Coming 2023